RETREAT

ALSO BY KRYSTEN RITTER

Bonfire

RETREAT

A NOVEL

KRYSTEN RITTER

HARPER

An Imprint of HarperCollinsPublishers

RETREAT. Copyright © 2025 by Krysten Ritter. All rights reserved. Printed in the United States of America. No part of this book may be used or reproduced in any manner whatsoever without written permission except in the case of brief quotations embodied in critical articles and reviews. For information, address HarperCollins Publishers, 195 Broadway, New York, NY 10007.

Designed by Nancy Singer

ISBN 978-0-06-333460-1

RETREAT

RETREAT

PROLOGUE

In the mirror, you study your face. Everyone does this, you think, practices different faces: pouting like a model, tightening your lips like you have a secret, hurling insults, or compliments, with only your eyes. Sure, you've been told you're beautiful—usually by those who want something from you—but you've also been called out for every little imperfection, torn down to nothing, piece by piece. Because when people look at you, what they see is a reflection of themselves.

You look and look and look until your features blur. You are everything and nothing. It's terrifying. It's thrilling. You smile. The mirror smiles back, playing the game you've played since you were little. You'd watch yourself laugh, which people loved. Because it made them funny, even if they weren't. You'd watch yourself cry: the downturned mouth, the blotchy skin. People loved that too, you realized. It made them strong by comparison. It made them caring, sympathetic. Or else victorious, if they were the source of your tears.

Like a mirror, you told them how to behave, who to be, what to do. *Mirror, mirror, on the wall . . .* Give everyone what they wanted, and you could leave with so much more. Everyone thought they knew you, when really no one knew you at all.

A little depressing, how easy it is to become invisible.

You'd be surprised, though, how easy it is to get away with murder.

PART I

PART I

1

Outside the massive windows, falling snow silences Chicago, leaves North Dearborn Street mute and white. Inside the Hartmann Gallery, it's loud and warm. Alive with the clink of champagne glasses, the clatter of Jimmy Choos, and the murmured sounds of self-congratulatory conversation. *Your eyebrows are to die. How is Billy enjoying Andover? You look even skinnier than when I saw you at Vail!* Large frames fill the thirty-foot-high walls with an array of abstract selections that remind me a little of regurgitated hospital food. Don't get me wrong, I'm not one of those people who can't appreciate abstract art, I just know the difference between good and . . . whatever this is.

Not that most of the people here are even sparing a glance at the art lining the walls. It's the middle of winter in Chicago, so of course everyone is trading resort vacation tips. Their glittering conversation and clothing are a stark contrast to the ostensible reason for the gathering: the annual gala for the Melanoma Foundation. There are about a thousand other places I'd rather be on a Sunday night than here, surrounded by this crowd, high on their own generosity, making sure you know they're platinum-tier contributors to the cause.

But I know it will be worth it, in the end.

"Thank you." I pluck a flute of champagne from a passing waiter's tray.

"My pleasure." He smiles at me as if we're old friends, and maybe, after enough Veuve, we could be more. He is handsome, even in his stiff shirt and clip-on bow tie. So, for fun, I level him with one raised eyebrow. The glasses on his tray wobble.

"Hit me again before I'm empty."

"I'll be watching." *I'm sure you will.* He offers his free hand. "Jason."

"Liz," I say, gripping his hand firmly so he doesn't spill. My silk slip dress stains if you stare at it too long.

A mic blasts static—must be time for the speech—and we both wince. I slide into the crowd and face the platform, where a woman in an ochre satin gown, probably the gala chair, thanks Bob Hartmann for the oh-so-gorgeous, newly renovated space. We all applaud and mutter in agreement while he bows and clutches his grateful heart. Next, the lady in ochre thanks her dear, dear friends, art collectors and philanthropists Mr. and Mrs. Reed. They've given more than expected to the cause, made this evening a success with their overwhelming commitment. "In honor of Grandmother Reed, who succumbed to skin cancer at too young an age . . ." We clap again and cheer like the Reeds gave a showstopping performance instead of a tax-deductible donation. I down my champagne, wave the empty glass until Jason returns, and switch it out for one filled to the top. *Cheers*, I mouth to him, and I can practically see the film reel playing in his head as he imagines other things these pursed lips could do. Across the way, Top Donor Lady Mrs. Reed blushes from all the attention. She waves off the praise, but I can tell she's loving every second of it. Move over, melanoma: this is Mrs. Reed's night.

And why not? She's earned it—spent the past few months leveraging her power to get the city's top donors involved. I know because I've had my eye on her for a while.

As the crowd disperses back to their dinner tables, I move to the edge of the room, where a collection of wannabe–Dorothea Lange photographs hang, mostly exploitations of the underprivileged: sullen-faced men and women, dirt-smudged children, boarded-up factories, and broken-down cars. Deep stuff. I study my reflection in the framed glass and wonder if I look like someone who's suffered loss and grief. My face is smooth, unburdened by emotion. My dark hair is swept into a chic twist, not a strand out of place. But there—in the corners of my eyes. A darkness. A hollowness.

Then a flash of ochre satin catches my attention. Mrs. Reed has left her inner circle and is making her way toward the restrooms at the opposite end of the hall. She's listing like she's on a boat, or like Jason's been refilling her champagne flute too. As she passes me, I turn away to wipe discreetly at the few tears that have collected.

"Dear . . ." Mrs. Reed turns to me, and it's like we're alone in the crowded room. She hands me her cocktail napkin to dab my cheeks.

"I'm here in honor of my mother," I say, as if blinking back an image: wan face, nose tubes, flickering hospital fluorescents . . . Mrs. Reed's bony hand touches my wrist.

"So sorry for your loss."

My mother is alive and well, living in Boca, last I heard. We haven't been in touch for years. And trust me, it's no great loss. But I know how women like Mrs. Reed operate. Her children are her life, and now they're grown. So whenever she spots someone in need of mothering—especially someone who lost her own, God forbid!— she swoops in like she's wearing a damn cape.

"Thank you," I say to Mrs. Reed, "for your generosity to the cause."

She offers a tipsy smile, her eyes sorrowful and wet.

"Anyway." I gesture. "I was also dying to see the gallery renovation."

"It really is something." Her glassy eyes brighten as she

appreciates the space, and the art, if that's what they want to call it, and the money she's raised to make it happen.

"These floating walls are brilliant," I say, taking her cue, moving on to creativity and aesthetics, the beautiful things, making the most of her champagne high. "They're the perfect shade of white. What is it? Chantilly Lace? Your son-in-law did an incredible job."

"Yes. Thomás is really making a name for himself in the design world. He's a true visionary."

I look for the handsome Spaniard who captured the heart of Abigail Reed's son. Their Mallorca wedding, featured in *Town & Country*, was an art-world palooza, a who's who of breeding and taste. Mrs. Reed raises her champagne glass toward the far side of the crowd, and I spot Thomás with Alan, her redheaded son.

"There they are," she says, pointing, showing off her large ruby ring. The smooth oval stone, snug in its gold classical setting, is like something Cleopatra would wear. It hangs loose on her finger. She really should have it resized. "Are you in art?" she asks.

"I dabble." I grin a small smile, humble embarrassment mixed with pride. I pull my business card from my clutch. It's vague but polished, only the word "Consultant," followed by my name, Elizabeth Hastings, and number. "Here," I say. "I know of a Haring that's severely undervalued."

"Oh? That's interesting . . ." She takes my card and studies it, then carefully studies my face.

"It is," I tell her casually. "I believe you and I share some friends in common. We should really chat sometime."

"I'd love that," she replies, her eyes lighting up.

"Great!" I say cheerily. "I'm off to a dinner engagement, but ping me soon! You know how fast these things can slip away." I grasp both her hands like we're relatives instead of strangers.

"Thank you, dear. What a wonderful turn of events," says Mrs. Reed. "You'll hear from me very soon."

I smile before blending back into the crowd. It really is that easy sometimes.

The night is crisp and clear when I step outside, snow hurrying through the glow of streetlights. I slip into a waiting town car. In the darkness, I pull Mrs. Reed's ruby ring from my clutch. Couldn't help myself. The color is just stunning.

2

Thursday morning the sun is out, but still bitter cold, when I reach the town house on North Dayton. The light glints off the FOR SALE sign bolted to its iron gate. I took a liking to it as soon as I saw the photos—it's $3.5 million, which is not unreasonable for this neighborhood. Snow still tops the iron sconces like little ice hats, and it's like something out of a fairy tale. *Beauty and the Beast*, maybe. First movie I went to alone. I was ten, and I used a ticket I'd picked up off the lobby floor from an earlier showing. I wanted to be Belle so bad—all those books and all that conviction, and then winning the jackpot with the sweet, rich, perfectly tortured beast. I was disappointed at the end when he turned into an ordinary man.

With a scarf and large black sunglasses hiding my face from the doorbell camera, I open the iron gate and hurry up to the double glass doors. I reach for the lockbox on the doorknob and punch in a few numbers, but the box stays stubbornly locked. There's a peeling sticker with the caretaker's info: *call in case of emergency*. I take off my right glove to use my phone. "Mr. Einhorn?"

"Yes, this is Don, how can I help you?" I figure he's in his fifties, and a smoker, from the gravel in his voice.

"Nice to meet you, Don. I'm Liz from Chicago Luxury Staging. We're staging 301 North Dayton." I worked for them briefly; if a house is on the market for more than three million, chances are,

Chicago Luxury Staging was called. If I'm wrong, he just won't let me in.

"Right, Liz." But I'm right.

"So, I'm at the Dayton Street property now. Final walk-through. It's gorgeous, by the way."

"Oh yeah, the Thacker place. You should see their house in St. Barts—they're there for the winter."

Just as I suspected. This part of Chicago is as nice as it gets, but anyone rich enough to afford living here still leaves for half the year. And I don't blame them. The brutal lake wind makes me shiver in my Burberry peacoat (a gift from the confused Mastro's coatroom attendant), and I want the St. Barts life too. I picture a beach, white sand. Palm trees and a warm breeze, a cocktail in hand.

I need to get out of town soon, and not just because of the weather. The Viceroy has given me a ticking clock on my bill—end of this week—and my loose ends are starting to catch up with me. Besides, I deserve a vacation too. I've played a long game in Chicago and won.

"I can't seem to open the lockbox." I rattle the key inside and finger the buttons at random. "I must have the wrong code. I've tried several times." The caretaker has to look it up, but it only takes him a minute. "Thank you so much," I say, memorizing it easily, then punching in the four numbers to open the box. The key works on the first try.

A huge chandelier hangs from the entryway's high ceiling, catching the sun pouring through the open door, spraying light across a palace of pale gray walls. I wipe dry the soles of my boots on the mat, unwrap my scarf, and toss it onto a post in the entryway.

While I'm unbuttoning my coat, an alert flashes across my screen. Fifty thousand from Mrs. Reed, like clockwork.

I heard from her the morning after the gala, and we agreed to meet for tea at the Peninsula that same afternoon. Someone was eager. In our cushy clandestine corner, I poured her Darjeeling while telling her all about the opportunity she'd be an idiot to pass up. "The seller has no idea what she has," I whispered conspiratorially. "She and Haring were friends in the '80s club scene, and he just gave the piece to her. It's literally in her closet. Can you imagine?"

Mrs. Reed looked aghast. "She should do her homework."

"Better for us that she doesn't." I gave her a wink—too much? Not at all, she was eating this up.

"Indeed," said Mrs. Reed, her eyes sparkling with understanding. I already knew she was familiar with this controversial little corner of the art world—dealers who operate more like stockbrokers, turning huge profits for their investors when they resell pieces at auction. The old guard hates these shameless flippers, who make more money on the art than the artists ever will. But Mrs. Reed is not one of those scrupulous types. She couldn't care less about "cheapening the soul of creativity" so long as she makes some serious money. I've watched her long enough to know this.

"I want in," she said. "How much do you need?"

"I already have a few investors on board, so I'd be looking for a fifty thousand buy-in. If all goes well, we're looking at a 5X profit."

Not everyone would have bitten at this—the Reeds don't need to play the risk for a mere quarter million, but the Reeds enjoy the game. Almost as much as I do.

I smile at my screen now. The funds for the Haring deal have been electronically deposited into my account. It rings like a register, loading my phone with electronic cash, and my heart does a little dance of relief. "Just in time," I say. I've had enough of the cold. And I'm ready for something new.

Through the app, I reply to Mrs. Reed's electronic deposit: Thank you! I'll be in touch as soon as the seller agrees to my offer. She's out of the country until next month. Once it's ours, I'll do the research to make sure we list the piece at the right auction. That's when things get fun!

I wonder how long they'll wait for the Haring that's never coming. How long they'll fight the fraud case to get the money back before deciding it's not worth it. *Oh well, fifty fucking thousand dollars down the drain, what can you do? We sure were wrong about Liz . . .* Don't feel bad—everyone is.

I move from the entryway into the living room. The Thackers' decor reminds me of a luxury hotel lobby—expensive but as inoffensive as possible. "Someone's got a flair for the boring," I say to a photo I pick up off the back of the black baby grand. The Thackers are a family of five: parents—together, in the photo anyway—and three children. As an only child, I always get a kick out of pictures like these. The three kids, stiff in their matching khakis and sweaters, artfully arranged around Mommy and Daddy like dolls in a curio cabinet. I imagine the siblings squabbling right up until the moment when the photographer says, "Smile!" But maybe I'm being unfair. Maybe they get along—or at least take comfort in one another's existence. Safety in numbers, after all. God knows I could have used some backup when I was a kid.

In the photos, the Thacker children grow into teenagers, then adults: family reunions at a lake house, high school sports, holiday portraits on these very stairs . . . The daughter went to Yale, as evidenced by the series of photos of her graduation, all showcasing the same tasseled hat. And the naïve pride of someone winning at life when they started at the finish line. Five years from now she'll be on some Women in Business Panel explaining how she "girl-bossed" her way to the top, and the next class of Yalies will eat it up. Acting as if I really were a home stager, I pull frames off the piano, saving a single tasteful black-and-white family shot taken at a ski resort—Park City or maybe Vail. The rest, I stash in the piano bench, out of sight.

I adjust the angle of the matching club chairs to create a more harmonious balance with the curved-back charcoal sofa and rearrange a few pillows and lamps for flow. No matter where I am, I

instinctively spot the flaws, the mistakes and missed opportunities—
it's a compulsion. But I resist the urge to keep fussing with the
space. It's not why I'm here.

The main bedroom takes up the whole top floor if you include
the gym overlooking the backyard. I can't help myself—I rearrange the pillows on the king-sized bed, then tidy the brushes and
makeup on Mrs. Thacker's vanity, pocket her Klonopin. Her half of
the walk-in closet is all various shades of beige. I laugh thinking
of her on St. Barts, wading in the warm pristine water in the beige
dress she wore to her daughter's graduation.

Mr. Thacker has a little more style. His neatly hung suits range
from almost black to seersucker, with a sea of blues in between. I
straighten his rack of colorful ties, many with funny patterns his
kids probably gave him for Father's Day, rows of golden retrievers
and old-timey cars. I bet he wore them to work to make them happy,
not caring if it looked like Hallmark vomited on him.

While I'm rifling through his sock drawer, my phone rings. *ED
NOBU HOTEL BAR.*

Fuck. I don't want to answer—I'm done with him. But Nobu
Guy—I mean *Ed*—can be relentless, and I've only known him three
weeks. We met while I was scouting the Reeds. What can I say,
I'm a sucker for a hottie with a well-cut suit and a penchant for
negronis—and after a few of them, the word "no" slips out of my
vocabulary . . . while his credit cards slipped out of his pockets.

Shit, is that why he's calling?

I let the call go to voicemail, and, like I knew he would, he instantly calls back.

He's either angry (happened to check his Amex bill off-cycle) or
needy (doesn't like a mistress who won't drop her panties the second he calls). I almost hope it's the former. God, I hate needy. I've
been on that side before, the one dialing over and over, unhinged,
praying for a response.

"Hey there," I say. If I don't pick up now, he'll never stop.

"What are you wearing?" he asks. Not even a *how've you been* first. Jesus.

It sounds like he's in a small space, maybe a bathroom, the way his voice echoes. Gross.

"Something tight." I check out my ass in the Thackers' full-length mirror, round and high in my fitted jeans. So what if I've charged ten grand on his cards so far? He got his paws on this.

Honestly, he had potential before he got desperate. He's rugged at the edges in the right way. And he's a hair-puller. Which I like when it's done well: the sharp tug, the hit of adrenaline. But now Ed—an aspiring crypto-bro in his late forties—is proving himself to be just another guy who thinks a woman's body is a code to be hacked. In bed, it's like he's doing an experiment, trying to get a specific result. *Did you try unplugging it and plugging it back in?* I've only stuck around for this long for the meals—oysters flown in from BC, caviar and crème fraîche . . .

"Fuck. I want you right now," Ed breathes over the phone. "I'll come to you. Tell me where you are, and I'll come," he says without irony. And I'm struck by a bitter hatred of men that goes way beyond Ed. They all just want what they want when they want it.

I hate it.

I can also relate.

"Save it for your wife."

"Wife? What are you talking about?" I hear his breath hitch. *Caught.*

"I'm talking about Pamela. She's probably at Pilates right now." I smile to myself in the mirror. Players are always so shocked when they're played. Especially men.

"What the fuck?" he asks.

I hang up. With any luck, worrying about me showing up at Pamela's workout class will distract him so he won't notice the charges I've made on his Amex: the gala dress, these jeans. Maybe he'll put in a little effort with the wife so she won't start wondering where he's been. He should send her the lame roses he sent me. And take her to Alinea for dinner. See? Move over, Mrs. Reed. I'm the fucking philanthropist.

Still, I can feel the heat behind me, like I always do when it's time to ditch town. For a moment, a wave of bitter irritation washes over me. How many more times will I have to city-hop until I can stop and just . . . rest?

I continue rummaging the Thackers' bedroom drawers until my hand finds what I came here for. Good stuff's always hidden with the socks, especially by men like Mr. Thacker, who would know better if he had watched a single segment of local news in his life. *Priceless family heirloom raided from unsuspecting moron's underwear drawer, aka the most obvious hiding place of all time. Details at eleven.*

I sort through a handful of credit cards, cash, and potentially useful business cards, the stuff you don't take with you to St. Barts because it makes your wallet too fat, the extra cards you forget you have because your wife only signed up for the bonus miles. I peel the top several hundreds from a silver money clip and snatch a card that hasn't even been signed. It's one of my classic low-risk maneuvers. If they're observant enough to notice the charges—everyone has auto-pay nowadays—their only concern will be getting their money back, not tracking down the culprit. That'd be like finding a needle in a haystack. Or having a bike stolen in a big city—it's not as if the cops show up and dust for prints. The bill for this brand-new card won't show up for at least a month, and if the Thackers do catch any fraudulent charges, their bank will just reimburse them. No harm, no foul.

My hands are still in the drawer when a text pings from an unknown number—the first few words make me pause. I stop what I'm doing and read the text again to be certain the words are real:

My name is Isabelle Beresford. Abigail Reed gave me your number. I need to hire someone immediately to manage an art installation in my new house in Punta Mita, Mexico. It won't take long—only a few days. Are you available next week? I know it's very last minute, but Abigail suggested I contact you. Hope you can help!

My heart races, and I glance up, almost expecting a camera to be watching me. Did this Isabelle woman read my mind or what? Punta Mita, Mexico. Never been, but a quick Google tells me it could be just what I need to get away from all this.

But then I think about how much I enjoy this game—the high of sneaking into people's homes, weaving webs of fantasy around easy prey and sucking them clean of a few precious items in the process. It really has become a game: How much can I get? How far I can go?

Abigail Reed: the gift that just keeps on giving.

It wasn't always this good. I was sloppier when I was younger, had full-on Shiny Object Syndrome, no impulse control whatsoever. Now, I like to think I can hold out for the longer play if I put my mind to it. Kid Liz would be proud I've reined in my hasty greed. But I always knew how to spot a mark.

When you've been evicted more than once, when you've had to change school districts a few times, you get practiced at finding that one girl. There's something sympathetic in her smile; she takes you under her wing right away, eager to share her knowledge. Who's got cooties (or, in later years, who's got herpes). Where to sit, who to like, how to swim with the other fish. She's the connector. The key. When I tracked down Abigail Reed at the Melanoma Foundation gala, I had a hunch she would be my way in for this part of Chicago. And sure enough, she just keeps serving me up opportunities.

A wave of electricity pulses through me once more as I reread the text from Mrs. Reed's friend for the third time. *Isabelle Beresford*. I want to celebrate. I should have gotten Jason's number, because I'd love to pop open a bottle of champagne and have a proper romp right here on the Thackers' bed. I feel giddy, like a teenager. *Thank you, Abigail Reed.* This opportunity in Punta Mita is exactly what I need. The last time I managed a tropical vacay—Bahamas, nice enough resort—was on the arm of a cute cardiologist. We met at a club the night before his annual conference, and he brought me along as his plus-one for the full six days. It was a decent little getaway, but for a cardiologist, he was light on the cardio behind closed doors.

This will be different.

A real retreat. An opportunity to detox a little from the fast pace of this life.

Trying to contain my excitement, I reply to Isabelle Beresford: I'd be happy to manage your art installation. My schedule is pretty tight, but I could move some things around. Anything for a friend of Abigail's. Before I hit send, I hear a sound coming from the foyer. *Shit.* Did I forget to lock the door behind me? Or could this be the actual Sotheby's Realtor coming to check on the house? I remove my boots and scurry sock-footed to the back staircase, which, I'm guessing from the style of house, will lead down to the kitchen. The servants' stairs, though they'd never call them that now. I perch on a step halfway down and listen as someone crosses from the entryway toward the main stairs. Must be the Realtor, a woman clacking across the polished wood in heels.

I slide silently up a few steps pressing my back to the wall. Any Realtor worth a damn will insist on taking the main staircase first. The knob turns and the door cracks, letting in a sharp sliver of light. Thankfully, the Realtor is worth a damn. As soon as I hear her hit the main staircase, I sprint through the kitchen and out the front door.

It's only after I've hurried down the street that I remember my scarf is still hanging in the Thackers' entryway. *Amateur move, Liz.* But who cares? This time next week, I'll be in Mexico.

3

"One more before we land?" the flight attendant offers me a final champagne.

"Thank you." It's only prosecco, but it tastes almost as good as the real thing while I drink the final first-class sips. The plane descends through a cloud, and it's like we're suspended there, motionless. But then the Pacific reappears, closer now, bluer, and striped with incoming bands of waves. "Cheers," I say to my ghostlike window reflection, barely there, like an etching, just the lines.

My cheekbones look sharper than ever. I'll never forget when my tenth-grade English teacher, Mr. Stafford, told me on the first day of sophomore year I looked good, "different." *I see you've lost the "baby fat."* Code for *you're old enough to fuck.*

Through the plastic window, my reflection dissolves into sunlight as I watch Puerto Vallarta appear, the beach resorts and hotels, the jungle beyond. I've never been to Mexico, and only know what I learned about Punta Mita on the internet: the gated peninsula is a private enclave for the super-rich.

It's been exactly three days since the text from Isabelle Beresford arrived. After my little visit to the Thackers', I returned to the Viceroy, where my welcome was about to run out—my card had been declined again, and they gave me three days to settle up or scram—and confirmed with Isabelle:

Yes, I can depart on Sunday, February 22nd. I'm glad Abigail connected us, and I'm happy I can help.

Isabelle told me that she and her husband, Oliver, closed on their new vacation home at the end of December. Over the past six weeks, Oliver has been down to Mexico a few times to oversee some renovations, but Isabelle herself hasn't even been down there yet—too busy with the holiday rush and her duties on the philanthropy circuit. *Must be nice to be so fucking loaded*, I thought to myself, reading her texts. After all, only the most obscenely wealthy would drop millions on a Mexican villa sight unseen, and at the tail end of peak season.

In fact, the Beresfords are apparently so nonchalant about their new oceanfront mansion that instead of soaking up the last of resort season in Punta Mita, Isabelle and Oliver are headed to Bali this week. To some bougie wellness resort that doesn't allow phones. She said they needed to unwind, but it sounded more like "rekindle" to me. She bought him a Rufino Tamayo oil painting as a birthday gift, something Mexican for the house. The painting needs to be hung, and the decorator has already left. Isabelle hasn't hired a staff and doesn't know anyone there yet. She wants to surprise him with the artwork. Romantic, I thought. Or desperate.

I'd need to be there to accept the delivery, then hang the painting on the one wall without windows in the living room. I promised I'd know the right height, which is trickier than you think. It was my almost-degree in art history that gave me a real breadth of knowledge, but it was a twenty-four-year-old interior design boyfriend who taught me years ago how to use a tape measure and my eye. She's lucky I know what I'm doing, because it sounds like she's so rushed, she'd hire anyone Mrs. Reed vouched for.

You're a Godsend, she texted when I agreed. I want everything to be perfect when Oliver and I first walk through the door after Bali. Do you have a middle initial? I'm booking your ticket now.

Thank you for asking, I replied.

Fuck me. I'd need to give up my real name to get on a plane. I didn't have a choice. Can you please book under "Elizabeth Dawson"? That's the legal name on my passport. There. Simple, vague. Let her think "Hastings" is my married name or something—as opposed to one of many fake last names I use on business cards for a few months before moving on to another alias.

No prob—will do!

A first-class boarding pass arrived via email within the hour. And the code to the house, which she said was finished; I could stay in whichever guest room I liked—I'll have the place to myself. Isabelle booked my return ticket for the following Sunday, in case the painting gets delayed. Which gives me an entire week to bliss out on the Beresfords' dime.

Of course, I immediately wanted to know everything I could about Isabelle—I'm nothing if not thorough—but even my best go-to sources on the internet didn't yield much on the couple. From what little I did find, I knew they were loaded; they spent most of their time in a stately home in Connecticut, or their chalet in Switzerland, occasionally the mansion in Newport or the Manhattan penthouse. That is, when not traveling. They donated to several museums and charities around the world, but nothing like the impressive global reach of families like the Reeds, who go back generations. No kids. Very little evidence of family whatsoever, in fact. There was a short wedding announcement too, but no pictures. They eloped to Niagara Falls, of all places, which turns out used to be a thing. Only people I've known that eloped were either poor or knocked up. I found no pictures of the ceremony, though, no proud in-laws posing with the happy couple, no cousins, no cute nieces and nephews running around in crisp child-sized dresses and suits.

Connecticut, Switzerland, Newport, New York, Mexico, yet they still needed to pay to go to a resort in Bali.

Because no matter who you are and how rich you get, everyone needs to reset. They've got something they want to change, or wish they could leave behind; a dream to manifest, or a past they're running from.

I did find one oldish-looking image of Oliver on a sailboat with a man who could be his brother—same jutting chin, same dark hair, though the other man's was more tousled and unkempt. LinkedIn told me Oliver was a venture capitalist with his own firm (aka money-making machine) called Beresford Capital. He went to Yale and Wharton. (Snore.)

But Isabelle was harder to pin down. All the Isabelle Caldwells (her maiden name) I found were too young or too old or too trashy to have eloped with a Beresford. Finally, after social media stalking everyone in their orbit, I found what must be Isabelle's Instagram. But the obnoxiously coy handle—@IForIsabelle—and the grid of vague but appealing shots made it hard to tell for sure. In one post, a brunette in a blue gown stood between two old men at a gala in Telluride. She wore frameless glasses, but half of her face was obscured by a raised glass of red wine. In another, a pair of long bronzed legs extended on a chaise longue in Positano. I paused on a dramatic shot of two catlike eyes reflected in a handheld compact mirror, then on one of the back of her head, her hair pulled into a short ponytail while she beat a boxing bag, with the caption: don't mess with us—women are strong. Clearly, she got off on being secretive and enigmatic, but she wanted the attention too. Like celebrities who won't allow their babies to be photographed, then post forty-five fucking pics a day of the little moneymakers, just with cheesy emojis plastered over their faces. But still, something about Isabelle Beresford struck me, like when you hear a few notes of a song you recognize but can't name.

I zoomed in on the picture of Isabelle in Aspen, so her face filled my laptop screen. We could be related; both of us with dark brown hair and practically the same eye color—hers perhaps a bit greener and mine more hazel. Her face shape's a little pointier, but we're definitely the same type. Judging from her style—that ultrasophisticated haircut (love!), the modest shape of her dress (meh)—she was probably a bit older than me. Face it, with that kind of money, she'd always be thirty-five. I scrolled through more posts: gallery openings and snowy glades and martinis in glamorous bars . . . Her life seemed so perfect, I wanted to hate her. I wanted to *be* her. And I wanted to be her best friend, the person she told all her secrets.

I showed her haircut to the guy at the salon. Hard not to be inspired by it, by her.

"That look's gonna be high-maintenance," he said.

"Exactly."

• • •

"Welcome to paradise," the pilot says over the intercom. And the bridal party behind us in coach—a bunch of women my age who are acting like they're still living in the sorority house they moved out of a decade ago—cheer.

Paradise, indeed, I think to myself. *This first-class seat, this sunshine, this fabulous Zimmermann sundress and Chanel espadrilles . . .*

"I love your whole look. You could go straight to the beach. Or, like, a fab cocktail party," the woman beside me says. Her name is Nance, and she's a mother of four from Evanston meeting her college pals for a week of drinking (and no doubt more). During the flight, our attendant kept pouring, and Nance kept talking. I suffered through her rambling about her shitty husband and her "wonderful" children, who, from the sound of it, have driven her to this moment: drunk with a stranger, venting too much truth. When she was in the bathroom, I should have swiped the Tiffany tennis bracelet ($46K) she thinks she's hidden in her purse, but I'm trying to make this a vacation.

"I'm headed to Punta Mita. We're staying at the Four Seasons," she says like that is a very big deal. "What about you?"

"Also Punta Mita. I'm decorating a villa."

"Wow!" She clutches her left breast. "I'm so impressed. Do you have a card?"

"Sure." I reach into the Row tote I acquired from a cubby at hot yoga and hand her the same card I gave Mrs. Reed. This time, "consultant" means interior decorator to the rich and famous.

"We should share a ride. My husband ordered a driver." She leans close and whispers, "He's such a worrier. Thinks if I leave the country alone, I'll get kidnapped."

"You do have to be careful," I say. Maybe don't bring a diamond tennis bracelet that screams *I want people to know I have money!* The pocket with her wallet isn't even zipped. It's a miracle she made it through O'Hare without it getting pinched. "I'm all set, thanks. My client provided transportation."

"I'm always telling my oldest daughter to pursue interior design—decorators have the best lives," Nance says while everyone rushes to gather their things as if the flight might take off again with them still on board if they don't hurry. "How long are you staying? I bet it's a big job."

"A week."

Isabelle said six days. Perfect amount of time to relax, make some cash, and maybe pick up a few leads.

"Lucky you."

It's not luck, Nance. Not everyone can do what I do. But I smile and nod.

We're in the airport now, filing down the endless hall toward customs. Ads for new condo complexes flash on the walls—YOU CAN LIVE HERE!—targeting everyone who wants to escape. When we reach the front of the line, I let Nance go first.

I've had my share of stressful moments at customs, lying to

uniformed officers about everything from how much cash I have, to the packed treasures I've neglected to declare. And there's always the fear that someone like Abigail Reed is smarter than she looks and has alerted the authorities. It's this underbelly of my lifestyle that gets to be a drag. The constant lurking anxiety of the clock running out on me.

While Nance practices her Español and the stout Mexican woman stamps her passport, I remind myself I'm here on business. There's nothing smuggled in my bag. The officer in lane eleven waves me over, and I stride to his station with my shoulders and facial muscles relaxed, channeling my best inner calm. Nothing to worry about here.

"Elizabeth Dawson?" the customs agent peers across his desk. My passport is six years old. The Liz in the picture was headed to Thailand with a biker maniac—it wasn't my finest hour. But the customs agent has seen it all before.

"Welcome to Puerto Vallarta," he says and waves me through. I'm safe.

Outside of baggage claim, I spot Nance with a uniformed driver holding a placard bearing her name, and a suitcase big enough for her whole family of six.

"Come to the Four Seasons for a drink—you have to meet my friends," Nance says while we're jostled outside in a stream of tourists and hustlers, grinning vendors offering tequila and *cerveza*.

"Of course. I'd love that. If I'm not too swamped."

"They'll all want to hire you!" she says. I see five-bedroom colonials on the lake, sprawling apartments on the Gold Coast, Nantucket summer homes . . . maybe, even, the potential of going legit for good. Is it too much to think it's possible?

We air-kiss. "*Hasta luego*," we both say. I wave as her town car pulls away.

"Miss Elizabeth Dawson?"

I turn to find a driver holding a sign with my name on it. For a second, I think of my dad. Imagine what he'd make of a first-class flight, a tropical vacation. I haven't even met Isabelle Beresford, but she's trusting me with her house, and a painting that must be worth over $200K. This is what winning looks like. Would he be proud? Or suspicious? Chuck Dawson, Follower of Rules, worked construction his whole life thinking it would pay off, but all it got him was two shot knees, a bad back, and social security that barely covers a monthly supply of Bud and Wonder bread. I couldn't get out of that life fast enough. He signed my scholarship applications, and I never looked back.

From the back of a black SUV, I watch as we drive past Puerto Vallarta's large resorts, gas stations, and strip malls. Thirty minutes later, the driver pulls into a gated drive through a dense green wall of waxy ferns, bushes, and trees. This is Punta Mita—the entire private peninsula that houses the Four Seasons, the St. Regis, and a handful of exclusive residential communities. He lowers his window to greet the guard he obviously knows. I took five years of Spanish, but they're speaking too quickly for me to understand anything except ISABELLE BERESFORD, KUPURI ESTATES.

"Esmerelda," he says. And we're in.

Cue the music because right away, it's like I'm on a movie set. Outside the gates, palm trees grow wild, busting upward at off-kilter angles through shrubs and strangling vines. But in Punta Mita, they're all erect and expertly placed. Wilderness tamed. We round a cobblestone circle filled with rows of precision palms, then circle roundabouts onto the peninsula that lead to immaculate roads where couples and tanned families drive golf carts. We pass a number of signs for residential communities, following the one that points us to Kupuri Estates. A golf course appears, dotted with quartets of unfuckable golfers in plaid pants and pink skirts. Joggers enjoy a dedicated path. The metronomic rhythm slows my pulse.

There's a second, separate guard shack at the entrance to Kupuri Estates. The driver easily talks his way past this one too. *Hola, hola, hola.* I like not having to sneak in for once. It's a good thing too, because while I know how to have my way with a Four Seasons, this place is unusually secure. We roll to a stop.

"Casa Esmerelda," the driver says, like he wants me to be impressed.

I exit the car and crunch across the gravel circular drive toward the front door, fluffing up my new Isabelle-inspired haircut. One thing I know about beach houses is that the real front is the side that faces the ocean. Even so, the jungle side of the house blows my mind. It's bone white, and modern—all rectangles and squares. Better than the photos, which doesn't happen often.

I approach the large wooden front door, repeating the code I memorized from Isabelle's text. I'm already sweating but can't tell if that's because the driver's watching me, waiting for me to prove I'm legit—or because it's ninety degrees. I enter the numbers, and the light flashes green. Then the lock clicks open with a stutter. I smile at the driver, turn the knob, and step inside.

4

When I was in elementary school, I had a recurring nightmare. A girl in my class had told us all the gory tale of an old man who lived down the block from her. His wife had gone missing a bunch of years earlier and when he died, they found her body buried in the basement wall behind the boiler, hacked up. I became terrified of the boiler in *our* basement. In the nightmare, I would find myself trapped down there, screaming for help, but no one was home. I'd stare at the boiler, which had a huge red dial on it, and I'd watch the temperature rise—up and up and up until I couldn't breathe. I'd wake up panting, covered in sweat.

Eventually, I stopped having that dream, but to this day, humid, dark places make my throat constrict, and that childhood scream rises within me. It's hot inside Casa Esmerelda—too hot, and too dark. I fumble and search for the AC control. Thankfully, it's easy to find. I blast it, punching the arrow lower and lower, then hit the switch next to it that opens the blinds. As the blinds rise, the mansion swells with a soft, buttery shade of sunshine I've never seen; it reflects off the pool, casting ripples of light through the giant open space.

The house is bigger than I imagined and keeps growing while I wander from room to room, each opening to either the Pacific or the jungle; many to both. It's insane. Earthy walls and floors show off the fixtures and bright modern patterns—aqua cushions and pillows on the living room sofa, bar stools upholstered in light blue. I open a few drawers at random—everything's in its place: silverware in the kitchen, cleaning products in the bathroom. I feel like I've slipped into a turned-down bed, all fresh and inviting and waiting just for me . . . but there's something unsettling about it too. Like the house is holding its breath, waiting for its true owners to arrive. It has cooled down, and I've opened a few doors so there's a fresh breeze clearing out that stale air, but there's still something creepy. Like those pictures you see of Pompeii—everything frozen in time.

A fluttering of ghostly white in the entryway startles me, but it's only a dustcover I didn't notice when it was still too dark and too hot. I remove it to find a striking bronze sculpture of a girl with a slab of long hair, a flat book pressed between her overlapped hands. She looks away, over her shoulder, as if she can see the past . . . It's familiar to me. Maybe I saw it in a Bonhams catalog. Or maybe it was featured in the one modern art course I took in college before I had to drop out. Either way, I'm transfixed, studying the soft curves of the figure—so smooth it almost looks like mahogany. Must have taken the sculptor forever to complete, but she appears to be of a moment's making, like the artist turned a real girl to bronze with a wave of a magic wand. It takes a certain eye to appreciate that kind of studied effortlessness. The empty crate beside the sculpture is addressed to Isabelle, not Oliver—so it was her purchase, not his. Every detail I learn about this woman makes me like her more.

Down an open-air hall, I reach what must be Isabelle and Oliver's room, where Net-a-Porter boxes stand stacked alongside moving boxes labeled *Lot 22 Esmerelda/Primary Bedroom*. Art will be needed in this room too. I make a mental note, something to pitch, maybe even a way to extend my trip. But, except for the boxes, everything else is in place. She told me to stay in one of the guest rooms, but this suite opens onto the back patio, which overlooks the pool and the Pacific. I slide open the glass doors and listen to the crashing waves and the buzzing jungle—insects and birds chattering away. An intoxicating scent hits me, and I throw myself onto the bed, making myself at home. What Isabelle doesn't know won't hurt her.

I open one of the moving boxes with a metal nail file I find in the nightstand drawer. Inside, are several framed black-and-white photographs: Oliver sailing, Oliver skiing with a bunch of bros. There's one from what must be their wedding—just the two of them dwarfed by the falls. It's backlit, and her sweet little veil is blowing across her face in the spray—all I can see is her smile. In the only other shot of her in the batch, she's shopping at what looks like a Moroccan bazaar. Wearing a wide hat, sunglasses, and a caftan, she could be anyone. She could be me.

I open the first Net-a-Porter box and select an orange Eres bikini from the pile of bathing suits inside. It's a perfect fit, and the pool is calling. Isabelle can claim it wasn't in the box when she finds it missing. That always works for me. And honestly, this suit looks too good on me to give it back.

When I reach the edge of the pool, the salty wind hits, and my hair flies behind me like a flag at full mast. How, I wonder, could Bali be better than this house? What the fuck is so wrong with their marriage that only the beaches of Indonesia, but not the beaches of Mexico, can fix it? They look in love in that wedding picture . . . Did all this money drive them apart?

I start for the deep end, ready to dive in, but before I touch the water, my phone pings with a text from a Connecticut number.

It's Isabelle's assistant, sending me over the tracking information for the painting, which is due to arrive tomorrow afternoon. She includes this little bit of advice:

Also, a Club Punta Mita concierge dropped off membership cards.

He said he left them in the golf cart. They're linked to the company Visa. Isabelle said to tell you to use the beach clubs, go to dinner or whatever. She won't care how much you spend, so enjoy yourself—I always do.

I shoot the assistant a Thanks! with a winky face, then dive into the pool. The water soothes me as I soar through the silence, bathing suit clinging to my skin, then emerge from the shallow end like I'm in a perfume ad—a woman with everything.

Lying on a lounge chair, staring out at the glassy waves, I'm overwhelmed by a sense of calm I've never felt. It's like someone turned off a high-pitched noise I'd grown to live with, and its absence allows me to hear the quietness of peace. The stifled reaction I had when I entered has blown away. This place is the opposite of my childhood nightmare. It's a fucking dream. And it's all mine for the next six days.

I could get used to this. I could really slow down here. Hide out from the world. Read some self-help books on the beach. Try to turn myself into one of those people who *live, laugh, love* or whatever. It's cheesy, but it's also exactly what I need right now. Maybe I could even meet a guy here. A hot tattooed chef to feed me *sopes* and talk to me about art while he rubs suntan lotion down my back. The fantasy of it all makes me want to cry a little with relief.

But voices catch my hazy attention. There's landscaping for privacy around the pool, but not enough to block the view—and I can see them when I crane: three women about my age strut north on the beach, toward Esmerelda, chatting and laughing, sandals dangling from their fingers—a statuesque Black woman, a petite blonde, and a willowy redhead. It's six p.m., the sun's starting to fall. They're probably headed to the Kupuri Beach Club. I watch as they pass by, walking the beach like it's their private backyard.

I could lie out here all night, but eventually, hunger forces me inside in search of something to eat. The bar is conveniently stocked, but no groceries. Luckily, along with the membership cards, the concierge dropped off a copy of *Punta Mita Living* magazine, which has the delivery menus. While I wait for my food, I slip into Isabelle's new loungewear set. (The cashmere is to die for. She'll have to report this missing to Net-a-Porter too.)

I collect my fresh ceviche from the delivery guy, grab the bottle of Siete Leguas Siete Décadas Blanco, and pad back out onto the patio. A flick of a switch and the whole place is cast in soft light. Wicker lanterns hang from the branches of a low-tree barrier between Esmerelda and the beach, the pool glows an eerie, electric blue.

The ceviche is divine, and the flowery tequila melts my whole body. I wonder if Nance is balling out too. Did she take off her wedding ring? Is she four cocktails in? I imagine her postfuck at the Four Seasons, satisfied for the first time in years. I wonder what name she used.

My phone pings with a Nextdoor alert: the Thackers have filed a police report after noticing some valuables missing from their home on Dayton Street. *Shit.* That was fast. Usually, with people like the Thackers, you have at least a couple weeks before they realize, if they ever do. That's the curse of having so much—takes a minute to notice when something's gone. It's why I was bold enough to steal that ruby ring right off Mrs. Reed's hand at the gala. After all that champagne, no way she'd feel her finger's nakedness right away. Probably wouldn't even realize the ring was gone until the next time she went to wear that ochre dress. No such luck with the inconveniently observant Thackers. They must have clocked the scarf I left behind the minute they walked in. *Damn it, Liz.*

I hear laughter again on the beach and tuck my phone—along with any fleeting concern about the Thackers—away. It's the women I saw earlier, returning home from the club, drunk now, and loud. I watch their silhouettes in the rising moonlight. I think of their jewelry, their wallets, their bank accounts, their husbands . . .

No, Liz. Stop.

They pause at my lantern trees and point up at Esmerelda.

"Someone's home," one of them says.

"Beresford . . ." floats up the beach steps. I hear feet on the stairs, and almost duck, but they wouldn't enter a private property uninvited.

Only people like me do shit like that. Not people who live here. Not people like Isabelle.

• • •

I wake up early the next morning, alert and focused. Usually, I'm immediately on the hunt for a new mark, but now I'm looking for something else. A sign. More opportunities to go legit? Maybe. A side piece to enjoy while I'm here? Probably.

What can I say. I'm never able to relax for long without seeking something.

But I try to tell myself that the only thing I'm seeking here in this beautiful place is fun.

You can still have fun without digging another hole, Liz, can't you?

"*Hola*," I say to the man at the desk of the Kupuri Beach Club, as I hand over the membership card. According to the Punta Mita magazine, there are several other equally stunning private-access-only clubs scattered across the peninsula, but the Kupuri Beach Club is the only one that faces the tranquil Litibú Beach—and it's walking distance from Esmerelda. While his fingers scatter across the keyboard, I take in the view: Sun blasts the ocean turning the waves bright cyan when they break on the sand. An array of umbrellas the same color as the sand, shade chaises beneath. There's a boutique to one side, and in the center of it all, a thatched-roof bar. A long swimming pool flows under a pair of footbridges. *Damn.*

"Welcome to Kupuri, Señora Beresford," the man at the front desk says, handing me back the card.

"Oh no, I'm . . ." I cut myself off. *No cons while here, Liz.*

But . . . what does it matter to this desk clerk whether I'm Isabelle or her guest? In fact, being Isabelle Beresford for a few hours this morning will probably open more doors than being Liz, the hired help. "Gracias," I say, my spine automatically straightening a bit. I tuck a strand of hair behind my ears—my new blunt bob inspired by Isabelle herself—to get into character. I think of her smile in the wedding photo at Niagara Falls and mirror mine to match—soft, genuine, though still a little enigmatic.

Getting into places like this is easier than most people think—anyone can slip past the bouncer, or fake being a hotel guest when really you're parked down the road. What's hard is knowing what to do once you're in.

My mother pulled tricks like that all the time when I was growing up. I remember going to Veterans Stadium for the first time when I was eight. My dad was content to just sit in the bleachers, but not Mom. She bought us the cheap tickets to get through the door, then marched me down to sit behind home plate. She scrambled down so quickly, it was hard for me to keep up. She grabbed a pair of seats that were still empty at the top of the third. "Go on," she ordered. "Sit." That's when I knew there were two different worlds. My mom said all we had to do was get past the usher, but she was wrong, and I knew it the minute her ass hit the seat. These front-row fans were wearing the same Phillies shirts we were wearing, but there was something different about the way they carried themselves. Crisp and polished—like each T-shirt was tailored to fit its wearer. My mom had plenty of confidence, but that day, trying not to get caught, I noticed for the first time all the ways she was rough around the edges. Her shirt was too tight and low-cut. Her red hair—which she dyed herself—had two inches of dark roots showing. I smoothed my braids, sat upright, and mimicked the cheers of these top-dollar fans, while my mom whistled at the players, two fingers from each hand shoved in her mouth. I'll never forget the way the kids my age watched us get kicked back to the nosebleeders. "Trash," a boy said.

The next time we went, I dressed us both. I even did her makeup, copied an ad I'd cut out of a magazine. She really was striking—and without all that blue eye shadow and hot-pink blush, people watched her a whole different way. I was only eight, but I could see the difference. A few minor tweaks, and my mom had class. After the second inning that day, she spotted the best vacant seats. "Let's do this," she said. I descended the sticky steps behind her with the entitlement of the brat who'd called me trash. I was him.

We were never kicked out again. Once I was in charge, we were safe.

On my way down to the beach at Kupuri, I channel that same energy. I'm a wealthy philanthropist who has the taste—and the budget—to fill my home with exquisite art. I pass two women with yoga mats (and yoga bodies), who give me a subtle chin nod of acknowledgment. I am one of them. I am Isabelle. An attendant covers a lounge chair with a towel for me at the edge of the residents-only section. I stretch out in the morning sun, and oh God, it feels good.

It seems like only one second has passed when the waiter returns with my cappuccino and the Wi-Fi login code. A young man passes with a board under his arm and the broad shoulders of a real surfer. "Morning," he says, while we check each other out. Millionaire Surfer might be my new type. I watch him walk down to the water, then paddle out into the shimmering waves. A nanny leads three kids with bright plastic buckets and shovels across the dune, and I think about the coexisting worlds again. The invisible line in the literal sand.

"We haven't met," says a woman sitting a few feet from me,

coffee in hand. "I'm Julia." She sets her coffee on the little table and lathers sunscreen all over her freckled skin. She's the redhead I saw yesterday on the beach.

"Nice to meet you, Julia. I'm Isabelle Beresford." The name rolls off my tongue easily, smooth and rich like melted dark chocolate. What's the harm? "I arrived yesterday."

"Is that you, in Casa Esmerelda?" she asks, and I nod. "Your house is spectacular. I've been dying to meet you. Dying!" I slip into my sandals, but she keeps talking. "This might be presumptuous of me, but my housekeeper's sister is looking for a new position. I don't know if you've hired a staff yet, but she runs a whole team, including a cook. And Martina's so nice. You'll love her."

I shield the sun from my eyes with my hand. I drink my last cappuccino sip.

"At least meet her," Julia says. "I can vouch for her. One hundred percent."

"Of course," I reply with ease. "Tell her to come by." Obviously, I have no intention of retaining a staff. Once I get the painting installed, it's only a matter of days before Isabelle and Oliver arrive, and I need to fly the nest. But that's still enough time to make a new friend . . .

"Yay!" she says, like the Midwestern cheerleader I'm certain she was. "There's a party here on Thursday night," she adds with that same *rah-rah* voice. "You have to come and meet everyone."

Bingo. Luckily, my flight out of town isn't until Sunday morning. I'm sure Isabelle won't mind me borrowing her name for a few more days . . .

"I wouldn't miss it."

And how could I turn down that smile? Julia's beaming, so thrilled to have made a new friend. She reminds me of the girls at St. Catherine's Junior High, the school my dad briefly sent me to the year my mom left, believing a bunch of preteen girls and nuns would help fill the female-role-model gap she left behind. I was just starting to master the skill I would later hone—how to fit in while still managing to stand out. The girls at St. Catherine's were desperate for me to join their cliques. They wanted me like I was that perfect accessory that completed their ensemble and made their whole look cool: distressed Frye boots or a vintage Chanel clutch. But I never was a joiner—it was always easier to float between them, easier to maintain that air of power they so coveted, and never get close enough to get hurt.

• • •

Julia must have Martina on speed dial, because the woman arrives at Esmerelda about five minutes after I get home from the beach club. "Señora Beresford?" she asks when I answer the door.

"*Sí*. You must be Martina."

That's as far as we get before the FedEx truck pulls into the drive. Martina jumps in to help me carry the large wooden crate inside, hustling like if she does this right, I'll hire her on the spot.

"I need to speak to my husband before I make any decisions," I tell her when we pry off the lid.

The wire is already installed on the large, colorful Tamayo, which is intensely Impressionistic—swirls of purples, golds, and reds—but it's still clearly a portrait of two blurred women who sort of smear into each other, and they're standing, so thankfully I know which way it's meant to be hung. Martina helps me measure out the center of the wall and hammer in the hangers that came taped to the inside of the crate. It's no easy task, and I'm thankful for her help.

"It's perfect," I say when we're done. "*Muchas gracias.* I will call you soon," I lie.

I open my phone to enter her number to complete the ruse and find three missed calls and a voicemail. For the moment, I ignore them, and after I've added Martina's number, I fire off a quick text to Isabelle's assistant with a photo of the painting.

Wow, she replies, seconds after the image is sent.

I know. Isabelle has amazing taste.

She does. I'll let her know it's all set. If I can reach her—she's way off the grid!

As I'm saying goodbye to Martina, my phone rings again, and I send it to voicemail. My pulse quickens, and the hair on the back of my neck pricks up—something isn't right. Once I'm alone, I take a deep breath and press play on the first message:

"Hello, Liz?" It's the voice of a woman. Refined, but needy, and on edge. "This is Abigail Reed. My son Alan would like more information about the painting. He'd like to touch base. He's interested in buying the painting for himself. Can your contact send us photos? Please get back to me ASAP. He's eager."

Settle down, Mom. I told you it could be eight weeks. And no, precious Alan can't just bogart the deal. It's not even real, so there *are* no photos, but I'm still rankled by his presumptuous arrogance—thinking he can snap up the painting directly. I bet he'd offer me half of what it's worth. I bet he thinks he deserves some kind of inside deal. *Think again, Red.*

All the other messages are from the same number . . . "Eager" is right. At least, I hope it's just Alan's eagerness to snag the Haring for himself that's causing his mother to phone me four times in a row. Obnoxious, greedy, wannabe art moguls I can deal with. But if *suspicion* is what's actually driving the Reeds' incessant calls, then I'm in trouble—*more* trouble. Because I'm already in deep shit with the Thackers filing their police report. The Viceroy hounding me for unpaid bills . . . Chicago had been a reliable home base for close to a year—a pretty long run, for me—but now it seems to be imploding with rapid speed.

This happened to me in Los Angeles, but I got out just in time. I hid in Tucson for a few months, then crossed the border into Canada. I wasn't too worried about the couple I'd conned in LA tracking my passport; like a lot of rich people, they were too shady themselves to call in the feds. Big-money crime. Government shit. Their son was arrested while I bartended in Whistler (tourist destinations are good places to disappear), and the couple gave up on the bling I'd swiped ($100K). I was the least of their worries by then.

I make myself a tequila soda to settle my nerves and step out onto the patio, collapsing into a lounge chair and letting the beating sun drive out the chill that's crept into my bones.

When I was hiding out in Whistler, a middle-aged man (whose watch I later pawned for $5K) asked me what I would do if I won the lottery.

"Take a nap," I said. I'd been lying all night, but that was the truth. I'd be done with this racket, over the finish line. I know I can't hide in the shade of this striped canvas umbrella forever. But for just this moment, I allow myself to feel safe. I still have a few days to enjoy this. No one will find me here. No one even knows I'm Liz here. They think I'm *her*.

Thank God for you, Isabelle Beresford.

5

With my back to the full-length mirror, I tie the strings at the bottom of my open-backed dress. It's Thursday evening, only four full days since I arrived in Mexico, but I marvel at my own transformation. I have a distinct glow and zero tan lines thanks to sunbathing topless by the pool. I look like someone without a care in the world.

Of course, that's not the case.

I haven't turned my phone back on since yesterday—I've been avoiding the obnoxious Reeds. I don't love that Abigail has gotten her son involved. Added complications are never a good thing, and I need to tread carefully. Families like the Reeds have their own ways of seeking justice. A wealthy family's fixer can be more of a threat than a seasoned cop.

But tonight I'm determined to put that out of my mind. To enjoy being Isabelle again for a few hours at the Punta Mita residents' party and to start formulating my next plan. Obviously, I can't go back to Chicago. And I'd rather avoid stolen credit cards now. Thankfully, I pulled that cash from the Thackers. That, plus some leftovers from Ed, should be enough to go anywhere.

I wish I could just stay here, though. But it's too late. I've already sown the seeds of a false identity. Sometimes, I feel like I've conned myself—out of what I really want, what I really need.

Mrs. Reed's ruby ring fits a little tight on my ring finger, but I think a ruby wedding ring suits Isabelle—classy, unusual, rare . . . The dress—another Net-a-Porter find—perfectly clutches my curves and shows off my bare skin. I feel alive—ready to find my next opportunity.

I turn toward the mirror till the slit opens and jut out my newly tanned leg, but not far enough to expose my scar. Isabelle sprang for the whole outfit, so the sandals (which probably cost more than my flight), match the dress. So does the clutch. Before I leave, I sit at Isabelle's vanity to touch up my makeup with the lipstick and mascara I packed. Inside the vanity drawer, I find an antique silver brush-and-mirror set. Isabelle must have bought the collection in an antique store, because the initials STW are engraved across the back of the oval hand mirror, in curlicued cursive amidst the etched flower vines. I sit for a moment on the upholstered stool, smoothing my hair with her brush. Then I pick up the mirror for a back-side view, and my image repeats infinitely, endless Isabelles about to be introduced to Punta Mita society, my tropical coming-out.

Poor Izzy is going to be massively confused when she arrives here to greetings of familiarity from everyone at the club, but hey, there are worse problems to have, like your private jet not being stocked with your fave caviar. And I'll be long gone by then.

I walk to the club on the beach while the sun burns an inch above the taut horizon, spilling orange-and-purple light across the rippling water. It's a gorgeous view, and I swear I can feel my blood pressure drop a few points just by taking it in. I try to never get too attached to any particular place, but I'll be sad to leave this little slice of paradise when my week is up. Only a few more days to go. And I'm going to savor the hell out of them.

Soon, I reach the beach club, and when I arrive, a small jazz band with a xylophone and a voluptuous lead singer accompanies my entrance. Julia and her posse, hovering around a firepit, look up when they see me. The blonde tilts her head like I'm a threat.

I walk toward them, cool and slow, letting the breeze rustle my dress and hair while they pretend not to watch. Part of me is so tempted to play this room like I usually would.

Here's how it works: You start small—Julia wouldn't be the entree; she's not even the appetizer, just the amuse bouche. You get into a group and that's when you figure out who the actual leader is. This person will be your biggest challenge, but if you win them over, you gain access to everyone. Once you've conquered the group, you use that position to make the rest of the social sphere come to you. It's simpler than geometry—and a hell of a lot more useful. Honestly, *this* is what they should be teaching kids in high school.

"Isabelle!" Julia leans in for an air-kiss when I'm near enough. Her multicolored dress is tiered like a cake, but she's so tall and thin, she pulls it off. "Everyone, this is Isabelle Beresford."

"I've met your husband—Oliver?" the blonde says.

"That's Palmer Kelly," Julia says. Palmer's clearly the enforcer in their gang. Her blue eyes narrow, her lips tighten, and smokers' lines appear on her otherwise wrinkle-free skin. *Careful, your face might stay that way.*

Aimee completes the trio. She's French Caribbean, and with the flickering glow of the fire illuminating her high cheekbones, she's the most beautiful. She offers me her delicate hand. She's the quietest of the three too, but I sense right away from how the other two watch her that she's the one who sets the tone.

"Yes." I meet Palmer's gaze and hold it. "Oliver's been popping down here to keep an eye on the renovations." I wonder if this woman is in love with Oliver, and jealous of me—or rather, Isabelle. Maybe she's just a bitch. "May I join you?" I'm not about to let her severe ponytail scare me away. Julia nudges Palmer to make room.

"We've all spotted Oliver here and around town this winter, but we've been eager to meet *you*." Julia's words slide between Palmer and me like a referee. "We hope you love the Kupuri." She's wearing over two ounces of what appears to be solid gold in the braided necklace wrapped around her freckled neck.

"So far, I love it. I had a massage and a facial here today. Don't tell Oliver." That gets a laugh from the squad. Our husbands' irritation at our spending is something over which we can bond. "Do you all live in Kupuri?"

"I do." Julia raises her hand. "I'm four houses south of you." That red hair blows across her face. She plucks away a strand stuck in her lip gloss. "Aimee and Palmer live in Ranchos Estates."

"It's on the other side of the peninsula, but still inside the Punta Mita gates," Aimee says. Heavy gold bangles clank on her arm. These women probably drop their jewelry in beach bags when they swim, leave earrings by their pools, purses unattended at all the clubs.

"It's quieter over there," Palmer says. "More private, how Neil and I like it."

More exclusive, she means. But "quieter" is also sometimes a word wealthy people use to deflect from their home's shortcomings. Like when someone says they chose to live on the North Fork because it's more "grounded," when in reality they just couldn't afford a place in the Hamptons.

"Ranchos is gorgeous," Julia concedes. "I'm pretty sure Jeff Bezos's new place is in there. The houses are unreal."

Ugh, fine. Score one point for Palmer.

"That's nice." I wish I had a drink.

Palmer holds her squint. "Where did you grow up?" she asks. "I can't hear it in your voice. I can usually tell."

Maybe she's more formidable than I'd guessed. "We moved around a lot," I say offhandedly. With so little on the internet about Isabelle, I'm improvising fiction now. The fire is too hot. I lean away from the flames.

"Did you meet Oliver at Yale?" Palmer has turned this into a chess game, and she's already brought out her queen.

"Oliver is older than I am, so no." It's a guess, but not a particularly risky one.

"Ah, right," she says, her eyes narrowing. "You're probably closer in age to his younger brother." She must mean the sailor who looks like Oliver in the picture I found online. It's useful information, but talking about the Beresford family is a minefield I'd like to avoid, especially now that I've got a drink in hand. Clearly, though, there's something here. Something Palmer knows that's giving her that triumphant little smirk. When she speaks again, there's smugness seeping out of her voice. "Oliver told me and my husband about all that family trouble."

I feel my veins hardening. "Oh, did he?"

She pouts her lips in the fakest version of sympathy I've ever seen. "Seemed sad that they aren't close," she says. "Such a shame, what addictions do to a family." Jesus, this woman is hardcore. She clearly wants me to know she's done her digging on my supposed in-laws, with her manipulative faux-pity. It's a power play, a warning shot. She's letting me know that she's aware of the skeletons in the Beresford closet—and she's not afraid to use them.

"Families are complicated," I say, pivoting as gracefully as possible. I don't need to know more about some long-lost troubled little brother—I can already imagine the rich-boy-fallen-from-grace saga, the string of stints in rehab. Who the fuck cares? "Anyway, Oliver and I met through friends," I add, hoping we can move on.

"Aw, that's so nice," Julia gushes. "Jeff and I met on an app," she says with a cringe. "And lucky Palmer here met Neil when they were practically babies."

"We were high school sweethearts," Palmer says with a little eye roll. But I can tell from the set of her jaw that she's gearing up to bombard me with more questions. "So, Isabelle—"

I cut her off with a laugh, trying to cover my irritation. "I was having too much fun to settle down *that* young!"

"Oh?" Palmer raises an eyebrow. "Were you wild as a teen? Where'd you go to high school?" This is getting absurd. What is her deal? At first, I thought she was just asserting her dominance, but her questions are so pointed, now I wonder if it's something more. What does she suspect? I rub the ruby ring with my thumb.

"I went to boarding school in Switzerland," I say, trying not to sound like a rushed contestant on a game show spitting out answers before a buzzer cuts me out of a prize.

"You're kidding—me too!" Aimee says, reaching across Julia to grab my hand. "Surval Montreux—you?"

"Monte Rosa." I rattle off the name of a school I learned about from an art dealer in New York.

"*Très bien*," Aimee says, joining my team—and clearly signaling to Palmer to chill out.

"I always wanted to go away to school, but my parents couldn't afford it," Julia says. "And now that I can afford it for my kids, I'd never let them go!" I envy the casual way she references her humble beginnings, her position in the elite echelon now so obvious and secure that her modest upbringing has become a quaint anecdote, not something she needs to distance herself from at all costs.

"Julia went to public school . . ." Palmer says.

"And I'm damn proud of it." She stands. "Come on, Isabelle. Let's get you another drink."

I've passed the test. But that Palmer woman is sure to go home and deep dive into the Monte Rosa Facebook page. Julia hooks her arm through mine and leads me away from that gauntlet. "Palmer will warm up to you," she says. "We really are excited for new blood. We need it—can't you tell?" Julia and I laugh. Palmer was about as pleasant as eating bugs, but I am here to play nice.

As soon as a cold margarita is in my hand, a man I assume is Julia's husband waves her over, and for the first time since I arrived at this party, I am free to really play. I move through the crowd, close enough to the band to see the beads of sweat on the pianist's forehead.

"Isabelle?" A man touches my shoulder as I dance to a Sade cover. "It's nice to meet you. I'm Neil Kelly." Ah, the dreaded Palmer's husband. He offers his hand like it's some kind of gift I might want. He's tall and there's an intensity to his gaze. His monogrammed white shirt is unbuttoned to his chest. The singer belts out "Smooth Operator," and the coincidence makes it almost impossible not to laugh.

"So glad you've finally made it down to Punta Mita," Neil says. "I've gotten to know your husband a bit this winter. Man's got a great golf swing! Actually, the last time we were on the links, Oliver and I were talking about going in on a little investment together," he adds, and I nod like I know what he's talking about, like I'm the kind of wife who's kept in the loop. But my mind is whirring. How many of these people know Oliver? Isabelle's texts made it sound like he'd only popped down a few times to check in on the work being done—and there's hardly any evidence of him living in the house. Maybe Neil is just one of those guys who latches on to new acquaintances. He certainly seems the type. At least I know for sure that Isabelle hasn't set foot in Casa Esmerelda yet, so I'm not moments away from coming face-to-face with someone who will instantly spot me as a fraud.

"Is Oliver here with you? I tried to reach him the other day—"

"He's on a retreat in Bali." Neil's eyebrows rise slightly, like he's having a hard time picturing his golfing buddy meditating. "Remind me—do you live in Kupuri Estates too?" I ask, changing the subject, even though I already know the answer.

"No, on the other side of town. Ranchos." He tucks his chin with intentional modesty, like he's embarrassed to admit to his own wealth. Yeah right. This man's dying to brag. "You must be thrilled with how Casa Esmerelda turned out."

I beam at him and place a hand on my heart. "It's stunning. We're so blessed."

Neil smiles. "Will Oliver be joining you down here soon? Palmer and I would love to have you two over for dinner."

What a dream, sitting across the table from that bitchy blonde, but I simply smile and nod.

"As soon as Oliver's back, let's get something on the books," Neil says. His grin is so big it looks like it's about to crack his face.

"Absolutely!" *Not a chance.*

I scan the room looking for something to pull me away from this conversation, when, from across the band, a man I noticed when I first walked in winks at me. I don't usually fall for obvious moves like that, but it's so ballsy I can't help but smile. "Great to see you, Neil." I toast his glass and move through the crowd toward Mr. Wink.

He's scruffier than most of these men, like he just returned from a backpacking expedition.

I swerve around gossiping women, beer-sneaking teenagers (who don't have to sneak—no one's watching), and thick cigar clouds to reach him, then "accidentally" bump into him with my shoulder.

"Oopsie," I say, turning to face him. His smile is bright and re-sponsive—a guy who is used to women finding threadbare excuses for hitting on him.

"Jay Logenbach," he says with a smile. "And you are?" Oh, good, that means he doesn't know.

"So clumsy," I answer. "Hope I didn't get your clothes wet." I gaze up at him, blinking.

He laughs at that. "Not yet." I can't help reflecting back his smile. This game is infinitely more fun than bitch chess.

I am pretty sure from his immediate vibe that he doesn't have any clue I'm supposedly Isabelle Beresford, nor any context on who the Beresfords are to begin with, but you never know with this talkative crowd. So just in case, I slip my knee out through the high slit to distract him from remembering.

He looks down at my leg and my foot, then all the way back up my body, until our eyes meet again. I use the time to check him out too: the muscles under his tight light blue polo, the narrowness of his waist. He has a swimmer's body. He pushes back his overgrown sandy hair, blinks his long-lashed brown eyes. This is a man who has never been refused. And I have no intention of being the first.

My fantasy from the other day morphs from hot tattooed chef to sultry scruffy swimmer. I let myself get lost in Jay's dark eyes for a moment, then force myself to focus on what he's saying.

"So . . . all alone on the most romantic beach in the world?"

There it is. Just as I suspected, Jay wants to play.

"For the moment." Isabelle wants to play too.

Jay edges so close I smell his peppermint shampoo. Men who don't hide behind cologne or aftershave are always the best in bed. Guys who drown themselves in Tom Ford are usually compensating for a lack of confidence—or a lack of something else. They're the ones who rush through foreplay just to get to a very underwhelming main event. But Jay would never do that. I can just tell from the cut of his jaw, the heat of his gaze, that he would take his time with me.

And I'd love every second of it.

"It's ironic," I say, "because my husband and I bought this place hoping to reignite the romance. And he's not even here." I figure he can know "Isabelle" is married . . . sometimes those are the most available types.

Jay's eyes trace my lips as I pout.

"Any house with you in it would ignite me." Even hot Jay Logenbach can't save that line from its cheesiness. But he continues with, "Could be anywhere. A shack in the jungle," which is nice, I suppose. He might even believe it. But if I weren't decked out in

Isabelle's clothes, if he'd met me on a busy street, or in a dive bar, instead of exclusive Punta Mita, would he still look twice? It's never just the person they want. It's the whole package. The illusion.

"Really?" I turn so the slit parts at the top of my leg. Playing the horny housewife suits me. "Wouldn't you get bored? Or distracted? Oliver is so easily distracted."

"Oh, I'm distracted." He stares at my inner thigh. He touches my waist. "I have a property at the Four Seasons. I leave tomorrow afternoon."

Perfect.

I may be playing Isabelle, but I doubt she knows this routine. A few quick lines, a flash of skin, that telling touch . . . and it's decided. I'm about to score the hottest man here. A mini-adventure within the adventure . . .

He still doesn't even know my name.

His fingers reach out and trace my collarbone. We need to move this off-site, stat.

We down a few shots of tequila, then agree to meet at his golf cart. I can't afford to get caught running off with this man. As far as these people know, I'm a married woman, and the last thing I need on this impromptu little vacay is trouble. So I say goodbye to Julia and Aimee—even Palmer gives me a terse little hug. I promise to join them for yoga, and paddle boarding, and hikes. I hope the real Isabelle's a joiner, because she's going to have a packed calendar when she arrives. "I can't wait!!"

Then, with the moon lighting the way, and fireflies teasing, Jay drives me through the tidied jungle like we're some resort version of Tarzan and Jane. We swig from the bottle of tequila he's stashed, laugh when the golf cart flies over the speed bumps, and kiss like teenagers every few meters, his hand always finding my exposed leg. For a moment, I'm Liz getting drunk and wild. Could be a stolen cart on a public course. "You're fun," he says.

"And we're still in the cart." I whisper in his ear, "Just wait and see how fun I can really be."

He can barely keep to the road as I swig some more. And some more. Letting him think he's the one tricking me into bed.

"I've never seen a woman like you drink tequila straight from the bottle."

"You've never seen a woman like me."

● ● ●

It's almost nine a.m. when I wake up in Jay's suite. He sleeps beside me, his arm draped across my hips, fingers barely grazing the scar at the top of my leg. I've made peace with my scar. It doesn't seem to lessen the power my body has over men—he kissed it for an hour. And I let him. I enjoyed it. Which is hard to believe, considering the shame it used to cause.

It wasn't like I was comfortable in my skin before the accident. I'd shot up six shapeless and stringy inches between seventh and eighth grades. Forget boys—I drooped over them like a broken umbrella. I had wide eyes and big cheeks but otherwise I was a reed. I'd look in the mirror and think, *Who even are you?*

And then the accident happened.

At St. Catherine's I met my first "horse girls." I was thirteen, and, with their matching riding boots and shiny double French braids, they were the epitome of what I aspired to be. I couldn't believe it when Megan invited me to her birthday party at the horse farm. I was thrilled. The problem was, I'd told her I knew how to ride. She and her friends said they rode English, so I said I rode English too. But I had no idea what that meant when the barn hand led me to the biggest horse I'd ever seen. Megan and Olivia and the rest all managed to mount their horses without help. I tried to copy them, but they were too skilled and quick for me to learn from watching on the spot. I stared at the stirrup as if it might shout out instructions. The first tip-off that I was a fraud was the barn hand giving me a boost. Though, for a split second, my legs wrapped around that giant horse, and I sat up straight, and I was one of them. Gripping the reins, I petted the horse's thick, brown neck. "Good boy," I said. "Good boy." Meaning: *Please be nice to me!* He didn't listen. Megan squealed, and my horse ran. The next thing I knew, I was on my back in the dirt, hoofs everywhere. And laughing girls. The shock of the fall was so intense, I didn't notice at first that I was really hurt—no one did. That barn hand had to carry me away. He told me I'd been thrown from the horse, but really I'd been thrown from the whole group. I was so embarrassed I begged my father to let me transfer to public school, promising I'd make the most of a new fresh start. But my father didn't need persuading—tuition at St. Catherine's was a stretch.

My mom had been gone for eight or nine months by then. And my dad was bitter and out of touch. Looking back, I don't blame him. I was bitter too. But he didn't realize I was depressed about more than the horrible, stifling cast. It was like when we were kicked out of the good seats at the ball game, except this time, I had only myself to blame. I was the loser who didn't know how to mount a horse. I couldn't wipe off some gaudy makeup or cover my poor background with a hat.

I let all the public-school girls sign my cast and told them I'd been in a car accident, that I'd almost died. One girl even cried. It was the first thing that made me feel good in a long time.

Not as good as last night with Jay, though. Pathetic young Liz had no idea what "good" really felt like yet. She had no idea she'd become *me*.

Slowly, I roll over, careful not to disturb Jay. My face is chapped and raw from the stubble I'm dying to rub up against again . . . but I don't want to stick around for goodbye. If he hadn't told me he was leaving today, I wouldn't be in his bed. I reach for the dress he tore off and recall the feel of his hands on my body, his mouth devouring my neck, his strained voice chanting, "Isabelle," over and over. It may have been another woman's name I gave him, but it was *my* body that made him come apart.

I don't take his watch (Panerai, $20K). Looks too good on him, and I'm trying, trying, to behave. But I do peek through the wallet I find in the pocket of his jeans, and snap a few photos: his license, his Platinum Amex, his health insurance card.

Just in case.

As I slip out of Jay's room, I notice a few texts on my phone from an unknown number. Opening them, I see a series of angry messages from Alan Reed, Abigail's son. *Shit.* Texts along the lines of "heavy concerns" and "second thoughts" and "honoring Mother's polite request to back out of the investment," and then they grow more demanding: "Miss Hastings, please know we do not take this situation lightly and you will be hearing from one of our representatives."

Representative. A word extremely wealthy families use to mean not an actual lawyer but a hired enforcer. No need to expose their shady deals to legal scrutiny.

Still, I'm surprised they're this antsy. Some of these cons can drag on for years, while I keep up the game of musical chairs, sending infrequent updates about the latest whereabouts and valuations of a piece, without the mark ever even considering the fact that it doesn't exist.

But no, Alan Reed has to meddle in his mama's plans—and thus, mine.

I wonder if they'll try and reach out to Isabelle and warn her about me. But I don't know that they're that close, or that Abigail even knows Isabelle hired me. Besides, Isabelle's off the grid in Bali anyway. I've got time.

I turn off my phone, thinking it might be best to simply drop it in the hotel pool. I almost feel bad for Liz Hastings. Isabelle Beresford is a much more enjoyable role.

I sneak out without making a sound and scurry down the winding resort path wearing last night's dress. No one will even notice. And if they do, they'll just be jealous, because I'm sure I have the glow of a woman properly fucked.

I wind through the lush grounds, nodding hello to the fast walkers like I belong. I pass the sprawling pool, where a sole swimmer is out doing morning laps, and continue on my way to the concierge in the lobby building to order a shuttle (on Jay—I'm sure he won't mind after last night), when I hear a woman's voice call to me from behind.

"Isabelle?" she says. "Isabelle Beresford? Is that you?"

6

I hear her run toward me, with her jangling bag and clunky sandals. "Isabelle," she yells. "Isabelle! I thought I heard you were here!"

My pulse skids. Someone who knows the real Isabelle. Someone who, so far, has only seen me from the back. I try to ignore the clomping and jingling headed my way, but it's not like I can run, especially not in these heels. I could deny it. *You have the wrong person*, I could say. Then collect my fee from the real Isabelle and move on—find another beach, latch on to another Jay Logenbach. Maybe Isabelle could line me up for another gig. I'm sure she's got at least one friend who needs help filling a chateau in Provence, or a bungalow in Bora Bora. I'll be on a flight out of Puerto Vallarta anyway in a few—

"Isabelle, it's me!"

I'm stuck dealing now. She's inches from me.

I turn, still not sure which way I'll go—will I be Liz or Isabelle? But the eager beaver with brassy blond hair makes the decision for me. She doesn't hesitate, just latches on to me with a tight hug, her big brown eyes nearly popping with excitement.

"Isabelle, how are you? I heard you arrived early." She touches the side of my arm like we're close. *Sorry, sweetie, you and Isabelle aren't that close, or you'd know she's not the one you're talking to right now.* But then again, we're all a little face blind. And context is everything. My own father once didn't even recognize me when we ran into each other at the batting cages (I was there on a date with a hot sophomore from the baseball team. We were laughing, kissing. I must have seemed like a whole other person to him. Someone older, cooler, happier. Not the lanky, angry, tangle-haired mess who he usually saw sprawled on the couch at home). People see what they're expecting to see, more than what's right in front of them. The mind edits details that don't fit. It comes down to the first interaction. If this woman doesn't catch the act now— the tiny differences of voice or how I move or the fact that I'm at least two inches taller than Isabelle (I can tell from the tailored dresses she bought)—then she never will. She'll lock me in as her new visual.

"Thank God you're here," the woman continues. "I've been *dying* for someone to play with." I smile. I wait. "It's Tilly! Tilly Endicott? We met at that Frick Collection event," she says, freeing me from an awkward: *And you are?*

She's animated and charged, like she needs to be liked, which could be useful to me. If I give her that, what will she give me in return? "Of course," I say, with the neutral closed-mouthed smile I use whenever I'm not quite sure what I'm getting into.

"This is pretty." Tilly runs a finger down the flowing fabric of my dress.

"It was a gift from Oliver," I say without thinking, my instincts kicking in.

"Gift-giving husband . . ." she replies. "Is he always so thoughtful?"

"He has his moments," I say, wishing she'd stop asking questions.

"It takes more than a moment," she says. "So, what are you doing here at the Four Seasons? Isn't your house finished?" Is that scrutiny I hear? Because I'm not in the mood. Maybe someone *did* notice I'm wearing last night's dress.

"I woke up early, so I came here for breakfast."

"I would have done the same," she says, and I wonder what she's implying. Would she have done Logenbach too? Then she leans in, lowering her voice to a whisper, and says, "I've wanted to apologize about what happened after New York. I know it's between our husbands, but still, I should have reached out when their deal went south. I had hoped we might be friends."

"No worries," I say. *Jesus Christ, is Oliver Beresford working on deals with every single person here?* I edge toward the concierge desk, needing that ride back to Casa Esmerelda ASAP.

"No, really." She clamps a hand onto my forearm like a boa constrictor. "Let me make it up to you. Join my private yoga session at El Surf Club—I'm here for a 'mental health break,'" she adds with air quotes. "I know, I know—it sounds kind of ridiculous. It's not like my life is so bleak I need to get away from it all." My tight smile grows into something a little more genuine. It's refreshing to hear someone wearing an entire Harry Winston boutique (large wedding ring, tennis bracelet, two-carat studs in her ears) acknowledge the fact that life has been pretty fucking kind to her. "To be honest," she continues, "what I needed was a break from James. Some distance so my heart can grow fond."

"I hear you," I say.

"Distance brings all the fondness." And I swear she winks at a passing young man wearing a rash guard with the words ST. REGIS BEACH CLUB stretched across his pronounced pecs. She follows him with hungry eyes as he makes his way toward the beach. Then she gives her head a little shake and turns back to me. "Is Oliver here too?" she asks.

"No. He went to Bali to relax, and, well, I wanted to come here instead. Just like you said. I needed a break."

"The longer you're married, the more you appreciate alone time, right?

"Amen," I say.

"Come to yoga. Then we can go into town, hit Mina for ceviche and cocktails."

"Maybe some other time, I've actually got to—"

"Liz!"

I whip my head around, but I can't answer to that name. Not now. *Shit.* It's Nance from the airplane, heading into the restaurant with her pals, who all look like they're three mimosas in, toddling on wedge heels and loud printed dresses they must have bought at the Four Seasons boutique, looking like overgrown tropical birds. I suppress an eye roll.

Luckily, Tilly doesn't seem to notice. "Seriously, we should do something. I have an idea. Do you hike?" she says, oblivious to Nance and company. "I was planning a locals-only hike today. I've got all the gear with me." I've never understood why anyone likes hiking, but there's a hopeful gleam in her eye like dragging me up a hill is an act of contrition she's been dying to perform. I'd sure love to know what happened in New York that she's trying to make up for now. "It's a trail with a waterfall—two, actually. Amazing view. You can see all of Ranchos Estates. Come with!"

"Liz!" Nance yells again. "Over here! Liz!" She's crossing the lobby now, waving like a lunatic. Automatically, my brain starts running through scenarios, ways to get out of this corner I've found myself backed into. I need to escape this hotel lobby. And fast.

"Liz! It's me, Nance!"

"Is that woman yelling at you?" Tilly asks.

"Who?" I say turning to look at a passing family, then at the concierge desk. "I don't think so." I spin Tilly so we're both turned from Nance. "A hike would be great. Let's go."

• • •

Tilly smiles at the guards as she peels out of the Four Seasons' circular drive. She's a fast driver, maneuvering her car's stick shift with surprising deftness. We rumble over patches of cobblestones and around circles filled with those mathematical palms before we finally reach the main gate and exit the safety of Punta Mita, heading into town.

Instantly, we're in another world. Sun-bleached cars jockey to park at what I'm guessing is the Mexican version of 7-Eleven; stray dogs meander across the potholed streets. Perhaps it's the jarring change of scenery, but I suddenly wonder what the fuck I've just done, hopping in a car with a total stranger. I'm off my game. I shouldn't have let myself run off early with Jay last night. He was hard to resist. But if I'd stayed at the party, I could have left with a lot more useful contacts—these types always need help with art and real estate; I could have put some people in touch with my "associate" Liz and gotten real work out of it. Instead, here I am, on the run from *Nance*.

This. This is why I needed a reset. Because I keep ending up in stupid situations like this, on the run from one or two minor bad decisions. Yet somehow, I can't help myself, even here in paradise.

I lean out my window. The ocean disappears and the jungle thickens when we head into the hills. I swallow the acid building in my throat. I've never been much of an outdoorsy type. Sure, I love a good view, but I love it more when I'm looking at it out of a floor-to-ceiling window.

Unfortunately, there's no going back now.

"I'm so glad I ran into you," Tilly says, as the car climbs a steep incline. "I've wanted to do this hike ever since the bartender at the Four Seasons told me about it. *Locals only* . . . It's not safe to do it alone. Too steep. Rockslides. Last rainy season, someone died. And they didn't find the body for weeks." *Fuck me.* "This is where he said to park," she says cheerfully as she cranks her tires into the hillside like a pro, then hops out of the car. "We have to walk from here," she says.

I follow Tilly past women sweeping their small square houses, then a new-looking *escuela* at the edge of the town. Cracked asphalt gives way to a dirt path, and I swat at mosquitos. My leggings—borrowed from Tilly because she claimed stopping at Esmerelda would take too long—are too short, leaving a swath of lower calf and ankle exposed to the swarming pests. "If we don't hurry," she says, "it will be too hot out to make it all the way to the lookout point."

I want to stop, say I'm sick, or fake a sprained ankle. I already feel blisters forming from the borrowed hiking boots—hideous galumphing things half a size too big. But she's determined. And fast. Even if I came up with an excuse to turn back, I'm too out of breath to speak.

"Come on," she says. "We don't want to burn alive in the jungle."

"Found it," she says now, gesturing toward a thick tangle of dark green leaves covering a rock spray-painted with the words LAS MELLIZAS. I jog to her as she slides into the opening I can't even see. This is crazy. What are we supposed to do, bushwhack our way up to the summit? But once we're through the gap in the foliage, the trail has a wide opening and a white arrow spray-painted onto a rock. "Keep an eye out for those marks," she says as if sprayed splotches are common signage I should know.

It's steep, and my legs are shaking. Rashes are threatening to erupt everywhere my sticky sweat pools. I'm afraid I'll pass out when the trail finally flattens for a stretch, and she stops.

"I keep getting missed calls from James," she says, holding her phone. "I should call back before we go farther and I lose reception."

She looks guilty, like she's been blowing him off for days. "Do you mind? I'll catch right up! I'm clearly faster than you!" she says with a grin.

What the hell? Now I'm stranded on this godforsaken trail alone? But I'm not going to hang around and eavesdrop on her marital drama.

"Okay, sure," I say brightly, half-wanting to shove her off the trail's steep ledge.

"Thanks! Sorry, I'm the worst. See you in a minute! Just follow the markings!"

"Got it."

"It's worth it for the view of the twin waterfalls, I promise," she says with a smile, beginning to dial her phone.

The sounds of the jungle grow loud as I leave Tilly behind: bugs and birds and Lord knows what else. Forget slipping and breaking my neck—which could easily happen; it's that steep—I could get eaten by a big cat, bitten by a poisonous snake. A blister swells on my left heel. A mosquito pierces my flesh. Blood streaks across my arm when I kill it with my other hand. The sight of the red streak makes my stomach churn. *It's just a bug bite, Liz. Get it the fuck together.* Birds squawk like they're laughing at me. *Fuck you too, birds.* When I turn to look back, Tilly's blond ponytail is long gone from view. But she's such an Energizer Bunny, I'm sure she'll catch up in no time.

I hear it first: rushing water loud enough to drown out the heckling birds. Then I see the waterfall, through the thickness of the jungle. But the path seems to splinter, and the one that appears to lead toward the sound of water is narrower and windier. Still, that must be the way—and it's mercifully less steep, so I head in that direction.

I'm at some sort of rocky lookout point now, though it's thick with overgrown jungle. At the edge of the cliff, the river plunges out of sight. Is this the right waterfall? I look up and see that, farther above me on the sloping terrain, there seems to be a bigger outcropping. Beyond it, I see a much larger waterfall cascading down from the higher point. Maybe I took the wrong path after all. The view from down here probably isn't as magnificent as the one above, but through the opening in the thick leaves, I sort of see the beach, and the houses—Ranchos Estates? I scan the row of mansions that must include Neil and Palmer's, wishing I had binoculars. I have to admit, they do look pretty spectacular, even from here; their swimming pools reflect the sun like blue diamonds—turn rays into shining crosses so radiant they reach my eyes through the muggy air. A whole world made of diamonds.

I know that the phrase "diamonds are forever" is the world's best marketing scheme, meant to drive up sales of one of the most ubiquitous gemstones on Earth, but in that moment, I'm stricken with longing. I don't want to temporarily squat. I don't want to be on the run, moving from city to city to escape the people chasing me down. I want the permanence of a forever diamond.

I back away, but the rock I step onto isn't secure. It slides, and I slide too. "No, no, no." Fighting gravity, I throw myself onto the muddy bank.

Nice one, Liz. It's nature giving me a little slap in the face for breaking my promise to myself to play nice on this trip. If I had stayed clean and stayed Liz, I wouldn't be lost in the hot, thick wilderness right now.

And while I'm thankful Tilly didn't witness my fall in the mud, I'm angry too. I feel like I did when those twelve-year-old bitches I thought were my friends laughed after I fell off a horse. I don't do animals. I don't do nature.

I grab hold of a branch and pull myself away from the water; the rocks I was standing on crash over the edge, thudding and smacking on their way down. I've caused a literal rockslide, just like she said. I bear-crawl away from the waterfall. When I'm safe, I clutch my knees to my chest.

Standing up gingerly, I turn my back on the cliff's edge and walk a few steps back into the jungle. I should go back to the fork in the path and try to make my way up to the other waterfall. Clearly, this dangerous spit of land is not the scenic lookout Tilly was talking about. But suddenly, I do not see any trace of the thin, winding trail—or what I thought was the trail—anywhere. Come to think of it, there wasn't any spray-painted sign when I went in this direction.

Where *am* I?

The hot, panicky feeling of being lost settles over my body. I walk a few paces parallel to the cliff edge, trying to find the path that will lead me back to safety. The roar of the larger waterfall grows louder. This can't be the right way . . .

That's when I spot something bright blue in the brush about fifty feet away, a color that can't be a flower, or water—a color that's man-made.

It looks like it's an anorak, muddy and torn. I'm grateful for this sign of civilization—it must mean the trail is nearby. I head in that direction, thwacking my way through waist-high, scratchy underbrush.

When I reach the anorak, I spot a hiking boot too. One boot with red laces sticking out from under the brush and . . .

"Oh my God."

It's a fucking *foot*.

The puke comes then, a waterfall of last night's cocktails and canapés splattering onto the ground.

I wrap my arms around myself, shaking. Time is too slow then too fast, like I've dropped into a warp. "Tilly!" I stumble backward and trip over another—different—boot. Two mangled bodies buried under rocks and strangled by ripped-apart roots. They must have fallen from that higher cliff.

Oh my God.

"Tilly!" My voice echoes back at me, broken. The waterfall roars and Tilly is nowhere to be found and I'm between corpses and a jungle and a cliff.

Kneeling in the dirt, I sob, then retch again. Wipe my face with the back of my arm.

I breathe, trying to calm myself down and think straight. This is not what I signed up for. I don't do death and danger—not real, life-threatening danger.

Competing emotions attack me like stinging bugs: panic and fury. Fury at Tilly for letting me wander off into this treacherous wilderness alone.

I feel cursed—this whole trip was a mistake. I pinch my eyes closed, but taunts from deep in the past echo in my ears. *Trash. Liar. Stalker. Freak.*

"Pull yourself together," I mutter. "Get a grip." I force myself to stand and get my bearings. And then I see it—a narrow strip of beaten-down plants that make up the "path" I mistakenly took. If I retrace my steps, I should be able to find my way back to the main trail.

My eyes are pulled back toward the bodies. What am I supposed to do? Can I really just leave them here? Someone must be looking for this couple. Their boots are muddy, but they're of obvious quality. And their bodies are still strong and lean, the woman in lavender bike shorts and sports bra, a blue anorak tied around her shoulders, a baseball cap with a letter *B* logo tangled in her ponytail. The deaths are recent; I'd guess one day, max, considering the jungle predators and the blazing-hot sun. My heart races as I squat closer. The woman's face is a complete mess. I can't look at it. Fully crushed by rocks, it's as if Mother Nature went on a bender and took it out on this woman—merciless.

Merciless.

The word triggers something in me, and suddenly I know exactly what to do. *Wallet. Always look for the wallet.* Call it survival. Call it innate curiosity. Call it criminal. Call me rotten to the core, I don't care. I've never taken anything it really hurt the victim to lose.

And nothing hurts when you're dead. I can't believe what I'm about to do. I've never touched a dead body—but my instincts take hold and I fumble toward the female.

She's stiff, but I will myself not to think about her flesh while I search for pockets. Nothing. I turn my attention to the man. Thank God, his wallet is in the first pocket I check. I look both ways, though obviously out here in the thicket, no one's coming, then pull out his cards and give them a quick look over. And I'm stopped cold.

I blink, check again. *It can't be.* But it is. According to the Amex Black card in my hand, the dead body a yard from me is Oliver Beresford. My God, does that make her . . . ? The face of the woman is unrecognizable, but the hair . . . She has dark hair, like mine. She's my size. Fuck. *Fuck, fuck, fuck.*

I fumble with her ponytail, adrenaline coursing through me like a drug. The birds whistle and shriek while I extract the baseball cap. I turn the cap over, and there, just above the adjustable strap, I see the words emblazoned in stitched white lettering: BERESFORD CAPITAL.

She's Isabelle Beresford.

And she's very, very dead.

7

Ten p.m.

Midnight.

Two a.m., and I am still awake.

It's like I have a fever, the way I've flipped and turned all these hours, tangling myself in sheets I've twisted into ropes that snag my limbs like those dangling, creeping jungle vines. I can't close my eyes without seeing Isabelle's smashed-in bloody face. It's like the women in the Tamayo painting Isabelle hired me to hang, as if their blurred features are some kind of prophecy I should have been able to read. Swaths of red paint, the color of Isabelle's blood, purple splotches like the bruises on what was left of her mangled skin. I sit up and stare at the sliver of moonlight that cuts through the edges of the blackout shades. I told myself I'd be so good on this trip, to use it as a retreat from all the cons, but I couldn't do it. And now I'm paying the price. If I don't sleep, I'll be a mess tomorrow, and I need to be alert if I hope to get out of here as planned.

I unwind the sheets and remake the bed as if I can wipe this week from my past and start fresh, get a do-over. Then I con myself back under the covers and fold my hands over my chest like I'm a woman without a trace of regret who sleeps without fear. But I just feel like a corpse eternally trapped in a casket. I squirm and writhe like I'm back in the jungle with Isabelle. *Dead* Isabelle. Bugs and birds and worms . . .

Get out of my head.

I close my eyes again, desperate for a moment of peace. I relax all my muscles—still sore from the hike—and visualize melting into the mattress. I picture myself on a chaise by the pool, the hot sun softening my every cell. But something draws me to the trees, music, and a ghastly flower smell . . .

In my mind I cross the patio and creep down the stairs and I'm in a funeral parlor like when my grandmother died. I'm behind all these tall adults I don't know, inching toward her open coffin, and I wish the line would move faster so I could pay my respects and leave. My throat constricts because I'm too hot, pressed between all those black dresses and suits, and I'm so impatient I want to tear off my skin and run. But finally, I'm next. The man in front of me touches Grandma's clasped hands and solemnly mutters a prayer. I step up to the shiny black coffin lined with satin the color of Punta Mita sand—crushed bone. And I scream, because it's not my grandmother in the coffin, it's Isabelle. Her battered face hasn't been mended. She hears me yelling and opens her swollen eyes.

Jesus Christ, I think when I bolt upright. My heart pounds; my breath races. I'd rather stay awake if that's what awaits me in my sleep. *Fuck this.* And all my churning thoughts: mostly that I wish I could turn back time. But how far back would I have to go? I almost told Tilly about the bodies when I found her unfazed at the bottom of the trail today—maybe if I had, the police would have come, and it would be in their hands now instead of my brain. But I couldn't tell her the truth. Because I'd already told her *I* was Isabelle.

"Thought I'd really lost you up there!" she said when I found her at the trailhead, looking like she hadn't broken a sweat.

"I—I took a wrong turn," I managed to mumble. As if the

scratches and dirt all over me didn't make that obvious. Or the look of complete terror in my eyes. I'm a good liar but not *that* good.

She scanned me up and down. "What we need now is a round of strong drinks."

There was no way I could fake composure—one sip and I would have fallen apart. "I don't feel so well," I said. "I think the heat got to me."

She sulked and pouted, but then came the part that tripped me out completely. As I started to back away, she said, "Oh, Isabelle, wait. You dropped your wallet on the trail. I saw it on my way down. Here!"

I stared at it for a second, stunned into silence. Had the real Isabelle dropped her wallet on her hike, before falling to her death?

Tilly reached out a hand, offering the wallet up to me. I held my breath as my fingers made contact with the leather, as if touching it would trigger some alarm, as if I was being tested. *How far are you going to take this?* Tilly's eyes seemed to ask. But of course, I was just projecting. Tilly had no idea I wasn't Isabelle. And clearly, she hadn't seen the bodies—she wasn't rattled or sickened like me.

When I got back to Esmerelda, I gulped the fine house tequila in privacy and tried to scald the horror out of me under a hot shower, tried to scrub the death from my hands like Lady Macbeth. *It will never come out*, I realized. *I'll always have a hint of her in my flesh.*

I skipped dinner—I was too busy packing my suitcase. Maybe I shouldn't have thrown in the Pucci dress and the silver brush set—I don't need any more karmic retribution. I can unpack them before I leave. I called the airline after my shower and changed my flight to Seattle, a city small enough to manage but big enough to get lost in, a city to which there's a direct flight—I wasn't interested in extra steps. I've made mistakes. Or I'm in a vortex of bad luck. All I wanted when I changed my reservation was to get the fuck out.

I thought that if my plans were set, I could relax. *No such luck.* The tequila didn't even soften the edge.

Now, accepting that sleep—restful sleep at least—isn't coming, I get out of bed and creep to the bar to pour myself another short glass, avoiding the Tamayo painting as if it had caused my nightmare. Then I wander onto the patio to stare at the bright half-moon. I stretch out on a chaise—maybe it'll be easier to sleep here than in Isabelle's bed. But the hard, narrow cushion brings me back to a dorm bed and the misery of college—and Bekka.

I'd gotten a scholarship to UMass-Amherst, and Bekka was my roommate. I met her on day one and couldn't look away. She was magnetic. She was from Manhattan and wore all black and knew everyone in our dorm within a week, the whole class within the first month. People were drawn to Bekka like they're drawn to a new band, or a scent they can't place but that makes them want more. Unlike me, Bekka never had to try. There was always someone knocking on our door, and her phone dinged 24/7.

When she asked me to join her table at lunch, beautiful students I'd seen on campus flocked to us like she was a pop star they'd been dying to meet. They bragged about their athletic wins and their wealthy backgrounds: boarding schools and country clubs and ski vacations at Snowbird, everyone agreeing Utah has the best snow on Earth. They were rich, but they couldn't get into Yale, or even Boston College, so they clung to one another like they could create their own exclusive island amidst the normals like me.

"That was fun," I said while we walked to the library, orange leaves swirling at our feet. It may not have been Ivy League, but it was pretty.

"We're only getting started," she said.

I knew even then that I could learn a lot from this group if I played it right. That Bekka was an entrance to an entire world.

At Halloween, Bekka invited me to party at Amherst College—

the more elite liberal arts school down the road from UMass. She wanted to dress up together as the *Shining* twins.

"We're so hot," she said when we tried on the dresses we'd ordered online, then had altered at the tailor in town. "Shorter—we're not nuns," she'd insisted while the old man knelt and pinned our hems. "You're gorgeous," she said.

"*You're* gorgeous," I said. Bekka also had long brown hair, but hers had tight, bouncy curls. Four inches shorter than I was, I thought she was the perfect height. While I tended to shrink down into a slight slouch, she walked with her back straight and her shoulders down like she was perpetually on her way to the podium to accept a gold medal she'd known she would win. After measuring her, the tailor said her curvy proportions were numerically perfect, but it was her big brown eyes and thick black brows and lashes that made me—and everyone else—stare. That chilly afternoon, dressed as her twin, was the first time I was more interested in my reflection than hers. My cheekbones had grown more pronounced since I'd arrived at UMass, and all the campus walking had added definition and shape to my long, thin legs. Even next to Bekka, I *was* gorgeous. I was *hot*! It was like we improved each other's looks. The sum of us greater than our individual parts. And Bekka knew it too.

"We'll turn every snooty head, even the nerds," Bekka said. I mimicked her as she turned to her left and then right. *I could master this*, I thought. "Everyone will want to fuck us tonight."

She was right.

"What's your name?" a guy named Josh yelled over the dance music.

"Bekka," I answered without hesitation, just like I seamlessly became Isabelle that first day at the Kupuri Beach Club. Bekka was across the room, and this wasn't our college, so no one would know the difference, I told myself.

"Bekka . . ." he said, "you lost your twin."

"But I found you." The words shot out of my mouth like Bekka had spoken them instead of me. I'd been too obsessively self-conscious to date in high school, but in that moment, I wasn't me, I was Bekka. And Bekka was bold; Bekka took what she wanted. I grabbed his hand and pulled him onto the dance floor. I shook my Bekka ass in the little blue satin dress.

"I like you, Bekka." Now I was the cool girl who'd seen all the best films and got all the references and could handle her booze and take charge of a six-foot man. I danced closer until I was grinding my hips into his.

"Bekka . . ." he said when he pulled me into the stairwell and paused to breathe after filling my mouth with his tongue. He slid a hand under my dress, and I gasped when he pulled down my panties. "I want you so bad," he said. I'd been admired, sure, but I'd never been *wanted* in this rabid, blind way. As Bekka, I found raw power.

When I returned to our room a few hours before dawn, Bekka was asleep in her *Shining* twin costume. I studied her posters while I undressed, and the photos of her friends she'd stuck to her wall: In her Manhattan penthouse, in front of the Eiffel Tower, on tropical beaches like the one I'm staring at now. When I was down to my bra and panties, the power I'd felt with Josh turned to dread. I was Liz Dawson again. I'd been Liz all along. *Trash.* I wriggled back into my costume and slept as Bekka's twin.

After that night, I was hooked.

• • •

Dawn light appears over the water, faint and gray. My tequila is gone, so I head back inside with the memories of that first year of college still swirling in my mind like the almost-melted ice cubes rattling in my glass.

I dated Josh for two entire months, the whole time maintaining the lie, adding to it even, filling in all the blanks with Bekka's life instead of mine. Thankfully, his roommate was some kind of royalty from Africa—Ghana, I think—and wouldn't know if I'd gone to Spence, because he didn't know what Spence was and he didn't care—he was a fucking prince. And Josh was from Arizona, of all places. I made friends with the kids on his floor, partied with them. Whenever I was put on the spot, I acted too drunk to respond.

Then Bekka invited me to dinner with her father, who took us to the most expensive restaurant in town. In his presence, she shape-shifted too: sat up straight, stopped cursing, placed her napkin properly in her lap. I learned a lot from her, now that I think about it. How to be rich ten different ways. I learned a lot from her father too. "Confidence," he kept insisting, was the key to his success (not his inherited fortune or penis). "Confidence and recognizing opportunities when they strike. That'll get you anywhere you need to go."

"What an asshole," I said to Josh when I sneaked into his room that night, exactly the words Bekka had said to me the second we got out of her father's Mercedes. "He's so full of shit." Even though she'd obviously absorbed his mottos over the years. If anyone had confidence, it was Bekka.

"It's still nice he took you to dinner," Josh said to me as he peeled off my shirt. His tone was slightly put out, like maybe I should have invited him to join.

"He wanted to meet my roommate, Liz." As soon as I said this, I realized I'd made a mistake. Heat rose to my cheeks, a buzzing filled my ears, a weight heavy as stone sank in my gut. It's the same way I feel right now, with my packed bag and my escape flight booked. The feeling that I was dangerously close to being exposed.

"I haven't even met your roommate. This is the first time I've heard her name."

"She's dating a senior who lives off campus. She's never around."

But I was the one who wasn't around, and Bekka wasn't as easy to trick as Josh.

"Where do you keep sneaking off to?" she asked when I returned the next day. *Another world*, I thought. *An imaginary land where I'm you and I hang out with my hot rancher boyfriend and a dashing prince at a school that's ranked in the top ten.* "You keeping a boyfriend secret from me?"

"Of course not."

"Liar. You banging a local? I knew it. You *so* would."

It was the first time I didn't like Bekka. It was the first time she admitted she thought I was trash. I couldn't help it. I couldn't resist. "He's a professor. At Amherst."

Up she sat, wanting to know more, jealous, impressed. "*Quel scandale!* When in the world did you find time to pull that off? And how?"

"I met him when I was studying. He was doing research in our library."

Bekka narrowed her eyes, in that same cold way that Palmer did at the party last night. Women like them will do anything to prove their snobby instincts are correct, but I didn't know that at the time. In the end, it took her only three days to break into my phone and track down Josh—whose name I'd changed to *Prof* the night I told that lie. I'd deleted our whole thread too, but by the time she'd managed to get to my phone, the texts had once again stacked up, including one about meeting my roommate, Liz.

Even now, all these years later, I can feel the shame of what came next. I never want to feel that way again. I stare out at the Pacific, dark and churning. An idea begins to crystallize. Without even fully knowing what I'm doing, I scurry back to my room, strip out of my pajamas, change into shorts and sneakers, and stare for a moment at Isabelle's wallet, laid out on the nightstand beside the bed. Then I head for the front door, stepping over my packed suit-case on my way out. I grab the emergency flashlight and hop in my golf cart, but even zipping alone through the eerie early morning gray can't stop the memories.

"You fucking liar," Bekka said when I returned from class the next day.

"What?" I played innocent. But Bekka was too smart. The look on her face said it all: *Dance if you like, bitch, but you're already caught.*

I floor the gas and race over the Punta Mita speed bumps, and those pesky cobblestones. I wave at the main gate guard, who's too sleepy to look surprised.

"*Professor Josh* filled me in on everything, *Bekka*. We have so much in common . . . even our names. Ew, Liz. Gross." The rage I'd felt when she assumed I'd been with a townie returned tenfold. She, who had everything, was taking my boyfriend, my social circle, my whole life. All I'd done was borrow her name.

"I don't know what you're talking about." I kept going. Though, of course, I knew I was fucked. Just like I know now.

"For fuck's sake, know when to quit," Bekka said. "My father must have left out that golden nugget of advice when he took us to dinner last week. I'm surprised—it's one of his favorites. *Know when to quit, Bekka . . .*" Her anger increased as she recalled her father's insults, her face morphing into his. "I've put in a room change request. I've reported you to the school." So entitled . . . just like her dad.

She turned her back on me like I was too disgusting a sight for her precious eyes. And for a split second, I wanted to shove her through the frosty window of our fourth-floor room and watch her blue blood spill onto the snow-dusted path below. I remember that vision now while I speed through the town of Punta de Mita.

The sky lightens, and the first roosters scream their wake-up calls, and I almost wish I *had* pushed Bekka, because that fight was only the beginning. After that night, I was completely alone. Aside from missing Josh, who never spoke to me again, Bekka told all our friends at UMass. Well, *her* friends. She moved out the next day and some other normal girl like me from Western Mass took her bed. I left at the end of the semester and never returned.

I park at the spray-painted arrow for Las Mellizas and race back up the awful trail like I'm being chased. Because I don't want to lose this power again. My flashlight catches the eyes of two Mexican raccoons, taller and slouchier than back home, but I don't have time to be scared.

I make it up the mountain so quickly, I can't believe it was such a challenge before. Within minutes, I'm shoving my way through the underbrush off the windy trail to the waterfall, its water tinged with the reds of the rising sun, spilling toward me over the rocks like blood. A faint rainbow rises above the top of the cliff, and I realize the vortex I'm in isn't bad luck, but good luck instead. This is my once-in-a-lifetime score. Opportunity is striking, and now is not the time to quit.

I thought what I needed was a clean break, but the promise of what I see now is something else altogether.

The con to end all cons.

My reignited anger toward Bekka is like an amphetamine that gives me the courage to do what I need to do next. I find Isabelle first—her blue anorak. *Eat shit, Bekka.* I've Googled her over the years, and she hasn't amounted to anything. Her father got reamed in 2009, lost his entire fortune. That was all Bekka had—the promise of inheriting his money had made her powerful. She was nothing without his wealth. *C'est la vie.* Now I'll have a life better than hers at its best.

I shoo away insects swarming Isabelle's corpse. I'm doing her a favor really—I'd rather be fish food than composted by worms. It's not like I killed her, but it still takes me a moment to rally for what's next. "Do it, Liz," I say. "She's already dead." Isabelle's as heavy as a full rain-soaked duffel bag, but I find the strength I need to haul her into the rushing river. When I release her into the water, that powerful feeling I had when I passed as Bekka at Amherst returns. The sun crests the treetops and turns the water gold the second Isabelle floats over the edge. *I'll make you proud*, I think while she plunges down. *I won't squander the gift of your life.*

I have zero emotional attachment to Oliver, so in some ways, he's easier to move; I had been gentle with Isabelle's body, like she could feel every rock and thorn I was dragging her across. Oliver is much heavier, though, so I have to lean and grunt and yank at his limbs. Halfway to the water, I drop him on the hard earth to catch my breath. "Come on, Liz. Move it." The dawn's almost daylight; hikers will soon come. I need to leave now. So I roll him like an old carpet, looking away from him as much as possible, blocking the feel of his hardening flesh under his Patagonia gear. *One more shove and you're free.* Down on all fours, I push him into the water headfirst. But he doesn't float like Isabelle—he's too heavy. I wade in, grab his arms, and back myself toward the cliff. I don't look behind me at the treacherous fall. I need confidence now or we'll end up a threesome broken on the rocks. I straddle his body and, with one final pull, send him crashing over the edge.

Colorful birds burst from the trees below, and the sun rises over the cliffs above. I thrash my way back to the main trail and run down it, giddy, light, and free.

PART II

PART II

8

TWO WEEKS LATER

The sky's a Rothko of reds and golds, and the Pacific air whips through my short hair, tickling my neck—I'm still not used to this length—as I lean on the railing of *La Natalie*—Aimee's sixty-foot yacht, named after not only her grandmother, but also the multimillion-dollar sustainable makeup brand Aimee started when her modeling career waned. She and Palmer and Julia caw over a story the Mexican bartender tells on the front deck, their laughter full of the abandon you experience only in the middle of the ocean, where no one can catch you being yourself. The water glimmers and winks, and I'm filled with a rush of joy. Our little girls' afternoon on the boat became a drinks-all-day affair, and my body is warm with wine, my skin pleasantly sticky with salt air.

It's a Saturday in mid-March, but I only know this from the varying yoga and surf instruction calendars, otherwise it's nearly impossible to track the passage of time here. I can hardly believe it's been nearly three weeks since I first arrived in Punta Mita—and two since I disposed of the bodies—but it's truly starting to feel like home. In the days that followed that horrific hike, I'm proud of how I gradually and meticulously brought Isabelle back to life. I used the credit cards from her wallet to order a new laptop, more clothes, some additional toiletries—practical necessaries for myself, but also to create a digital trail that "proves" Isabelle's still alive. I hired Martina, the housekeeper, and also Lupe, a cook. I sent Martina into town to get me a new Telcel phone, one not trackable by the Reeds. The first text I made as Isabelle was to her assistant. She had already sent my $5K painting hanging fee, so I didn't need her anymore. And I definitely didn't need her poking around and looking for the real Isabelle. *Hey, it's me, Isabelle. I lost my phone and had to get one here.* When she replied, I spun some New Agey bullshit to explain why I was letting her go, texting how Bali really changed my perspective, how I'm trying to be more present in all of my endeavors without intermediaries, blah, blah, blah. It wasn't entirely a lie, anyway. I *have* been on a retreat, and I have definitely had a personal transformation.

She replied with a curt text, thanking me for the experience and hoping our paths cross again. Girl had no idea I was still at Casa Esmerelda, nor that her former boss was lying at the bottom of a waterfall.

Little by little, I began running into Julia, Palmer, and Aimee "by chance" at the beach club to solidify my friendship with them. I even joined Tilly for her private yoga classes and surf lessons a few times, after which we always grabbed drinks. "Work hard, play hard," she said without irony, which, to be honest, I loved her for.

But while I got a kick out of Tilly, it became clear Julia and the other women weren't her friends. When I asked what they knew about her, after a sound bath on Julia's back patio, they all exchanged glances. "We don't really know her that well," Julia spoke up. "You're the only person she's tried to befriend here. Other than . . ."

"A couple of the hotel bartenders and a surf instructor," Palmer said.

"What!?" I asked, faux-scandalized, but secretly impressed. I remembered Tilly winking at the hot guy in the hotel lobby that first day we met. And how she always seems more interested in chatting up our servers over brunch than mingling with the Rich Crew. Maybe that's why I like her. She seems to have very few fucks left to give.

While I stroll the circumference of this insane boat, I think about Tilly's running commentary on Punta Mita's celebrities—the race-car driver (big engine, small . . .), the reality stars' ever-changing proportions, the South American pop star (and her child groom)—and laugh out loud.

That said, her mood swings can be a bit much to handle. And she often invites herself over to Esmerelda to raid the Beresfords' well-stocked wine cellar and complain about the latest slight from her husband, of whom she's apparently not growing any fonder with all this distance.

"He told me to stay another month. A month!" she cried last weekend, sloppy at my pool. "If he only knew," she said, her admission slurred. "These husbands think only *they* can find a side piece. I mean . . . Look at us!" She strutted and gesticulated like she'd won a wet T-shirt contest, hands clasped together over her head for the victory lap.

She got so plastered I couldn't let her drive her golf cart back to the Four Seasons. "Stay here," I said. "I have three guest rooms."

"I want to see *your* room," she said. "I bet it's pretty." She started for my room like she knew the way, but then paused at the Tamayo and blinked several times as if to make the blurry paint sharp. "I'm drunk," she said.

"Come on." I led her to the nicest guest room and into the bed.

She giggled while I tightened the blanket around her body. "I always wanted a sister who'd tuck me in."

"Me too, Tilly," I told her, meaning it.

Now I sit on the steps that lead up to the bridge from the aft deck and think about all the nights I wanted the same. Even before my mom left, she wasn't the type to comfort me at night or tuck me in—looking back, she must have been checked out long before she actually split.

Then in college, before Bekka turned on me, there were nights I wished she'd brush my hair off my forehead and curl around me in the narrow single. For some reason, a man's company never did that for me—it has never been a comfort, only a fun distraction from the endless stretch of complete aloneness.

Not that I don't love being alone; I do. It's where I've learned to live. Where we all have to learn to live, anyway.

That doesn't mean I don't also like to be seen. To connect. To feel like if I drowned off the side of this boat, someone would care.

That night Tilly stayed over, I stood in the dark, watching her breathing even out, wondering what she saw in me—in Isabelle— that made her feel a kindred sense of sisterhood. Wondering if she also felt achingly invisible to everyone in the world, like she too had to wear a mask to be seen.

I'm back on my (bare) feet now, returning to the party I've drifted away from. I'm greeted by Julia's warm smile and her cheery Midwestern accent calling out, "There you are, Is!" and the main reason I continue to hang with Tilly becomes crystal clear: Her belief that I am the real Isabelle adds credibility to the illusion— people see what they want to see, yes, but people also believe what *others* believe. It may not last forever, but for now, becoming Isabelle feels so right. Like it's what she'd have wanted: for her house, and this boat trip—her fabulous life—to be enjoyed. I might never convince myself that Liz deserves to be happy, but there's no doubt in my mind that Isabelle does.

I reach the bar at the bow and pour myself another glass of wine, because I need to catch up with this boozy crew. They're stretched out on the cushions drinking and venting away.

"Ugh, it feels so good just to relax. I love my kids." Julia kneels and reaches for her drink. "But I should have brought the au pair."

Palmer nods sympathetically, while Aimee clicks her tongue in mock disapproval.

"*Non, non*—bring the au pair to a tropical paradise? *Never.* It's too tempting."

"Oh, please, Jeff would never cheat on me." Julia rolls her eyes.

"Ah, ah—but it's not always the husband who shags the nanny, is it . . ."

"What happened?" I ask, edging closer in on the cushions.

"Lacey Tuttle—"

"Mother of three," Julia says. "Ran off with a twenty-two-year-old from Portugal. They haven't been heard from since."

"That was just a rumor." Palmer waves her hands like she's swatting a bug.

"Well, I believe it," Aimee says. "Not everyone is cut out for motherhood. I know I'm not. I'm too selfish. I want to do whatever I want whenever I want."

"Ha!" Julia laughs.

"What about you?" Palmer turns sloppily to me. "Don't you want children?"

I take a long pull from my wine, obscuring my face in the glass while I consider her question. The truth is, I've never wanted kids. With a childhood like mine—and an adulthood—there's no way I could offer the kind of stability a child deserves. But *Isabelle* has the money to hire a nanny. She'd never be overwhelmed by bills and work and the struggles of parenting. She'd never throw a hairbrush at her whiny eight-year-old and scream, "I can't deal with you right now! Braid your own fucking hair!" Meaning: *I never should've had you. It ruined my life.*

There's an awkward pause, which Aimee breaks by saying,

"How gauche, Palmer. *Mon Dieu.* Everyone knows you don't ask a woman in her midthirties about having children."

"Maybe someday," I say with enough sorrow to shut this convo down.

"Sorry," Palmer says, though there's not much contrition in her voice. "I don't mean to be rude." She tips back the rest of her wine.

"Ah, please, rude is your favorite color," Aimee says. And Palmer laughs. Finally. It's taking forever to break this bitch.

Then some old song pipes through the boat's speakers and Julia squeals and strips down to her string bikini, removing her outer layers like a pole dancer, while the rest of us applaud. It's contagious, the stripping, and soon we've all wiggled out of our carefully chosen outfits to the smooth grooves of yacht rock. I don't blame them for wanting to show off the bodies they've worked so hard to acquire to someone new. Like always, I'm an illusion. I'm the woman they wish they were. I'm the "thin mirror" in the dressing room, reflecting a reassuring image they crave.

"You know I need your love. You got that hold over me!" Julia points at me, spitting a little when she sings, spilling her third drink onto my toes.

"It's been you, woman, right down the line . . ." I muster a few verses, words I know because I'm alive. They think these songs were written for their yachting pleasure, and I don't ruin it with the truth, but my mother, whom they would not let wash this deck, raised me on this shit.

We cruise away from the mountains and across Banderas Bay toward the Marieta Islands.

A few hours and a few bottles of sauvignon blanc later, the sun has finally dipped below the horizon and Palmer's adversarial edge has dulled, but it's still there, like the lip-lift scar I spot when we're together on the upper deck drinking shots and the sun spotlights her face. "Another," I say. *"¡Vamos!"* After we drink, we stumble back onto the large round bed-like sofa at the back of the boat.

"I . . . I . . . A friend of a friend went to . . . What is it school? Switzerland." Her hot drunk breath blasts my face. "Monte Rosa! Monte Rosa! I asked if . . . You know. Don't you know?"

She can't finish a thought. "Have you been to the Marieta Islands?" I ask.

She gestures to the uninhabited rocks. "Fish . . ." she says. Then she's out. *Thank God.*

I hope she's killed enough brain cells to forget this exchange when she wakes up. Because part of me is starting to worry. Palmer seems intent on catching me in a lie.

I leave her passed out on the sundeck and make my way back to the bow, where Julia lounges on a deck chair as the yacht heads back to port. "Where's Aimee?" I ask.

"Napping in her cabin."

This is my moment.

"Can I tell you a secret?" I say.

Julia perks up. "Of course."

I lean against the rail while I gear up for my reveal. "I didn't go to boarding school in Switzerland."

"Oh, I don't care where you went to school. I went to public school. State college too. I was waiting tables in Detroit when I met Jeff."

"But I told Palmer . . . and she's been trying to find someone who can prove I lied."

"Palmer can be too much," Julia says to me. "She's very inse-cure. I don't know why. She's always had money. She's beautiful. She has a successful husband . . . I mean, Neil can be a lot too—he gets so hotheaded about the dumbest things. Maybe that's partly to blame for how she acts, I don't know. But I wish she'd stop hassling you."

"I do too." The wind whips at my hair, too short for a ponytail now. I push it behind my ears, trying to make earnest eye contact with Julia. "It will be so awkward if she calls me out in a group. I don't want to revisit school. That's in my past." It feels good to merge Isabelle with Liz, to tell one truth to my new friend.

"You know what I used to say when I first met Jeff's friends? That my father was in the CIA! Can you believe that?"

"Maybe I should use that on Palmer."

Julia laughs, her giggle turning into a snort. "I'll tell her to stop asking. She may not listen to just me, but if Aimee and I gang up on her, she will."

"Thank you so much." I hug her. And she hugs me back. It feels nice.

"Your secret is safe." As we pull out of the hug, she reaches for my hand. The ruby in my "wedding" ring glows against my tan skin. In that moment, the ring is a talisman. A reminder that I *am* good at what I do. That I can handle the Palmers of the world.

Julia stares at the ruby lustfully. "It's so exquisite . . . You have the best taste." She looks into my eyes. "Can I ask *you* a favor?"

"Yes," I say. "Please." Whatever she's about to admit makes her skin flush.

"I know we haven't known each other that long, but I was wondering if you'd be willing to help me with the charity gala after the regatta? It's at the end of March. There's an auction, and we need donations—maybe you could help with that? I really want it to go well. I love your style and taste . . . If I could bounce some of my decor ideas off you, I'd really love your help."

"Of course!" I say.

"Really?" She grabs me and squeals. "I'm so happy you moved in. You know how you don't realize what your life is missing until you have it?" she says. "That's you. You're different from the other women here. You're real."

I smile.

• • •

A few days later, as I enjoy my morning coffee and Lupe's perfectly baked eggs (a celebrity chef I hooked up with for a few months made me an egg connoisseur), I am once again replaying Julia's words in my mind. Because I do feel more real than ever, like this life, *Isabelle's* life, needs me as much as I need it. I'm someone these women can talk to. Someone they admire and trust. Lounging poolside, it's hard not to believe this was my destiny. Not that it was easy—nothing's easy. The universe didn't push Isabelle and Oliver off that cliff to give me a new life. But it did send me on that hike.

Most people who win the lottery end up bankrupt. Many take their own lives. Getting your hands on the dream isn't the hardest part. Plenty of people stumble into it. The trick is knowing what to do once you've gotten what you want. And making sure you don't let it go.

"Señora?" Martina asks when she brings me another cup of coffee, already keyed into my routine. "I would like to hire another housekeeper before Señor Beresford's arrival—when is he expected to join you?"

I pause, a forkful of baked eggs halfway to my mouth. I've been casually brushing off questions about Oliver from the staff for a while now, hinting that our marriage is on the rocks, but I know I'm going to have to pivot soon. Give them something definitive. I'm not an idiot—I have questions too. Like why the fuck Isabelle and Oliver arrived early from Bali without even telling their assistant—or the stranger they'd invited to stay in their home. And why in the world would they go on that dangerous hike together, instead of heading straight to their glorious new digs?

Imagining the real Isabelle so close to waltzing through Casa Esmerelda's front door and catching me prancing around in her clothes sends a shiver down my spine. She could have caught me floating in her pool, sipping her tequila. She was right here, and I had no idea! Luckily for me, that never happened. But where did they stay between landing in Mexico and dying on that hike? Maybe they didn't come to Casa Esmerelda right away because they wanted to fly under the radar. Didn't want anyone—even the random woman hired to hang their art—to see them return home from Bali with their tails between their legs, their marriage on the ropes. Because my hunch tells me the purpose of the Bali trip—to rekindle their marriage—must have failed, and that's why they'd returned sooner than planned. And if I've learned anything in the past three weeks here, it's that the Punta Mita gossip mill can be vicious. Was that ill-fated hike a last-ditch effort to bond? To rekindle the spark and reclaim their power-couple status?

"You know," I say back to Martina, assuming the face of a disappointed, lonely wife, and hoping it's enough to cover my anxious thoughts, "I think Oliver may have to go straight from Bali to attend to some business. I'm not sure he's going to make it down to Mexico at all this winter."

● ● ●

It's raining after breakfast, so I slip into the cashmere sweats and log into Netflix, hoping to indulge in an hour or four of blissfully mind-numbing content. But before I can pick a show to binge, my new Telcel phone rings: *Caller UNKNOWN.* I feel a prickle of unease. Who would be calling me from an unknown number? I have the beach clubs saved to my contacts, as well as Tilly, and Julia and her gang . . . No one else should even have this number.

UNKNOWN could be the police.

UNKNOWN could be the morgue.

UNKNOWN could even be someone from the Reed family. That *representative* Alan warned me I'd be hearing from.

"Hello?"

"Mrs. Beresford?" a man asks. "This is David Morrow. I work with Oliver at Beresford Capital."

"Oh yes, hi, David," I say, while doing a quick Google search. Apparently, David Morrow is the VP of portfolio management at Oliver's company. Which is all well and good, except there's no way an employee of Oliver's should have this Telcel number. How did he get it? "Sorry," I say to David, "I have a new phone, so your caller ID didn't come up." I pull my knees up to my chest. A clap of thunder sounds.

"No wonder the number we had on file went straight to voicemail. I tried your assistant, but she didn't answer either. Thankfully, Oliver had told me about your new property. I got this number from the main office at Kupuri Estates."

Well, aren't we resourceful.

I suppose that explains how he got this number, but still that hint of unease simmers under my skin. This Morrow guy seems like just a needy middle-management type who works for Oliver—not much of a threat to me. Except why is he anxious to be in touch with Isabelle? And also, what *did* happen to the real Isabelle's cell phone? I assumed it was smashed to smithereens, like her face, and was now lying in pieces at the bottom of the waterfall—or else had washed all the way out to sea. But she could have dropped it on the trail, like her wallet. It could be somewhere in the jungle, waiting to be uncovered, inches from the path.

"Yes, I lost my phone and got a new number here in Mexico," I tell Morrow, figuring that's a simple enough explanation. "Now how can I help you, David?"

"Can you put me in touch with Oliver? It's urgent."

"He's in Bali," I say, dropping wariness into my voice. "We were meant to be there together, but I had a last-minute change of plans."

"No, he's not. At least, he's not at Soori Bali, where his assistant said he would be. I've checked."

"Oh," I say, acting surprised—Isabelle never told me the name of the resort. I'm out of bed now, pacing the room. "He often extends his trips. He was there to relax."

"Mrs. Beresford, your husband never even checked into Soori Bali."

Never even checked in?

I knew they'd left early, but her assistant would have let me know if they hadn't even gone.

He wasn't in Bali. *They* weren't in Bali.

The whole trip was a lie.

Each time I catch my reflection in a mirror—the three in the vanity, the wall in the closet—I look more like Liz. Less delicate and less refined. Like seeing a photo of myself that captured the worst angles of my jawline and nose. I'm Cinderella after the ball, and the spell is wearing off. I sit at the vanity and watch my expressions change: annoyance, concern, fear. I stare at Isabelle's driver's license until I find our likeness again. A flash of lightning appears in the glass, reflecting from the windows behind me like a gothic effect. I tear my eyes from the mirror and return to Isabelle's bed.

"I'm not the only one looking for him," Morrow says. "Do you know a Neil Kelly?"

Palmer's husband? What does he have to do with Oliver not being in Bali?

"We've met, but I don't know him well," I tell Morrow. We've never said more than a few words—in fact, I always got the vibe he didn't like me. I think back to that welcome party, when I first met Neil. He *did* seem pretty curious about when Oliver would be joining me in Mexico . . . Come to think of it, the few times I've run into him with Palmer at the club he's always asked after Oliver. And always with that slightly intense look in his eye. I didn't think much of it—just figured he was going insane with boredom without his golfing buddy. But now . . .

"Neil says he's been trying to reach Oliver for weeks," Morrow says. "I guess they were in the middle of some kind of investment deal? I don't really know the details—which in itself is strange because usually I'm looped in on anything Beresford Capital gets involved with . . ." Morrow sounds whiny, but also genuinely concerned. "Honestly, Mrs. Beresford, I'm starting to suspect foul play."

"Foul play?" I say, adding a convincing tremor to my voice, which isn't hard because I don't like where this is going. "I—I'm sorry, I don't know anything about this. Oliver told me he needed a rest . . ."

"If the screaming phone calls I've been getting from Neil Kelly are anything to go by, Oliver might end up with more than a rest."

"My God, what are you saying?"

Morrow sighs. "I'm sorry. I don't mean to upset you," he says. "But I've looked into Mr. Kelly. He's been known to align himself with some . . . questionable business partners. If Oliver is avoiding them, he must have a good reason. Or he's in serious trouble."

Him and me both.

Morrow clears his throat. "Mrs. Beresford, if you hear from your husband, please let him know I need to speak with him. Urgently. Otherwise, if Oliver doesn't surface within the week, I'm opening a missing person case."

9

I used to practice keeping my heart rate steady the way I'd practice holding my breath underwater as a kid. Appearing calm is half the con sometimes, maybe more. And here I am, in the middle of the biggest play of my life, losing control.

"Come on, think," I chant as I lap the bedroom, then the bath, then the closet, all the exquisite objects and dresses and views mocking my predicament. It's paradise . . . unless you're me. I rack my brain trying to think of a move that will salvage things. But it's like working a muscle that's begun to atrophy. I've been so focused on passing as Isabelle, I've forgotten how to be Liz. *You got yourself into this—don't be a little bitch. Get yourself out.*

If Morrow files a police report, I'm fucked. I thought dead Oliver was my ticket to freedom, but his corpse—or what's left of it—is about to send me to a Mexican prison instead.

Unless . . . I bring Oliver back to life.

I think of all the ways I've reanimated Isabelle over the past two weeks. Using her credit cards, making purchases and reservations in her name—and, of course, becoming the physical embodiment of her to everyone here in Punta Mita. Obviously, I can't do that last part for Oliver. The best I can do is weave a digital trail. I reach under my mattress for Oliver's wallet, where it's stashed alongside my Liz passport and phone. I need to find a better hiding spot—Martina's always one bed-making from uncovering the truth. And I can't afford to be sloppy now.

The first thing that anyone will check to confirm whether Oliver's alive is his credit card activity. I sit cross-legged on the floor with my laptop, pull out his credit cards and ID, and arrange them like they're tarot cards: *Tell me, Platinum Amex, what does Oliver need? A new pair of Versace swim trunks shipped to a random address in Bali? What next?* I ask the Upside-Down Driver's License, signifier of miraculous rebirth. I order a telescope and ship it to the Beresfords' beach house in Newport. Then send an Amazon office supply order to their Manhattan digs, both purchases that will seem totally normal for a very alive Oliver to make. But now I need something bigger. Something that will explain why Oliver is unreachable.

I try to think of what type of excursion Oliver Beresford might enjoy, but aside from fighting with his wife and potentially screwing over his business partners, all I know is that the man likes to sail and ski. *Real original, Ollie.* Then I remember something I heard about while I was hiding out in Whistler: remote heli-skiing in Canada and Alaska, rich dudes risking their lives for a few thrilling rides. Seemed crazy to me—I don't like being cold, and I *definitely* don't like hurtling to my death over a mountain range. But that's the kind of shit people buy when they have so much money, they need to manufacture danger and stress.

I'm still Liz as I research companies who peddle these extravagant adrenaline trips, ultimately deciding on a company in Alaska that drops restless millionaires onto some of the most remote and dangerous mountains on Earth. With Oliver's Platinum Amex, I order a matching jacket and ski pants and mail them to Alaska Heli's operations base north of Anchorage. When the charge is approved, I feel my breathing slow down. I'm back in control. But I'll need more than a few credit card charges to make this work.

I step into my slippers and poke through the various rooms of Casa Esmerelda in search of traces of Oliver I might have missed before now. Anything I can use to help sell the illusion. If Oliver really had been staying here while the house was being finalized— and already starting to do business locally, at least with the likes of Neil Kelly—then surely more of his stuff would be here too. It's never made sense.

I wander into the in-home gym. But there's nothing but unused equipment: treadmill, elliptical, spinning bike. Yet-to-be-inflated rubber balls. A rack of presumably never-lifted weights.

In the living room, I open all the drawers in the built-in book-case, which holds mostly artful objects for display instead of actual books, but I come up empty again. It's like the guy was a ghost long before he was actually dead. "Come on, Oliver," I mutter while paging through a coffee-table book about English gardens, "where the fuck did you—"

"Señora? Someone to see you."

I need to give this woman a bracelet with a bell—she's so damn stealthy.

Martina leads Tilly into the living room then excuses herself back to the kitchen. My mind is still frantically cataloging all the places where Oliver could have been storing his belongings, so it takes me a minute to greet her.

"I'm on my way to the Kupuri Beach Club for a massage and wanted to say hi," she says. But then her brow crinkles and her smile flattens into a line. "Are you okay?"

"Fine," I say, closing drawers and replacing the knickknacks I'd moved.

"Is it about Oliver?" she asks, and I nearly shatter a blown-glass vase.

"Why would you say that?"

"I heard you say his name on my way in." Tilly gives me an odd look. "Isn't he supposed to be here by now?" she asks, crossing the living room to the wide doors that open onto the patio. The rain has petered into a drizzle. The storms here are intense but brief. Almost as if Punta Mita needs to remind us every now and again that even paradise has a dark side.

"I can't reach him," I say to Tilly, wondering if I should mention Morrow's call. I don't want to raise the alarm to anyone else that people have begun to think Oliver is "missing." I cross the room to join her and lead her out onto the covered portion of the patio. "As far as I know, he's still in Bali. I did expect him back by now, but he's probably just moved along to another adventure without bothering to tell me. Last year he disappeared into the Dolomites for a spontaneous ski trip, and I didn't hear from him for ten days. You just never know with Oliver . . ." I trail off.

"What? Do you think it's something more?" she asks while digging into the fruit plate Lupe has just set out. "You can open up to me, Isabelle," Tilly says once Lupe is out of earshot. "I've heard rumors." She leans over as if someone's trying to listen, though we're alone on the patio.

For a moment I freeze—are there rumors circulating that Oliver is dead? But I look into Tilly's eyes—sympathetic but also slightly catlike; she looks like she's relishing something she knows she shouldn't—and suddenly I think of the women on the yacht, the gossip. I realize what she must mean.

Of course Oliver stepped out on his marriage.

I should have figured this from the start. It's another twist I could do without. I'm sure Isabelle felt the same.

"I feel like such an idiot," I whisper. I try not to lay it on too thick. After all, Isabelle would have some pride—at least, my version of her would.

"Well . . ." Tilly draws out the *L*s. "People are talking . . ."

Bingo. Thank you, Punta Mita gossip mill.

"Tell me," I say.

"They're saying Oliver has a lover in Sayulita."

I keep my face neutral, but it makes sense—it explains why Oliver doesn't have any stuff here: he was shacking up with his mistress. "Apparently, they were pretty brazen about it while he was down here working on the house," Tilly continues. "Going out to dinner, pawing each other at the beach club, the whole nine yards. Oh, Isabelle, I'm so sorry. Men are horny dogs."

Of course, I couldn't care less about the sex he had. But I have to worry Oliver's lover will show up any minute and demand to know where he is—or worse, that she'll open a missing person report like Morrow threatened to do. Plus, if Isabelle's a scorned wife, she has a motive to kill, making Oliver's prolonged absence from Casa Esmerelda seem a lot more suspicious. For a moment, my mind fills with images of flashing lights and sirens and police banging down my door to arrest Isabelle for her husband's murder. But I shake the thoughts away. No one is going to find his body. I made sure of that. And now I just need to make the world believe Oliver is still alive. This info from Tilly will help. "Do you know her name?" I ask.

Tilly pauses to think. "Homewrecking Bitch?" This gets a little smile from me. "Sorry, it's not coming to me," Tilly says. "I can try to find out for you?"

"No, that's okay." I don't want to seem too eager, and I don't want Tilly asking around and drawing attention to Oliver being MIA. If everyone in town knows about the affair, I'm sure I'll be able to get the information from someone else.

"Shit," Tilly says, glancing at her phone. "I'm about to be late for that massage. I wish I could stay here with you and toss back a bottle of wine from your fantastic cellar, but this masseur books six months out. They say he has magic hands, if you know what I mean." She winks and tilts her head forward into a leer. Once again, I think of Julia, Palmer, and Aimee, and what they said about Tilly. Running around with all sorts of men. No wonder she keeps extending her break from James.

I walk her to the front door where she gives me a reassuring hug, squeezing me tight with her deceptively strong arms. "I'm sure you're right about Oliver. He probably took off on another adventure and didn't tell anyone. Men are lying assholes. But at least we have each other, right?"

And in that moment, I couldn't agree more. It feels good, I realize, to have an ally in this shit storm, even if I can't tell her everything.

"Absolutely. Now go enjoy that massage, if you know what I mean," I say as she heads toward her golf cart. And then, shocking even myself, I call out, "Love ya, babe."

She turns back to look at me, betraying a momentary look of surprise, then winks and blows me a kiss.

• • •

"Martina? I'm looking for the original plans for the house—have you seen them anywhere?"

If he was overseeing the renovations at Casa Esmerelda, Oliver would have had a set, and probably would have kept it here and not at the mistress's place. Blueprints don't make great foreplay (though I do find them kind of a turn-on). They could, however, give me some clue as to where he stashed his laptop and other personal effects. I don't buy that he came to oversee the renovations and didn't leave *anything* here at the house. He was clearly working, or at least cooking up some sort of investment with Neil Kelly. Something's not adding up.

And I know from staging many homes (whether asked to or not) that guys like Oliver love their man caves. I once stumbled on a whole hidden bunker beneath a politician's mansion I was decorating in Montreal, mostly full of canned goods and porn.

"Plans?" Martina asks, stumped by my English for the first time.

"You know, like a map of the house. It's what the builders use. Sometimes they're kept rolled up?"

"Ah," she says, and I follow her into the kitchen. *"Esto?* Is this what you're looking for, Señora?" She bends down and pulls a long cardboard tube out from under the sink. The contractor must have stored them there.

"¡Sí! Gracias!" I say, taking the tube.

"De nada." Martina returns my smile. The tube has probably been in her way under there with the cleaning supplies.

I slide the plans from the tube and unfurl them on the dining table. *Casa Esmerelda/Lot 22* . . . There are several pages, and all the writing is in Spanish. *Come on, Oliver. There must be some secret hiding spot in this place.* It's not till the third page that I recognize what I'm seeing as a straightforward floor plan of *Primer Piso*, which I'm guessing means *first floor*. There's the kitchen, with its perfectly drafted sinks and stovetop. Finally, I turn the page to *Planta Baja* . . . Google translates the words to *lower floor*. There are two distinct rooms drawn, with a staircase in between. The larger room must be the wine cellar, but what's that beyond it?

With the unwieldy map stretched between my hands, I pass behind the kitchen and through the pantry. Lupe's there taking inventory. He sees me heading toward the door that leads down to the wine cellar and gives me his usual warm smile and calls, *"¡Vino!"*

The narrow staircase opens to rows and rows of storage for wine. Some of the shelves are filled, but several boxes remain unpacked on the floor. The thermostat is set so low, my arm hair stands on end. Being a tequila girl myself, I've barely spent any time down here, save for when Tilly dragged me down to grab bottles of Blanc de Blancs. I consult the plans again, then look up at the room, trying to visualize where the second space would be. Eventually, I spot it—a discreet door at the back of the cellar, nearly indistinguishable from the basement's stone walls. I rush up to it, and of course, that's the first door in this house I've found locked. It's frustrating, but also encouraging. I can tell I'm close to something, like that game kids like to play: *You're getting warmer, warmer, hot, hot, HOT.*

I'll have to let Martina in on the secret room if I hire a locksmith, which wouldn't be ideal. Then I remember a detail from the blueprints—the hidden room has windows on the south side of the house. Windows you wouldn't be able to see from either the driveway or the pool.

I grab the plans and a bottle of wine for cover, then jog upstairs. Lupe approves of my selection when I set it on the counter. *"Ah, muy bien. Una selección excelente."* But I'm on a mission. I hurry to my room and change into running clothes.

"Hasta luego, I'm going for a run," I call out. When the door closes behind me, I sneak around to the south side of the house and find the windows, which are narrow, and only inches above the ground, and obscured by a freshly planted hedge. I expect to have to shatter one with my foot, but the first window I try opens in. When I shimmy through, I feel like I'm diving under the ocean for a treasure chest, like I've finally spotted it, open and overflowing with gold coins and jewels.

And in some ways, I have. I land on what I soon realize is a desk. Because this is Oliver Beresford's secret office.

10

It's a jackpot bigger than a pirate's cache. The room looks like Oliver spent hours here, and only recently stepped out for a cup of coffee. It's like he evaporated midtask, like aliens took him instead of that deadly cliff.

The furnishings are ultramasculine in a way that doesn't match the rest of the house: mahogany built-ins, a leather upholstered chair, a clunky green-and-brass lamp, even a gold-plated trophy tucked into a crowded bookshelf. The trophy looks recently polished. *Narcissist.* I read the engraving: OLIVER AND BRADEN BERESFORD, VOLVO OCEAN CUP. 3RD PLACE. I pull up that photo from my earlier Google searches—Oliver and another man sailing. "Brother Braden . . ." I say to his sunburnt and salt-stained photographed face. Beside that, a big ugly glob of something—copper?—that is apparently meant to be sculptural but looks more like a bludgeoning tool. The taste choices here truly baffle me. He should have asked Isabelle for help.

I don't have time to linger on every trinket on the bookshelf— I'll return later to gather intel (and stash my phone and passport behind his leather-bound Hemingway set). But right now, I need to stop Morrow from filing a report. I need Oliver to return from the dead.

His laptop—the Holy Grail—sits open and plugged in amidst a

pile of bills and papers with Oliver's letterhead: Beresford Capital. And beside the laptop, his phone, just lying there for the taking, dark-screened and out of juice. I plug it in, knowing the effort's pointless. Even the police can't open cell phones without the passcodes.

Laptops, on the other hand, are a different story. It's a little-known fact I picked up from IT guy Jared, who thought rambling about computer security liabilities was effective dirty talk. In his defense, I was pretty enthralled by the tricks he taught me. I place a finger on the trackpad to wake up the sleeping machine. Thank God Oliver didn't enable the FileVault. If he had, I wouldn't be able to reset the password in Recovery Mode using the magic keystrokes I've memorized for moments like this. The screen goes black and then makes the sound I want to hear.

I spin in the ergonomic chair, which costs more than a week at the Four Seasons, while I wait for the laptop to finish rebooting. He must not have expected anyone to enter his underground domain, because his desk drawers are unlocked. Hello, cheating mother-fucker. "What do we have here?" I ask his smug, winning smile in the photo still on my phone screen. "Box of condoms can't be for your wife." For a second, I'm Isabelle, so angry I want to smash his stupid privileged face with that trophy I bet he cheated to win. But the computer dings to life, the screen lights up, and suddenly I'm Oliver. And I'm alive.

David Morrow's email autofills when I start to type his name into the "send to" field of a new message. This needs to be personal. And threatening. No *Hope you're well*, no *Best regards*.

Stop harassing my wife! This deal between me and Neil Kelly is none of your business. Isabelle doesn't know I'm skiing, and I'd like to keep it that way. Don't forget how many secrets of yours I've kept. You know I can destroy you. And I will.

Men always have secrets, and they never remember who they've told. Morrow's soul-searching (read: pants-shitting) will buy me at least another week. I hit send.

I want to find evidence of his mistress, but Oliver doesn't have the messages app installed, and I don't know her name. I try searching a few keywords—"dick," "wet," "hard"—and nothing comes up. Whatever sexts they exchanged must be confined to his cell phone, locked there till the end of time.

Who else might come looking for Oliver? My eyes drift back to that engraved trophy on the shelf. OLIVER AND BRADEN BERESFORD. Palmer hinted that the brothers were estranged, but I should make sure. I type "Braden" into Oliver's inbox search field, and sure enough, there are no recent exchanges to be found between them— all that pops up are mass-distro Beresford Capital emails.

Oliver's assistant, Chelsea Edwards, is up next:

I read a few of their exchanges to get a feel for his cocky style.

Hey Chelsea,

Sorry to leave you in the lurch, babe, but I had an opportunity to ski Alaska. YOLO! We hardly get a signal out here, but I'll check in next chance I get. Thanks for holding down the fort.

You're the best,

O

It's not as fun to be Oliver as it is to be Isabelle, but sitting in his hidden space, I do feel powerful, ordering everyone around, being Mr. Big Shot, Mr. Trophy-Winning, Mistress-Fucking, Heli-Skiing Asshole. He probably thought he was untouchable. Cozy in his lair, it's easy to forget he didn't get away with his clandestine life. I recoil, remembering the weight of his decaying corpse.

He's dead, but I still feel like he's a step ahead of me. And there's nothing I hate more. I've made strides with my digital deflections, but I don't feel like I'm fully in the driver's seat yet. I'm waiting for the other shoe to drop. Because something is still eating at me—the fact that, according to Morrow, Oliver and Isabelle never even checked into the Bali resort . . .

I type "Neil Kelly" into the search field, and a handful of emails come up—including Oliver's very last email, sent on Wednesday, February 25, just days before I would find him dead on the trail. I once again feel unnerved knowing that Isabelle and Oliver were here in Mexico at the same time as me. That I could have so easily been caught pretending to be Isabelle at the beach club.

The message is mostly bro stuff—setting up tee times and talking surf reports. There's no mention of Bali, so it's hard to know if my growing theory—that the whole trip was a misdirect—is accurate. But I feel confident that Oliver and Isabelle never planned to go—they just wanted people to *think* they had. Instead, they were lying low, nearby. And David Morrow seemed to think that Oliver was avoiding *Neil*, in particular . . .

I reread that final chain between them. Scrolling down, I finally catch it. We still haven't circled back on the accounting issue, Neil wrote, and Oliver replied, Let's discuss on the golf course. I swear the wife can hear through walls.

What "accounting issue" did Oliver need to talk to Neil about in private? Something tells me they aren't referring to a little bookkeeping mishap. They're talking about money that was supposed to arrive somewhere, and never did.

What kind of shady shit were you into, Oliver? And did Isabelle know?

I scroll and scroll.

My eyes blur from staring at the screen, so I turn my attention to the papers scattered on the desk. One is a bill from Strauss and Schwarz Law Firm. The statement is for over $10K, but it includes no useful intel, only billable hours. I search the name on Oliver's computer, and several files and emails pop up. The emails go back several years, but there's a flurry of them from the months leading up to Oliver's death. The folder titled *S&S* requires a password to open, so I try the emails. But when I try to click them open, they're encrypted too. I Google the law firm—*specializing in estate planning: wills, inheritances, life insurance* . . .

I feel sick. What kind of husband needs so much privacy that his office is literally buried under the house, hidden behind a secret locked door? At first, I thought maybe Isabelle's superior taste had relegated his man-cave-loving low-brow shit to this sad little corner of the house. But now I wonder if Isabelle knew this office—Oliver's fantasy secret bunker—even existed.

What else didn't she know about? She clearly didn't know their trip to Bali was a ruse—after all, if she knew she was going to be in Mexico the whole time, why would she go through the trouble of hiring me to hang the painting for her? No. That fake-out must have been Oliver pulling the strings. Maybe he told her last minute there was a change of plans. Rich people do that all the time—lost deposits don't matter to them. Then he picked her up from the Puerto Vallarta airport and drove her right to the hike, packed clothes and sneakers for her, and forced her up that hill with some false promise of reconciliation, like he was going to get down on one knee at the top and present her with a wedding-renewal ring . . .

But why? Why manipulate her like this? *I swear the wife can hear through walls*, Oliver wrote to Neil. Clearly, Isabelle was starting to figure something out. Some secret.

I think about what I've learned about Oliver so far: there's the chick in Sayulita . . . Maybe Isabelle found out and threatened to leave him—taking half of everything with her? (Because surely Isabelle would have been savvy enough to make sure the prenup was fair.) Then there's whatever "accounting issue" he was emailing with Neil about . . . David Morrow said Neil was in bed with sketchy people. Isabelle might have known Oliver played dirty in business too. Known all sorts of shady stunts her husband had pulled over the years. Shit the lawyers are no good for. Things you need to keep quiet any way you can.

One gnarly hike, and a well-timed push, and she's gone. All his problems are solved.

Oliver Beresford: not just a smug asshole, but a murderer.

When a woman turns up dead, it's nearly always the husband. What does that tell you about the state of marriage these days? Doesn't matter how goddamn rich you are. As a woman, you're still replaceable, interchangeable, disposable.

Fucking disgusting murdering prick. If it's true. Which is a big "if," but still. Now that this version of the story is in my head, I can't see it any other way. He killed her—or tried.

But if he did, then how the hell did Oliver end up dead in the jungle too?

I think of Isabelle's Instagram post, a blurry image of a woman in a ponytail: don't mess with us—women are strong.

Did she see it coming and fight back?

I picture Oliver and Isabelle wrestling on that lookout point, falling together in the scramble, rolling closer and closer to the edge. I think of Isabelle and her legs, powerful from all that kick-boxing, lunging and shoving and fighting for her life.

Isabelle, taking her lying scumbag husband right down with her in the end.

If that's what happened, then *fuck. Yes.* And she deserves to be fought for now.

I go back to scanning the emails one more time. Oliver asking Neil Kelly to talk on the golf course, where his prying wife won't hear. If anyone knows more about what Oliver has to hide, it's him.

I grab the key and climb back out through the window. It's time for a visit to Neil and Palmer's house.

• • •

"I will get her, Señoras," I hear Martina say when I open the front door. Julia and Aimee have stopped by for a walk.

"Did you go without me?" Julia asks, after our mandatory greeting hug. (Double kisses for Aimee, of course.) I realize I'm already in my running gear, and sweating from breaking in—and out—of Oliver's lair, so I tell her, "A few blocks to warm up." I'd completely forgotten we'd made plans. But this is great. I think better when I'm moving, and I need to come up with a smooth way to get myself invited to Palmer and Neil's house. Palmer's a nightmare to deal with, but there's too much at stake here. I have to find out what Oliver was up to. What Neil knows. What liabilities need to be taken care of.

My life as Isabelle is on the line.

We fast-walk on the beach, pounding the hard sand at the water's edge, dodging waves, as I listen to stories about Aimee's new lipstick line and the upcoming regatta and auction I've agreed to help Julia with. I'll not only help with decor, but I also committed to donating a piece of art for the live auction. It's what Isabelle would do. But as I nod and smile, my mind remains focused on how to get into the Kelly house. It can't just be a girls' night either—I need the cover of a large crowd . . . What's that Gatsby line about large parties being more intimate? *At small parties, there isn't any privacy.*

"Can I ask you both something?" I say when we reach the rocky patch where we always turn around. "Is everything okay with Palmer?"

"What do you mean?" Julia asks, her brow crinkling with genuine concern.

"I couldn't help but notice she was acting a little strange on the boat the other day—"

"She doesn't have a drinking problem, if that's what you mean." Julia cuts in, defending her friend. "She just has a really low tolerance. I think maybe she has an allergy to the tannins or something."

Uh-huh. Sure, hon. But I file away this supposed allergy as a mental note.

"No, it's not that," I say. "It's just, when she and I chatted alone on deck, she kept dropping hints—unintentionally, I'm sure—she was plastered—that things were . . . tight for them. It made me remember something Oliver told me: his company was having issues with Neil's . . . and, well, I hate to say it"—I lower my voice, forcing Aimee and Julia to lean in to hear me better over the waves—"but it sounds like they might be in some kind of financial trouble."

"Really?" Julia runs a few steps to avoid a rush of white water. "I mean, I guess it's possible. Neil *is* a bit of a gambler. He used to be this big music producer, but now he's semiretired. He's always investing in different things. There was that protein bar company—"

"Titan Bars," Aimee supplies. "He made a good profit on that one. But he took a bath on that Ethereum-alternative company he put money into. Founder was a lunatic, it turned out, and the whole thing went belly-up."

"It's true . . ." Julia looks worried.

"Well, I only bring it up because just the other day I overheard Martina and Lupe—"

"Everyone talks so much here. The walls have ears." Aimee rolls her eyes. She's making it out like the house staff are the ones with a gossip problem, but really, the big talkers are the arrogant American homeowners who don't realize the help understands English. I've heard these women say some pretty personal shit in front of their staff without thinking twice.

"What did she say?" Julia asks.

"I only understood a portion of it, but it sounded like maybe his latest investment isn't panning out." I think of Morrow, describing those "screaming phone calls" from Mr. Kelly. "I mean, think about it: they never have people over."

Julia covers her shocked-open mouth. "Do you think they're selling?"

"Oh dear," Aimee says with a sincere frown.

"That would be so sad," Julia says.

Yeah, I'm crying a river. I toss a rock into the waves, watching the water rush over my toes.

My indifference must show on my face because Julia says, "I know she can be a bitch to you, but she's a good person. And if she's really stressed, and has to move . . . maybe that explains why she's been so catty lately."

I give a little shamefaced nod. Classic sweet, Midwestern Julia will run right to Palmer's to make sure she's okay. And I know exactly how Palmer will react to the notion that all is not well in Kelly-land.

They're nice women. I like them, I do, but they're so predictable; it takes only a couple days for an invitation to arrive to a party at their house, in "Celebration of all their recent success." I run into the group at the Kupuri Beach Club that Friday and find Palmer holding court. "I never give Neil the credit he deserves—he works so hard," she says, explaining why she's hosting a last-minute *look at how much money we have* party tomorrow night. It's so hasty it would reek of desperation to the rest of the Punta Mita crowd except that no one around here ever has much to do when they're here but show up to the clubs and dine out anyway. It's all slow-motion leisure time. Last-minute Saturday soirees are not uncommon, I've learned. They are a power flex. "I'm throwing this for *him*. Neil deserves to be celebrated!"

"I'm so excited!" Julia chirps—though the look of relief in her eyes tells me she's really saying, *I'm so glad you're not moments away from poverty after all!*

"You're welcome to come too, Isabelle," Palmer says, leveling me with a look that suggests she knows exactly what I've been saying about her and Neil and their supposed money problems. "Of course, you'll have to come by again in the spring—after we put on the addition." Her face strains into a self-satisfied smirk. She thinks she's one-upped me. That she's proving me and my nasty gossip wrong.

"I wouldn't miss it for the world," I say.

After all, the guest of honor must attend. Palmer doesn't know it, but the truth is, she's throwing the party for me.

11

"Isabelle Beresford," I say to the guard. The name feels different on my tongue tonight. More mysterious, more vulnerable.

He consults his list then waves me through the gates of Ranchos Estates enclave. The villas here are larger and set farther apart than the ones at Kupuri Estates. The real estate website I consulted earlier today claimed that this neighborhood offers "the ultimate villa experience" and that "no detail is too small"—a motto I happen to agree with. As I pored over the listing for Neil and Palmer's home— Villa Ranchos 25—I tried to catalog every detail of the layout. The party will likely be hosted on the back terrace, complete with a wade-in saltwater pool and thatched-roof cabanas sprinkled across the sprawling lawn. But it's the interior rooms that interest me most. Nine bedrooms, including two primary suites. One of which might contain information about Oliver and Neil's secret dealings.

What sinister shit were you two boys up to?

The circular drive is packed with golf carts and luxury cars when I pull up. Live music drifts from beyond the house as I float through the grand entryway—which has, no joke, a couple of guards carrying machine guns standing on either side.

I've barely crossed the threshold when I'm offered a pale pink drink with a flower garnish on the edge of a salt-rimmed glass. "Palmer Paloma?"

Suppressing an eye roll at the cheesy custom cocktail, I thank the waiter and take a sip—frothy and sweetly acidic, with a sting of salt. Just like Palmer. Old Liz would down this instantly and a few more as well, letting the tequila warm my veins and liven me up. But I'm too aware of those armed guards. Tonight, I need a clear head. After another sip, I ask, "Would you please bring me Topo Chico with lime, instead?" and send the waiter back to the bar to switch out my drink.

The house is modern and tasteful, a series of wide doorways opening into room after room. Must be at least ten thousand square feet, and it's empty except for the bustling staff and a stray guest or two looking for the powder room. I take a quick moment to wander the first floor, aiming for an air of mild curiosity—studying the painting in the dining room, running a hand along the credenza in the hallway—while I scan every surface for information. I feel the familiar urge to sneak straight to the bedrooms, but I sense the eyes of the household staff on me. And, anyway, I know better. This isn't about pinching a few credit cards and pricey rings. The stakes are higher tonight. And the task more difficult. I need to find a lead. It's not like Neil left a sticky note on his bathroom mirror that reads, *Tuesday 9am: commit white-collar crime w/Oliver.*

"Señora?" the waiter says when he returns with my drink. "The party is out back. This way, please."

"Of course." I follow him through the living room and onto the pool deck. Outside, sunset shines magic-hour light on all the guests. I breathe in the evening air: a mix of salty ocean breeze and expensive perfume.

Palmer has indeed gone full-on Gatsby, flaunting money to attract a beautiful crowd. There must be at least fifty people here milling around the pool and spilling onto the lawn beyond. Perfect—for her purposes, and for mine.

I immediately clock Julia near the pool, chatting with a woman

I recognize from the yacht club. I turn the other way. Last thing I need right now is an hour-long convo about the status of the regatta and the charity auction I stupidly offered to help out with. Off under one of the cabanas, I spot Aimee cozied up to a handsome man whom I vaguely recognize as a famous race-car driver. She's laughing coyly at his every word, and he's clearly getting off on the attention. *Atta girl, Aimee.* Let her have her fun. It's Neil and Palmer I have my eye on anyway. And there he is, hovering near the pizza oven in a crisp linen suit, chatting with a cluster of similarly dressed, clean-cut fortysomethings.

I make my way toward the raw bar set up on the far end of the pool deck, keeping an eye out for Palmer's blond ponytail. Bouncing around, playing host, she'll be distracted, which makes her an easier place to start.

The back of the Kellys' home is almost entirely made of glass. Looking up from the pool deck, you can see the outline of each dimly lit room, giving it a kind of dollhouse effect. I like to think I'm the little girl playing with her pretty Punta Mita doll set, pulling the strings and manipulating people into doing and saying what I want them to. But I don't want to get carried away in the fantasy and forget that behind all the twinkling bullshit, glamorous worlds are the most fucked up and ruthless of all. How many men at this party would push their own wives over a cliff, if given a chance? How many of these women would kill too?

Speaking of ruthless women, here comes Palmer.

"You look stunning." I kiss her cheek. Her hair's down and wavy like it air-dried after an ocean swim. It's much less severe than her usual ponytail. It probably took two hours, but her stylist made the right choice.

"So do you," Palmer says, eyeing me up and down with sincere admiration. I think back to Julia's comments on the beach—that Palmer's a bitch, but she's a good person. I remember thinking that about Bekka, even after she fucked me over. Some part of me still wanted another chance. I'd used her to get a guy, to reinvent myself, but what I missed the most from those days, once they were over for good, wasn't the parties with Josh and his royal roommate. It was all those times we went out together, when she made me feel like the two of us could conquer anything.

"Your house is fantastic," I say. Which is sincere too. But I would have said it anyway because I know what that compliment means to Palmer, and I want her to like me tonight.

She's empty-handed, so when the waiter nears, I grab her a drink.

"Thank you," she says. "The host is always the last one served, right?" She downs her tequila, closing her eyes from the alcohol burn, and the waitress repours.

I hook my arm through hers and lead her inside. "Give me a tour!"

We walk from room to room, poking our heads into the various bedrooms, and I pause a few extra seconds on her and Neil's suite. But Palmer doesn't let me linger—we have to see the gym and the playroom and the sauna. Finally, we circle back to the pool deck and step out into the steady breeze. I'm a little shocked when she pulls me close and gently settles her head on my shoulder with a deep sigh. "Beautiful, isn't it?" she breathes. "I'm so glad you came down to Punta Mita. Things were getting so boring before you got here, Isabelle."

She's buzzed. Time to start making my move . . .

"Looks like he's having fun too." I nod to Neil, who smokes a cigar with a cluster of cigar-smoking men around a firepit in the sand. They've corralled a shot waitress: every time one of them raises his glass, she refills it to the top.

"Ugh, I hate that shit-eating grin." Palmer laughs. "You'd think he had something to do with this party. He didn't lift a finger. He was all, 'I have to close this deal. You have no idea how much pressure I'm under.' And I was like, 'Well, I've been singled-handedly organizing this massive party *by myself*, so yeah, I think I *do* understand what pressure is, Neil.'"

My ears perk up at the news of a stressful deal, and I start thinking of ways to get more info out of Palmer without seeming too interested. But before I can come up with something, she continues on with her rant. "I even had to hassle him to get dressed. Hello, the only thing you have to do is show up, and you're making *that* hard? He couldn't decide between two belts. I almost strangled him with one." She finishes her drink. "Just kidding," she adds as we watch him smile at the cute waitress's low-cut shirt.

"Actually, suspenders make a much better murder weapon, because of the elastic," I tell her.

She looks at me in surprise, then laughs again, for real this time.

"What was I thinking with the shot girls? Lord help me if my husband gets a boner in public."

Now it's my turn to laugh for real. Tequila Palmer rules.

While she glares at Neil, I wrangle two more shots. "To Neil *not* getting a boner," I say, raising mine.

This time, I dump my tequila into a potted plant.

Palmer drinks her shot, then sighs. "He really is a complete jackass sometimes. But I love him. And he's a great dad." Her face softens as she looks across the yard at Neil. Even for all her complaints about him, she's still looking at him like he's the hottest guy in the frat and he's all hers. It's clear I'm not going to get her to turn on her husband and expose his dirty secrets. And judging by her starry-eyed expression, there's a good chance she doesn't even know about any of his shady dealings with Oliver. Still, I need to try. Maybe I can lead her there. Expose my own vulnerability and make her eager to help. Make her feel like it's the least she can do, given how perfect her own marriage is.

"Palmer," I whisper, "I love Oliver, but sometimes I feel like I don't really *know* him, you know?" I catch her eyes, and something passes between us, unsaid. It leaves a cold, sick feeling in my gut. She *does* know something. She swallows a lump in her throat, glancing back over at Neil, and then back to me. She looks like she's about to tell me something, but she's not quite sure how to say it. *Come on, Palmer. We girls gotta stick together.*

"Isabelle, I—" But the band starts playing a tropical version of Madonna's "Borderline," and Palmer lets out a scream and pulls me onto the dance floor.

Aimee and Julia join us, and after a few songs, everyone's ready for another drink. I don't even have to fake it at this point—they're too drunk to notice if I drink my shot or not. Palmer can't weigh more than a hundred and ten pounds. I'm impressed she's lasted this long, but I can see by her sloppy moves, she's about to crash. If she gets too drunk, she won't be of any use to me. I just wanted to loosen her tongue a bit. Maybe Julia was right—maybe she does have some kind of allergy to alcohol. I nudge her aside. "Let's get you some water."

It takes Palmer a few seconds to understand my words. She wobbles on her tall wedge heels. "Yeah," she says. "I don't feel so good."

"I've got you." I hold her around her waist for the walk back inside, because otherwise, she'll fall. *Fuck.* I need her to open up to me, not open up the contents of her guts. "Come on," I say as I help her up the stairs. "You can do it."

"I'm gonna . . . I think I'm . . ." She lists in the direction of her room.

"I got you." I rush her down the hall, then through her bedroom, through the pass-through walk-in closet, where makeup and hairbrushes clutter her vanity. Neil's stuff is everywhere too. They got dressed in a hurry—clothes and shoes and belts litter the floor. I can just imagine the argument that played out, the nastiness that went on behind the scenes before they both emerged coiffed and sparkling, ready to be Mr. and Mrs. Host. I maneuver Palmer to the toilet and find a hair clip. I twist her hair away from her sweaty face and she drops to her knees just in time to puke.

"Thank you," she manages to say with her face on the toilet seat. She slides down onto the tile floor.

"Come on," I say, trying to lift her. "Let's get you in bed."

"No. No, no, no . . . I like it here." Her eyes close; her mouth goes slack. I jostle her—I don't want her to fucking choke and die on me. I'm relieved when she lets out a moan. I try to move her, but she's so heavy, her body limp, leaden. She's barely conscious, but she's digging in. "Let me stay here." So I roll up a towel and place it under her head, then I wet a washcloth with cold water and drape it across her forehead. *We girls gotta stick together.* It's not just a line. Maybe if more of us were paying attention, we'd be less likely to get dragged by the wrists, pushed against walls, cornered in dark offices—shoved off cliffs . . .

"Thank you, Isabelle," she says before fading out.

The music from the party thuds through the floor, and I get to work. The mess in the walk-in closet is an unexpected opportunity— they won't notice anything moved. Palmer won't remember anything at all. I find his wallet in the back pocket of his discarded jeans, crumpled in a ball on the floor like they're Wranglers and not Givenchy. I grab a few pesos—I'm low—and a couple of hundreds, then photograph his cards and IDs since you never know.

I move back into the bedroom and can't believe my eyes when I spot a cell phone charging on a bedside table that appears to be Neil's. (It's empty save for the phone, a lamp, and a pair of glasses— the other is covered in Palmer's rejected party dresses.) A quick check of the lock screen—some preset abstract background— confirms my suspicions. Palmer's phone is plastered with pictures of her kids. This must be Neil's.

But of course the phone is locked.

I peek into the bathroom at Palmer, who's rolled onto her side and looks like a child curled around the porcelain bowl.

"Palmer?" I whisper. "Palmer?"

"Okay . . . I'm okay . . . I'm alive . . ." She doesn't move or open her eyes.

I'm out of options, and soon will be out of time. Julia and Aimee are bound to come up here to check on our tipsy host; they saw me guide her off the dance floor. "Palmer?"

She grunts.

"I have to make a phone call."

"Phone . . ."

"But my phone is dead. Neil's is here, but it's locked. Do you know the code?"

I know it's a risky move, but whether it's an allergy or not, she didn't remember interrogating me about Monte Rosa on the yacht last weekend. She didn't remember anything at all from that champagne-soaked day. I'm betting she won't remember this either.

She grunts out a response. "His birthday. So stupid." She's out again, but luckily I have the motherfucker's driver's license. I type in his six-digit birthday then swipe away the screen saver so all his apps are revealed. I would kiss Palmer if her mouth didn't reek of vomit. I kneel beside the bed and dig in.

This is Mexico, where everyone uses WhatsApp. If Oliver and Neil were discussing "sensitive" information, that's where they'd be doing it. I open the app, and the first thread is between Neil and Palmer. I can't help myself:

Where the hell are you? Golf doesn't take eight hours?

For fuck's sake! Stop busting my balls. I'm making deals out here. Deals that pay for your fucking lifestyle.

Fine! Also, Cynthia forgot to get milk.

Goddamn marriage noir. On the next scroll down, Neil shares

a series of photos with Palmer titled *Dinner in Sayulita*. The first shot is a view from their table of the beach at sunset, the waves dotted with surfers, tourists strolling past the restaurant in the sand. There's a bottle of champagne and four glasses, half-filled. In the next shot, Neil and Palmer raise those glasses to toast. It's like I know before I see the next photo. I've been Isabelle so long, I've tapped into her intuition. And I'm right. Across the table from the Kellys, Oliver and another woman raise champagne glasses too.

She has long brown hair and suntanned skin. She's a little younger than Isabelle, maybe, but not enough to make a difference. Perky little body, flat chest . . . She looks like a yoga type. Oliver's hand is on her shoulder, his arm wrapped around her back. She's looking at him like she wants to devour him whole. Maybe that's what attracted Oliver to her. That blind adoration. From what I've learned about Isabelle, she had her own life. Charities she served on, vacations she took without him. Oliver probably even resented her kickboxing classes. Sixty minutes when her focus was on something other than him.

I replay the scene from that harrowing outlook again in my mind: Oliver pushing Isabelle over the cliff, thinking he was about to be free of his ball and chain; Isabelle taking him down with her. *Sorry, Yoga Boobs, you'll have to pay for your own Dom Perignon now.*

I glare toward the bathroom, where Palmer is still lying in misery on the floor. All this time she knew my husband was a cheating dick. She smiled in my face and rested her head on my shoulder, when all the while she knew about Oliver's mistress. Drank fucking champagne with her. Were they toasting my impending death? Were they all in on that too?

It all brings Palmer's iciness toward me into perspective. Her allegiances were made prior to my arrival here. She'd never met me—never met Isabelle—but she'd already chosen her side. She was privy, probably, to a bunch of shit Oliver said about me—about Isabelle—behind her back. Maybe he railed about how nosy Isabelle was, how jealous, unhinged. I wouldn't like the sound of me either.

Not that this excuses Palmer one bit. Never believe a husband if he tells you his wife's crazy.

I send myself a screenshot of the smug mistress picture and delete the outgoing message. I need to commit this girl's face to memory, on the off chance she comes sniffing around Casa Esmerelda looking for him.

I can't stay in here forever, though, and while I want to dig into this affair as if I were the one he cheated on, I need to focus. I need to uncover Oliver's dirty secret—the one he was worried Isabelle had found out about. Because I don't have time to read their whole WhatsApp thread, I screen-record the exchange so I can play the video in slo-mo when I get home. Palmer moans softly in the background while I catch snippets of the two men's conversation as they roll by.

Hey what's the hold up on Beresford Capital coming onboard with the Cobre Vista deal?, Neil texts.

Sorry, been tied up. Dealing with the Isabelle situation, Oliver responds.

The "Isabelle situation"? That doesn't sound good . . . Is he talking about all the legal paperwork I saw on his desk? Or is he talking about a more *permanent* solution to his "Isabelle situation"? One that would end over the edge of a jungle cliff?

I continue reading and find several unanswered texts from Neil in a row:

Ok—confirmed that the minimum buy-in is 40M a share. How much can Beresford Capital go in for?

Ollie—You in man?

Told the guys at Cobre you were in.

What's going on? Need the $ bro.

Hello?

Finally, Oliver surfaces.

Hey you around to talk today? Having some second thoughts on Cobre.

WTF? This is an amazing opportunity! You're lucky I brought you in. We're gonna make BANK!

Not sure copper is the right investment for BC right now.

Dude what the hell? You can't let me get fucked over. This isn't funny—these guys don't mess around. And neither do I. You gotta pay your share. Or you'll regret it, trust me.

"What the fuck do you think you're doing?"

I whip around and stand, nearly dropping the phone. It's Neil—I should have locked the door. I should have left Palmer and just taken the phone.

"What are you doing with my phone?" he repeats.

"I—I needed to call for help . . ." Standing in the doorway, Neil's body, wide like a football player's, blocks my escape. "I couldn't leave Palmer . . ." Neil pushes off the doorframe—toward me. The door slams behind him as he advances. He doesn't head toward the bathroom, doesn't even check to see if his wife is okay.

"Neil?" Palmer moans. "Neil?"

But he's headed for me. "I don't like when people snoop around my personal things, Isabelle."

Shit. Shit. Shit. I keep my eyes on Neil, while I reopen the photo app with a tap of my thumb. "I knew it," I say, shoving the picture of Oliver and his lover in Neil's face. The image jams his brain like I'd hoped. "When was this taken?" I'm back in charge, winning on offense. "When did you and my husband—and his *lover*—all have dinner together? When?" I simultaneously whisper and yell. I make my eyes water. I shake my head like I'm crushed.

He's confused now, disarmed. But then he snaps back. "Oliver told me you were a loose cannon," he steps closer to me, taking possession with his tequila-and-fish stinking breath. "Come on, Izzy. We both know he wasn't the only one stepping out."

"Neil?" Twenty feet away, almost unconscious on the floor, Palmer tries again.

"I saw you leave the welcome party with Jay Logenbach." His eyes narrow. "You women are fucking hypocrites. You all like to bitch about how we're the dogs, but you're just as bad. So you can spare me with your woe is me bullshit."

Inches away now, he douses me again with his hot, disgusting tequila breath. I try to get past him, but he blocks my path.

"I've been wondering which one of you was to blame for Oliver's little 'change of heart.' The wife or the mistress? Which one of you had him so pussy-whipped you got him to renege on a very, very lucrative deal?"

I back into the edge of the bed and nearly fall onto it. "I—I don't know what you're talking about."

"No one else at Beresford knew what we were up to." Spit sprays from Neil's mouth. "We were sworn to secrecy. And now, all of a sudden, he has a change of heart? The only explanation is that he squealed, and one of you talked him out of investing in Cobre Vista. Now we're all fucked." He leans toward me. "I need Beresford Capital to make good on their share of the deal. And if Oliver's not here to fix it . . ." He grabs my wrist. His phone falls to the floor, but he doesn't let go.

"Palmer!" I yell. "Help!" Neil covers my mouth with his hand.

"Shut up," he says, though Palmer didn't hear me. She's dead to the world. I'm cornered in this bedroom while that party rages outside. Trapped.

But then light blasts into the room—the bedroom door bangs open.

Neil backs away before I've even let out my held breath.

It's Tilly, framed in the bedroom doorway, smiling in a sleek black dress.

She takes it all in: Palmer on the bathroom floor, me against the bed, terrified. "I didn't realize this is where the party was at," she deadpans.

12

I've never been so happy to see another human being. Neil stumbles away from me with an asinine *I didn't do anything* look on his face, and I discreetly check my own in the closet mirror. Thankfully, I still look like me. Like Isabelle.

"Party . . ." Palmer manages one word. Neil magically transforms into a husband who cares and runs to her aid.

"Come on, baby," he says. "I'll carry you to bed." Then he lifts her like he loves her and cradles her in his arms.

Palmer manages to open her eyes while Neil transfers her to her bed and her gaze lands on Tilly. "I didn't invite you," she murmurs.

"She came to get me," I say, though I had no idea she'd be here—it's like she felt my fear and came to my rescue. I take Tilly's outstretched hand. "We have another gathering to get to, right, Till?"

"Yeah. We'd better get going. Everyone can't wait to meet you," Tilly says, playing along.

FOMO momentarily rouses Palmer. With her head hanging back over Neil's arm, and her sloppy vomit mouth open, she mumbles, "Maybe I'll catch up with you there later," before her eyes drift shut again.

I pull Tilly by the hand and flee the room without a backward glance at Neil.

Outside, the band has long since stopped, and the DJ spins loud dance tracks to the drunk crowd. I hope for a quick exit as we race down the stairs, but Aimee and Julia catch us by the front door.

"You can't leave so soon," Julia says.

Soon? It feels like I've been trapped for days.

"It's too early," Aimee adds as she air-kisses me goodbye.

We pass the armed guards and I have the ugly conviction they're staring at our asses, but I don't turn to confirm the theory. We walk to Tilly's golf cart without speaking, and she floors the gas out of the drive. Once we're past the Ranchos Estates guard, and on the long road back to the other side of Punta de Mita, speeding toward the little underpass that leads to the peninsula and to Kupuri Estates, I exhale. The blinking fireflies and night jungle sounds steady my pulse.

"Are you okay?" Tilly asks.

I can only nod in response. I'm still processing what happened. He covered my mouth with his sweaty hand; an inch higher and I wouldn't have been able to breathe.

"Neil is such a creep." Tilly shakes her head. "I can't stand men like him. They've gotten everything they've wanted for so long they don't know how to handle women like us."

"Women like us?"

"Women who find men like him disgusting." She laughs, but it sounds like a bark. "Women who can't be played."

I appreciate her vote of confidence, but right now, shaking in her golf cart, I can't help but remember past incidents with equally narrow escapes, like Tuck, the bar manager in Vancouver who hated that I wasn't interested in him, so he started threatening to turn me in for a lapsed work visa. One night, when we were closing up together, he caught me coming out of the bathroom and pushed me from behind. He'd been drinking during the shift, but I was sober, so when I hit the beer-sticky floor, I had the wits to flip around. When he jumped on me, I kicked him hard in the balls. Fuckface cried like a fucking brat. But I was too naïvely taken aback by Neil's aggression to think to knee him in the balls, or bite his hand. If Tilly hadn't shown up when she did, who the hell knows what might have gone down.

I glance at her profile against the moon, thankful for her divine timing. It's almost like she's been watching out for me. That's a foreign feeling—someone worrying about me even when we're not together. Someone caring enough to come find me. How *did* she find me?

The moon disappears while we drive under the bridge. Tilly's uncharacteristically quiet, and I wonder what she's thinking.

"Why did you come tonight?" I ask when we're circling the roundabout that leads to my house.

"I was looking for you. Martina told me you were there. I came to apologize."

"Apologize? For what?"

"For suggesting Oliver was having an affair. It was only stupid gossip—I should never have repeated it. I was a bad friend." She glances at me. Her tone and her wide brown eyes convince me she really believes in our friendship. That it matters to her to make things right.

"No. You were a good friend," I tell her. "And you were right. Sometimes, it feels like you're the only person here who actually tells the truth." I think again of Palmer and Neil, and God knows how many more people at that party, who knew about Oliver's affair and didn't tell me.

"You know," Tilly says, "I'll never forget the conversation we had at that gala at the Frick."

I want her to stop driving over the noisy cobblestones so I can hear every syllable of what she's about to reveal.

"That was a great night," I say, doing my best to sound like I was there.

"I'd never met a woman who didn't bullshit before."

That makes me smile.

"You said you hated Oliver—"

"I must have been in a mood," I say, admiring Isabelle even more than before.

"Well, *I'd* certainly had a lot to drink—you know me!" We both laugh. "You said it wasn't even specifically Oliver you were so mad at. That what really pissed you off was feeling unseen. Which I *so* relate to. I hate the idea of being one among many. Like I'm moving through a crowd and I could be anyone there, interchangeable. Sometimes, I just want to scream, you know?"

"Yeah," I say, because I do. She's captured how *I* feel, to a T. I've spent my whole adult life learning how to blend. After a while, you start to wonder where you end and the person you're pretending to be begins.

"There's something else you admitted," Tilly says.

"I can barely remember," I say. "I guess I had too many as well."

"You said you wanted out."

I picture the inside of the Frick Collection on the Upper East Side, where I've only been once. I see myself, as Isabelle, with Tilly in the fountain atrium, spouting the kind of deep truths that only spill after several flutes of champagne. If I didn't already know Oliver was a lying, cheating son of a bitch, I might have waved off Tilly's memory as the vapid griping of two privileged women. But I *do* know that about Oliver—and more. If Isabelle said she hated Oliver, and wanted out, she clearly had good reason. I wonder how long ago this interaction between Isabelle and Tilly took place, and for how many years Isabelle was miserable, trapped, maybe even afraid.

We roll into Kupuri Estates, and I unlock Esmerelda's front door, not even realizing Tilly is right behind me until she speaks.

She drops her beaded clutch on the sofa and heads for the bar, reaching up to grab glasses and the Siete Leguas Siete Décadas Blanco. But my stomach churns at the sight of the clear liquid sloshing in its sleek bottle. I raise my hand.

"Actually, no more tequila tonight." Not after smelling it on Neil's breath.

Tilly seems to understand. She grabs my hand, pulls me toward the wine cellar instead. It's late. Martina and Lupe have gone home. Our footsteps on the stone stairs are the only sound. The cellar is cool and dark. I hang back at the foot of the steps while Tilly trails her hand along the shelves, walking the length of the long narrow room as if there's some specific bottle she's looking for. When she reaches the end, my heart stutters, wondering if she'll spot the door to Oliver's secret study. I hid my Liz Dawson passport and phone behind the Hemingways as I'd planned, and now I'm terrified she'll find the room, open the door, and spot a book out of place. But she just kneels to grab a bottle and says, "Aha, I knew you'd have this! Come see."

When I lean over her shoulder to see what she's found, I smell her musky and masculine shampoo. Something expensive. "Okay, what am I looking at?"

She tinkles out a laugh. "You really know nothing about wine, do you?" She looks up at me like I'm her adorable little pet project. "This is a really special bottle. They only make like twenty of them a year."

"We should probably save it, then, right?" Normally, I'd be all for downing some rich asshole's precious vintage, but everything feels off tonight. I feel like I'm walking on eggshells, still unnerved by Neil's threatening words, his hand tight on my wrist . . .

"Why?" Tilly asks, pulling me out of my thoughts. "Because *Oliver* is saving it?" She says his name with so much disdain it's like she was the one he was cheating on. But she's right. There's no use saving the bottle out of some twisted loyalty to the Beresfords. Isabelle and Oliver are gone. I'm the only Isabelle now.

"Fuck it. Let's drink."

• • •

"I love that painting," Tilly says several glasses later, while we lounge on the sofa under the gaze of the women in the Tamayo painting, their blending macabre shades—purple and red, just like the dark wine stains on Tilly's lips.

I top her off.

"Thanks," she says with a giggle, looking at me like a giddy schoolgirl at a slumber party.

"Thank *you*," I say. "For saving me tonight." She beams at this like I've given her a prized gift. I take a sip from my own glass, letting the liquid linger in my mouth. I've come down from the edginess of the party, and everything feels looser now, softer.

The Tamayo swims a little in my vision. It has creeped me out since I first arrived to unload it, but now it seems like it's talking to me. Like it's telling a story of disappearance, the story of me becoming Isabelle, one form blending into another, seamlessly. It's a transformation, but also a kind of vanishing. I think about what she said earlier, what she and Isabelle talked about at the Frick. "Do you really feel like no one sees you? The real you, I mean?" The words leave my mouth before I even know I'm saying them. Before I even really know what I'm asking.

Tilly sets down her glass and leans toward me.

"All the fucking time."

Her eyes are startlingly lucid, while mine feel hazy and heavy. I let them drop shut and sink into the cushions.

"I think we're a lot alike, Isabelle," she says. "*I* see you."

I nod, but I'm suddenly so tired I can barely remember what

we're even talking about. Tonight was a lot. The warnings from Neil, both in his texts to Oliver and to me in the bedroom. It's making me dizzy, the number of people Oliver Beresford managed to wrong. Or maybe it's just the wine. I need to sleep it off. Let these new details settle in my brain so I can figure out what to do next.

"Time for bed?" Tilly asks, as if she's read my mind. "Do you want me to stay the night?" She wiggles closer to me on the sofa. Her body is warm and soft next to mine, and I'm tempted to just crash out right here. Tilly strokes my hair. But the gesture is more agitating than soothing. And the heat of her body is too much after what I've been through tonight. The fermented taste of wine in my mouth is too much too—like rotten grapes.

I collect our empty glasses and stand. "No, I'm fine. You should go home."

"Are you sure? You seem upset. I'm worried about you."

"I'm sure." I walk her to the door.

"I'll check on you in the morning," she says after I nudge her outside.

"Drive safely." I lock the door as she leaves.

• • •

I close my eyes and try to count myself to sleep. But I have the eerie sense that someone is standing over me *now*, watching me while I sleep. *I see you, Liz . . .*

I gasp, my eyes flashing open—but no one is there.

It's getting lighter already. But I still feel that same sense of unease. I'm so fucking over this feeling of being watched and pawed and trapped. I grab my robe and slip out to watch the water turn pink when the sun rises over the mountains.

I sit on the chaise outside my room and try to focus. What red flags am I missing? If Oliver killed Isabelle—and she brought him down with her—he's obviously not a threat to me now. But I still feel on high alert. I watch the waves crumble into sherbet foam on the white sand. I should be blissed out, but instead, I feel hunted, like someone—or something—wants nothing more than to take this all away from me.

My brain flips and tumbles like the waves that inch closer with the rising tide. Here's what I know: Oliver had a mistress, and there are several encrypted docs to and from lawyers on his computer. Possible divorce plans, but that's just a guess. He also had enemies. He pissed off Neil Kelly—owed him money for some investment deal that Neil wanted Beresford Capital to go in on. Neil said the guys they were working with "don't mess around." And David Morrow implied the same thing. Whoever Neil was wrapped up with was sketchy as fuck. And then Oliver apparently grew a conscience at the last minute and decided to get out? It doesn't seem likely, based on the vision of him now firmly established in my head—arrogant, brash, a risk-taker. But I guess it could be possible. I know better than most that sometimes, you just get tired of running.

My phone is still in the bedroom, but I need to Google Cobre Vista, the company Neil was trying to buy into . . . Oliver's text mentioned copper—an industry I know nothing about. But the details of the deal matter less than this new question that's been haunting me: Is it possible Oliver didn't kill Isabelle, but rather *someone else* killed them both?

Did Cobre Vista come looking for their money? Or was it Neil who snapped?

I can still see his face when he came at me in the bedroom—all screwed up in rage. Julia said he gets hotheaded, and David Morrow said Neil called Oliver's office screaming.

And suddenly I can picture Neil up there on that hike, following on Oliver's and Isabelle's heels. Harassing Oliver to reconsider, demanding it, wheedling the same way he did in those texts, until things got heated, and Neil grew violent—reckless. I picture Isabelle screaming for him to stop, which only made him angrier, and then . . .

But if Neil killed the couple . . . then he must know they're both dead.

Which means he knows I'm not Isabelle.

He could expose me as a fraud, extort me for the Beresford money he's so desperate to get his hands on. And if I don't comply? Well, he's already killed Isabelle once . . .

The sun inches over the mountain range where Oliver and Isabelle died, and it floods the pool on the deck below me with searing yellow rays.

Swimming always focuses my brain. I grab my bikini and head to the pool. I dive in and swim a few lengths, hoping for clarity. But there's pressure in my ears, pressure in my head. I dolphin-kick back to the shallow end underwater, when suddenly, a figure appears at the edge of the pool. It's a man, I can tell that much, even from below the surface. Deep brown hair and khakis, white shirt. How was he able to get past Martina into the back patio? But it's barely seven a.m.—she doesn't get here till eight. I'm trapped. Again. It's like another recurring nightmare.

It could be someone from Cobre Vista. It could be Neil. Back to finish whatever he'd been about to start with me last night.

No, wait, this man is slimmer, and taller. I stop kicking and the blurry figure kneels and bends over the pool like he's about to catch me in a net. A flash of strange familiarity moves through me. I've seen the shape of this face. For a moment, it feels like I'm seeing a ghost through the rippling haze of the water. Because I suddenly realize I *have* seen that face before. I recognize that Beresford chin.

Oliver? I almost choke, bursting up to the surface for air.

But, of course, it's not Oliver standing here before me. The man smiles, pushes a messy lock of hair from his brow. Sleeves rolled up, strong tanned arms. It's the man in the photos from Oliver's study. It's . . .

"Braden." The long-lost brother.

He offers me his hand as if to help me from the pool. Our fingers touch, and fear lurches into my throat as he studies my eyes.

"Isabelle," he says with a slow grin.

13

Fuck me. Oliver's brother, here in the flesh. I do recognize him—from the sailing picture, though he's aged (well). This is the man Palmer mentioned, the bad-boy brother Oliver wasn't close to. But just *how* estranged were they? Enough that Braden wouldn't recognize an imposter posing as his sister-in-law?

I drop his hand like I've been burnt, grabbing onto the pool wall for support. Even on zero sleep, my brain's still running the rapid calculations that have, so far, kept me alive. Why is Braden here in Mexico? My gut says he's not just stopping by because he happened to be in the neighborhood . . . I feel that familiar constricting in my throat—a warning that something is off, that I need to tread lightly.

I squint up at him, and take in the glow of the pool reflecting in his deep brown eyes, and the sun on his sinewy arms. *My God, Isabelle, you sure chose the wrong brother.* Oliver's good looks were more polished, almost Ken doll–esque. But Braden's are a little rougher around the edges. He's like the bass player in the band. He doesn't need to be in the spotlight because he gets plenty of attention in the shadows—at least, from the girls smart enough to notice him.

I venture a simple—and truthful—greeting. "I'm surprised to see you here, Braden."

He says nothing in response. His eyes are fixed on me, his gaze penetrating. Normally, a look like that from a guy like him would send a flush of heat to my cheeks. But this is not the stare of a man who's spotted me across the bar and likes what he sees. No, this is more scrutinizing. Braden is studying me. Searching my face for traces of the Isabelle he remembers.

Confidence, I remind myself, *is half the battle*. I take a deep breath and climb out of the pool in one fluid motion, allowing Braden to get a quick look at my body—the high-cut bathing suit clinging to my skin, the water droplets dripping down my chest—with my right hand covering my scar (in case he's not distracted by everything else). Sure enough, a bit of leg and boob is enough to jolt Braden's brain into a reboot. He shakes his head slightly, his sharp-eyed gaze softening into something more friendly as he hands me a towel.

"It's good to see you, Is. For a minute there, I almost wasn't sure it was you." I flinch at that and wrap myself tightly in the towel. "It's been a minute since we last saw each other."

"It has." I spot a pair of sunglasses I've left discarded on a lounge chair and slip them on to better shield my face as I navigate this conversation. "It's been . . . what . . . ?" I trail off, hoping I seem like I'm just racking my brain for the precise number of months—years?—it's been since Braden and Isabelle last met. Luckily, Braden supplies the answer—

"Coming up on two decades, right? Since the wedding."

My head whips around to his before I can stop myself. *Twenty years?* I guess the brothers *were* pretty fucking estranged. I think back to what Palmer said at that very first club party. *Such a shame, what addictions do to a family.*

My stress levels recede. If my disguise has been effective enough to convince someone like Tilly, who has interacted with the real Isabelle much more recently, then I should be able to fool someone who hasn't seen Isabelle since she was in her early twenties.

"Look, I know we've lost touch over the years . . ." He struggles with whatever he's trying to say. "But I wanted to apologize for my behavior that night. I was kind of a mess back then. And the open bar didn't help . . ."

Oh? Clearly, something juicy went down at Isabelle and Oliver's wedding. A drunken brawl over the family inheritance? Some deep-seated childhood rivalry re-sparked after one too many whiskeys?

"You were pretty smashed." I keep my voice neutral, allow a little smirk. I can't help but sense a warmth between these two. Braden called me "Is" just now . . . The way he looks at me is almost unsettling. Too intense for an estranged brother-in-law.

"I'm sure Oliver's told you plenty of stories about me over the years," he says.

"A few," I say. "But I've only ever heard his side of the story . . ."

"Well, from my side of things it's pretty simple: we just never liked each other all that much." There's no bitterness in Braden's voice, just acceptance. "There were times when things were better between us, but even when we were sailing together, we were always competing. We were just so different, you know? He was the golden boy, and I was the wild screwup."

The lead guitarist versus the bass player, I think to myself. I know which one I'm picking every time.

"Oliver never trusted me. Not that I can blame him." Braden turns away for a minute, staring out past the perimeter of the estate, to the ocean, as if remembering transgressions from his past. "I know I burned some bridges with him, but I always liked you, Isabelle. Right from the first time we met in that dive bar. I couldn't believe you'd gotten Ollie to go somewhere so chill." He gives a little chuckle, then his deep brown eyes are back on me. "I remember thinking you were something else." There's that heat again—but this time, it doesn't feel like he's scrutinizing me. It's like he's *hungry* for me.

Well, well, well. Maybe Isabelle *was* smart enough to recognize the bass player bad boy after all.

Did Braden come on to Isabelle while she was dating his brother? Was there some drama over it at the wedding? There are clearly some serious vibes going on here. I'm pretty sure Isabelle and Braden fucked—or at least wanted to.

If they did have sex, Braden will have seen *all* of Isabelle— making him a major liability for me now. But maybe there's a way to play this to my advantage. Clearly, he's still holding a bit of a torch for her. If I give him just an ounce of feeling back—a soft hand on his arm, a gaze infused with a smidge of lust—I could have him eating out of the palm of my hand. Braden's memories of Isabelle have had twenty years to fade, to get tangled up with fantasy and longing. It's actually the perfect scenario for me to work my magic.

I lean into him, my voice a breathy whisper. "It's good to see you too. But why are you here, Braden? With no warning?"

"I tried to call you, Is. You wouldn't answer. Which I under-stand, but—"

"Oh, I lost my phone. I didn't even see the calls," I say hurriedly. "You came all the way here?" *What's so urgent, hot brother?*

"Isabelle. I'm here because Oliver called me."

It's a cold-water shock to the system. I lean back, tightening the towel around me once again.

"What? When?" I sit down on a lounge chair, and he takes one beside me.

"A few weeks ago—maybe a month? It was completely out of the blue. You know he and I are hardly ever in touch anymore. I can't remember the last time we had a full conversation in over a decade."

I start counting back the days to my arrival here in Mexico, to when I found Oliver's and Isabelle's bodies on the hike . . . Based on what Braden's saying, he might have been one of the last people to hear from Oliver before he died.

"What did he say?"

"We didn't speak—he left a voicemail saying we needed to talk, urgently. I tried to call him back, but never got through. And then I couldn't reach you either."

"Is that why you're here?" I say. "To see Oliver? Because he's not here."

"I know. David Morrow called me." My stomach churns. This is not good. Clearly, this Morrow guy is not going to stop until he finds Oliver. Braden mistakes the concern on my face for confusion and says, as if to clarify, "Technically, I'm still on the board of directors for Beresford Capital. And I guess Dad wanted to make sure the company stayed in the family, because the bylaws make me president if anything happens to Oliver." Braden runs a hand through his thick hair, clearly agitated by that possibility. I hardly know this man, but already I can sense that he's not the type who'd relish a desk job—even one that paid handsomely.

"Apparently, Oliver's AWOL," he says, "so now I have to clean up some mess that has Morrow bent out of shape. Ironic, huh? Now I'm the one cleaning up after Oliver instead of the other way around."

He smiles at me with a one-sided dimple, and I have the weirdest feeling of nostalgia, like we really do share memories of inside jokes, knowing looks exchanged across a crowded room, an ill-advised night where we took things too far . . . *Jesus, Liz, get ahold of yourself.*

"Good morning, Señora!" I break my gaze from Braden when Martina slides out through the patio doors. "Would you like breakfast?"

"*Sí, gracias.* And coffee," I say. "For two, please." I nod toward Braden.

"Señor Beresford?" she asks with too much excitement for my taste. Everyone wants to know where the man is.

"Well, yes." I stand. Braden does too. "This is Oliver's brother, Braden."

"*Mucho gusto*," Braden says smoothly, reaching out to shake Martina's hand. It's obviously something like "nice to meet you," but that's more than anyone here has said to their staff in Spanish since I've arrived, including me. I'm impressed. Not only is it a turn-on, but it could be useful. "*Gracias*, but unfortunately, I can't stay for breakfast."

As soon as Martina's back inside, Braden turns back to me, shrouded in seriousness once more. He squints at my face, and I again have the fleeting fear he's going to immediately spot me as a fake. But all he says is, "Morrow said Oliver was supposed to be in Bali?"

I look past him, over the pool, and out to the beach beyond. "We both were. But then he asked for *alone* time. Sent me here to open the house. I didn't even question it—you know how he is."

"I do."

In the distance, I watch an overeager gull tangling itself in a wave, confused, as if it's forgotten it has wings. But then it snaps back and flies easily to a cluster of its pals on dry sand.

"Anyway, I haven't heard from him since he left for Bali—or wherever the fuck he's actually gone. You know, last winter he told me he had a conference in France? Turned out he was in Alaska heli-skiing. For two weeks, I had no idea where the man was." Oliver will never be able to contradict me, so why not? "Morrow called me too," I tell Braden. "That's when I first realized he wasn't at the retreat in Bali."

"Well, we have to find him. Or I do, anyway—I can't let Beresford Capital fall apart. Whatever unfinished investment deal

Oliver left lingering is my problem now." Braden pulls out a pack of Marlboros. "Do you mind? It's the one vice I have left."

For a second, I linger on that, wondering what those other vices were.

"Go ahead," I say. We walk toward where the patio steps down into the sand. I notice he's not wearing a wedding ring, and he's here on his own . . . smoking . . . which, in my experience, is more of a single-guy thing. Wives and kids want Daddy to live. Most of the time, anyway. He relaxes a bit as we touch down into the sand, warm between my bare toes. He watches the waves and that flock of water-splashing birds. I watch too. When he finishes his cigarette, he puts it out in the sand, then slides the butt into his pocket. He'll litter his lungs, but not the beach . . . which is oddly endearing. If I weren't playing Isabelle, I'd make a move on him now.

"Can I take you to dinner tonight? I'm staying at the St. Regis."

"You're staying here in Punta Mita?" I say, genuinely alarmed. Braden might be easy on the eyes and fun to play off of, but I don't like the idea of him sticking around too long—especially not if he's going to be digging into Oliver's whereabouts.

"At least for the next few days. Morrow told me that Oliver was dealing directly with a guy named Neil Kelly, who lives down here. I need to connect with whoever Oliver was doing business with before he disappeared. Plus . . ." He turns to me, tosses the red-and-white box between his hands while he looks right through my sunglasses, into my Isabelle-green eyes. "I wanted to keep an eye on you."

I go rigid, all my muscles tensing. He wanted to keep an eye on me? As in, he's suspicious that I had something to do with Oliver's disappearance?

But then Braden continues, "I'm worried about you, Isabelle. It seems like Oliver might have made some bad decisions, and I don't want you paying the price for the mistakes he's made."

Braden's tone, and the way he's looking at me, like he's really afraid I'm at risk, makes it all seem more real. The concerns I've had ever since reading those threatening messages between Neil and Oliver grow.

"You really think something might have happened to him? That there might be someone out there who wants to hurt Oliver . . . to hurt *me*?"

"Maybe . . ."

Fuck, fuck, fuck. I was right, then. Oliver didn't push Isabelle and tumble down with her. They both were pushed. And whoever did it is still out there, possibly watching my every move.

"Isabelle, when was the last time you heard from him?"

I swallow. "I guess around the same time as you—about a month ago."

"That's a long time for a person to be completely off the grid, even for Oliver. David Morrow mentioned reporting him as a missing person—"

"Did he?"

"I told him to hold off—let me get down here and try to figure out what's going on first."

You and me both, I think. I need a minute to wrap my head around all of this. And to dig deeper into Oliver and Neil and Cobre Vista, and Braden too. I haven't even Googled him yet. So when Braden asks again about meeting up tonight, I suggest we do a late dinner.

"Sounds good." He rubs the wrinkles out of his khakis when he stands. "I'll pick you up around eight thirty?"

I escort him to his rental car, studying his movements from behind. I'm torn between fearing this man and lusting for him. That's always a potent combo. But I'm not Liz at a sketchy bar. I have to play this right, stay three moves ahead.

"*Hasta luego*," he says before driving away. And I'm struck by a brazen wish that I could scrap the whole charade and jump in his car.

I'm not even inside the house when I hear tires again on the gravel. *He's come back*, I think, like a needy schoolgirl. I'd be lying if I didn't admit the letdown of seeing Tilly instead behind the wheel of her golf cart.

"Hiya." She pops out of her cart. "You don't look ready for yoga . . ."

"Yoga? Did we—"

"Yes, we did. Yoga and Sunday brunch. We made plans last night." She sighs and paces a bit, her silver Birkenstocks crunching on the gravel. "Are you bailing?" she asks. She stops and faces me with her hands—balled into fists—on her hips. It's almost like she's angry at me. Which seems an overreaction to a friend forgetting plans, especially a friend who was in a shitty situation just the night before.

"Right, of course. Yoga. Sorry."

But I have no clue what she's talking about. I barely slept after that run-in with Neil, plus Tilly kept me up all hours drinking. Now my head is filled with Braden and his dead brother. My brain is fried. Yoga can't hurt. "Will you wait while I change? I'll be right back."

"I'll be here," Tilly says, and I wonder if I'm just imagining the edge in her voice.

• • •

I try to get into the practice. Clear my head, level out my breathing, all that shit. But it's not working. I'm too distracted by Braden's arrival. Not to mention the fear that someone out there might still have a target on Isabelle's back.

Beside me, Tilly's going all out. So instead of achieving Zen or whatever I'm supposed to do, I use all my energy trying to keep up with her. "Go at your own pace," our instructor, Amanda, says. I collapse into child's pose like it's called "dying animal" instead. Meanwhile, after an hour and a half of vinyasa, Tilly looks like she could easily sprint back up that fucking hike. She works out all the time, and it shows in the tight ripple of her abs; her arms, which aren't just toned but *hard*; her powerful, cut calves. It's hard to believe James doesn't worry about her down here. Looking like that, hanging out, as she does, at the hotel bars, making eyes at other guests, leaning in to flirt and gossip with the bartenders.

Thankfully, whatever was up her ass this morning couldn't keep up with her yoga either. All those down dogs and planks wiped away her bad mood. "I can't wait for brunch," she says, now practically skipping back to the cart.

We're seated under an umbrella at the Kupuri Beach Club patio facing the infinity pool. I order two eggs, like a normal person, but Tilly orders two entrees: French toast and huevos rancheros. I still don't understand how such a small person can have such a ravenous appetite. She must burn hundreds of calories just breathing.

"So, how are you doing?" she asks once our mimosas are served. (Tilly's health regimen includes drinking at noon.) "After last night, I mean."

I take a sip from my mimosa and nod. "I'm okay." I'm also not naïve. What happened last night could have been a lot worse. "Thank you again for saving me."

She reaches across the table and gives my hand a squeeze. "You know I have your back, right?"

Somehow, I don't find this reassuring. Neil didn't give a single fuck that his wife was half passed out right there in the bathroom. He implied *someone* would have to pay for Oliver's last-minute decision to bail on the deal . . . Now Braden is here wanting to talk to Neil too. Not only that, but both men could easily expose me as a fraud. Not for the first time in the past twenty-four hours, I consider packing my bags and getting the hell out of Mexico on the next flight I can find. I'm not stupid; I know all about the sunk-cost fallacy that keeps people chasing a bad idea because they've already invested so much of their energy. The most successful gamblers are the ones who know when to fold.

But something about this whole situation has snagged its claws into me. Braden's smile, hinting at the secrets he and real Isabelle obviously share. All the layers of deceit around the wealthy couple's obviously-*not*-accidental death. And, let's face it, the ongoing rush of being Isabelle. I just can't give it up. Not now. Not when there's still so much I want to do with this life.

"Actually, there's something I wanted to ask you about. I was so shaken up after . . . well, you know . . . with Neil, I completely forgot," I say truthfully.

"Do tell." She leans on her elbows, as if awaiting some juicy bit of gossip.

"How much do you know about Neil's investments? Specifically Cobre something?"

Tilly frowns, lowers her sunglasses. "Cobre Vista?" I nod. "I know a little. Why?"

"Neil said something to me last night . . . about Oliver owing him money for an investment they were going in on together? Honestly, it kind of scared me."

Tilly's mouth forms a grim line. "Isabelle." She lowers her voice and glances over her shoulder to make sure no one else on the patio can hear. ". . . Neil Kelly is bad news."

"How do you mean?"

"He's like an overgrown child, always needs to find a new toy to play with. He'll invest in anything and everything, but if you ask me, his real business is money laundering."

I choke on the sip of mimosa I'd just brought to my lips. *"Money laundering?"* The words make me think of drug dealers and human traffickers. Not exactly something I would have pictured a bougie couple like Oliver and Isabelle Beresford involved in. But, of course, it makes sense. Oliver had an entire bunker of a hidden office. Obviously, the guy was mixed up in stuff more incriminating than just an affair.

Tilly raises an eyebrow at me, swirls her drink so the orange juice mixes into the champagne, then gulps half in one sip. "Oh, come on, Isabelle," she says. "Why else would he be based down here?" I think about how Palmer's been such a bitch from the start, lording her money over me like it wasn't illegally earned. Maybe that's why she's always after me. Maybe she has something to prove.

The waiter arrives then with our breakfast, and Tilly immediately digs into the buttery, crunchy bread.

"I'm not saying Oliver was involved in *that* side of Neil's business," she says while chewing. "Cobre Vista is a mining company. They're opening lots of new copper mines all across Mexico. It could be a totally legitimate investment opportunity. I'm sure it's nothing to worry about."

• • •

Brunch with Tilly bleeds into lunch, bleeds into cocktails—or rather, me nursing a Bloody Mary while Tilly flirts with a heavily inked bartender. By the time I get back to Casa Esmerelda, it's already six thirty. I take a shower, slip on Isabelle's simple blue low-back silk dress, and do my makeup as quickly as I can. I need to do some research before my dinner with Braden.

I pass through the kitchen and mutter something about looking for a bottle of wine to bring him as a gift, but Martina doesn't care about my flimsy excuse for why I'm heading down to the basement. She's too busy vacuuming sand off the patio.

I return to the hidden entrance of Oliver's office and slip inside. On his laptop, I search Braden first because I can't get that man off my mind, but Google doesn't give much—just his age (forty-one), and where he lives (New York, New York). If I want his phone number, I'll have to pay. The only image that pops up is the same sailing picture. Leaning back in Oliver's high-backed leather chair, I take a moment to admire Braden's face. The little brother who couldn't resist getting drunk and screwing around with his big brother's bride . . . I zoom in till I can feel the ocean spray, smell the salt in the photographed air. I chew on my pinky finger while I stare into his pixelated eyes. *Focus*, I tell myself. *There will be plenty of time for that later.*

Next, I Google: "Cobre Vista. Money Laundering. Mexico." An article pops up from a few years back about how the cartels have been targeting local mines, extorting them for massive payments— sometimes they even go in and rob the mines, taking the minerals for themselves and selling them on the black market. The reporter cites a specific incident where workers at a Mexican copper mine were held up at gunpoint. I spring to my feet and grab that strange blob of metal I thought might be ugly abstract art. It's raw copper, according to the images on the screen.

Neil's message to Oliver said, *These guys don't mess around*. That doesn't sound like a run-of-the-mill mining company. It sounds like Neil was working with the cartel itself. Which would explain why he's losing his mind trying to get the money he promised them: he's trying to avoid ending up decapitated by a fucking chain saw or dissolved in a barrel of acid.

And I'd like to avoid that too, thank you very much.

This was supposed to be an easy job, a vacation. And yeah, of course, I'm the one who took it to the next level, but the opportunity was too good to resist. A chance to shed Liz and bask in the luxurious simplicity of Isabelle Beresford's life. I should have known. No one's life is ever as simple as it seems on the surface.

Maybe I can pay Neil off. How much would it take? I pull up the screen-recording I took from his phone and reread the messages he sent to Oliver: Ok—confirmed that the minimum buy-in is 40M a share. Jeez. Even if Oliver was only on the hook for half, that's still a fuck-ton of money. But still, the Beresfords are loaded. If I part with a good chunk of change to make Neil happy, I should still be plenty comfortable living off the rest of their fortune.

I return to Oliver's emails and search for bank statements. A handful pop up, some from Chase, and some from Inbursa, which Google tells me is a legitimate Mexican bank. I go to Inbursa's login page. Oliver's username is saved to the site, but it still prompts me to enter a password—which, of course, I have no shot at knowing. I click the "forgot password" button, hoping they might send a reset link to Oliver's email. But instead, a handful of security questions pop up. *What is the name of your first pet?* I look around the study, like I'm hoping to find some pathetic urn dedicated to the loving memory of Fluffy the cat, but there's nothing here to help me. I lean back in Oliver's plush leather desk chair and close my eyes, willing my brain to come up with another way to get into his bank account.

While my eyes are still closed, a man's voice comes from the doorway. "What is this?"

14

My eyes fly open. "Braden!"

Shit. How is it already eight thirty? And why didn't I remember to lock the fucking door?

Braden enters the study, still wearing the white shirt and khaki pants from earlier. "Hey. Martina told me you were down in the wine cellar. I'm so sorry I startled you. If I'm on edge over Oliver, you must be beside yourself. Don't worry, Is. It's gonna be okay."

He only knows half the reasons for my stress, but his concern still lowers my heart rate. Along with the warmth of his hand.

"So, what is this place?" Braden asks, crossing the small room toward me. "Oliver's man cave? What are you doing down here?"

"Hi, sorry, just give me a second—" I start to close the laptop, but Braden has already reached the desk. He leans toward the screen. His shirt grazes my shoulder and scatters my thoughts.

"Oh," he starts, but then stops when he registers what he sees on the screen. I tense, waiting for him to demand to know why I'm trying to hack into Oliver's bank accounts, but Braden just says, "The answer you're looking for is Murphy. He was an Irish setter."

I swivel in the desk chair until my eyes meet Braden's. He's got a crooked half smile, mischief sparking in his brown eyes.

"I tried to get into his Chase account earlier today," he says sheepishly. "I had all the info—his social, mother's maiden name—but I still got rejected by the system."

"Some banks use voice-recognition software now," I say. But my voice is faint, laced with confusion and, honestly, a little amazement. I can't believe it. Braden fucking Beresford. A man after my own heart.

"Yeah, apparently so. But come on, scooch over and let me help you with the rest of these questions. We have to get into his accounts."

"We do?" My brain is still a half step behind my mouth, which I blame on the heady scent of sandalwood and Marlboros that bombards my senses every time Braden leans toward me.

"We have to track Oliver's recent charges to see if we can figure out where he's disappeared to. That's why you're looking, right?"

No, I was planning on using your dead brother's money to pay off his enemies so I can keep living as your equally dead sister-in-law.

"Yes, exactly." I slide over to give him more room to see the screen. "Favorite sport?"

"Sailing," we both say. And it's like we're on a team and we've won a point. I want to give him a high five. Or a kiss. And we're in. He sits on the arm of the chair, gets comfortable while I click my way into Oliver's account.

The last transaction was made on February 23, the day I flew here. Oliver transferred $250K to an LLC called VH Inc. in the British Virgin Islands. "Shell company," I say.

"Yep," Braden agrees. "See if there are any more transactions to the account."

I scroll back in time, and find the same payment, again and again and again. It adds up to $10.5 million. *$10.5 mil?* Is that what he's already paid Neil? Or was he siphoning funds, building himself a secret nest egg so he could slip away—away from Isabelle, and away from Neil and his cartel buddies?

"There don't seem to be any clues that tell us where Oliver is now. But I'll see if I can track down who's tied to that shell corp, VH Inc.," Braden says. "This investment Oliver was making with Neil Kelly was clearly some under-the-table shit. I wouldn't be surprised if that shell corp ends up being in Neil's name. If it is, we'll be able to prove that Oliver did complete the deal before he fucked off to who knows where. Maybe this whole thing is just a misunderstanding."

I nod, but Oliver's dead body flashes into my mind, along with Isabelle's gruesome, smashed-in face, and I'm filled with growing certainty that Braden's dead wrong. There's no way any of this is the result of a mere misunderstanding.

• • •

There's a particular tree at the roundabout that leads to the St. Regis. Lit from below, it looks like a children's book illustration: magical and otherworldly. Every time I pass it in my little golf cart, I find myself swerving toward it like it's pulling me into its fantasy and away from my life. I almost ran off the road one time, I was so transfixed by its web of long, outstretched branches, reaching limbs intertwining into a gigantic half globe, and twisting together into a short, fat trunk below. On our way to the St. Regis, the pull is stronger than ever. Luckily, it's Braden behind the wheel tonight and not me. My head is full of thoughts that twist and turn more than those slim branches.

I excuse myself to use the restroom when we arrive at the resort. I need to calm my nerves. I don't need people whispering about how unsettled Isabelle Beresford seemed, or to draw attention to my dining with a man who is not my husband.

When I return to the restaurant's dining room, I spot Braden waiting for me at a table with an ocean view. A tall man in a tan suit begins to approach the table. For a second, I think it must be the sommelier, because of the man's serious, studied expression. I can't hear what's being said, but when the man thrusts his phone in Braden's face, Braden turns his head, and waves the man away. A waiter hurries up to the table and the man in the suit backs away, hands up in an apologetic gesture. When he saunters out of the dining room, something swerves in my gut, but I push the wariness aside.

"What was that?" I ask, when I reach the table. Braden hops up and begins to pull out my chair for me, again making me feel special, doted on, loved.

"He said he's looking for a missing woman," Braden says. My gut flips again. No one but me knows Isabelle's missing, since as far as they know, *I'm* Isabelle. But Braden's tone is reassuring. "He was talking to another table before. Probably a scam. He kept trying to get me to look at his phone—"

"What was on it?" I interrupt, my anxiety getting the better of me.

"I don't know, I was focused on waving over security. I assumed he just wanted to distract me so he could steal my wallet or my watch." (TAG Heuer, navy face, dinged stainless band. $5K.)

Our waiter returns, and I order tequila on the rocks, and Braden does too.

I raise an eyebrow at him. "I thought you gave up all your vices."

He looks a little caught out but tosses me a roguish grin. "I'll be good, I promise. You can keep me in line. Wouldn't want to risk getting thrown out of a nice place like this." He gestures at the white linen tablecloths around us. "I should have stayed in town—that's more my style. But I thought you'd be safer if we stayed inside the gates."

The reminder of the dangers that might lurk outside the peninsula gates creases my brows. I use my fingertips to rub it away.

I'm overreacting. No cartel thug is going to pop out from behind the oyster bar.

"You've been here before?" I ask.

"Years ago. I was engaged once. That fell apart," he says with a huff of a laugh. "On the trip, she and I got in a huge fight, and I headed into town on my own. Punta Mita . . . Such a cool little spot . . . Great point breaks. After we split, I came back down a few times on my own to surf."

I almost snort into my tequila. A legit millionaire surfer? Really? It's like God is making me pay, presenting me with a perfect man I can't have. Or can I? He eyes me in the blue silk, and I suspect he can tell the effect he's having on me, which won't do for his brother's wife. I straighten up.

"It's definitely more laid-back than the vibe here," Braden says, gesturing at the elegant oceanfront dining room. "It's where regular people live. Probably not your scene."

I raise an eyebrow. "Oh? You don't think I could survive among the 'regular people'? This wasn't always my way of life, you know." The tequila's making me speak truths.

"I do know," he says. His voice is earnest, but not in a cringy way. Just simple, matter of fact. Like there's no need for bullshit between us. "Look, Dad always thought you married Oliver for his money. But I know it was more than that. Besides, everyone's gotta do what they have to do in order to survive. And with growing up the way you did . . . Hell, I was born into this life—I'm in no position to judge." He throws back the rest of his drink then signals to the waiter for another round.

The waiter arrives with our food just in time. I need the distraction.

"Let's walk on the beach," he says when our entrees are cleared. "More private."

"Okay." I'm trying to control my tone and my expression and my body temperature as he signs the check and I follow him outside. We stroll past the long, straight swimming pool that juts toward the waves, night birds and insects accompanying our walk like a movie score. The night air is cool against my flushed cheeks.

"Do you mind if I . . . ?" When he reaches for his pack of cigarettes, his hand grazes mine and I don't know how much more of this I can stand.

"No. I don't mind."

He lights up; it smells like my youth. I first tried cigarettes with the popular girls in the parking lot of Jefferson High. It made me feel mysterious, like one of those badass female antiheroes in noir films, Stanwyck or Dietrich. But every time I smoked, my father would go ape shit the second I walked in the door. Nothing made my father madder. He'd smell it in my hair and ground me for days. I think it reminded him of my mother.

I almost ask for a drag, but at the edge of the sand, Braden snuffs it out in one of those ashtray trash cans. Then he takes off his shoes, so I take off mine. When we're close to the water, alone on the dark stretch of beach, he says: "Oliver doesn't know what he has."

"He doesn't know a lot of things," I say, letting the water surge over my feet and ankles and shins.

"That night at the bar . . ."

Don't stop. I need you to keep talking. Though whether it's because I need the info to keep my front, or because I want to live vicariously through Isabelle, I'm not sure.

"You were so vulnerable with me. You lost a lot, and it taught you how to survive," he says, and it's like he knows I'm Liz too because, maybe for the first time ever, I feel seen. I walk faster to keep up with my racing pulse. I'm both captivated and terrified.

Whatever happened between them—whatever's happening between *us* right now—it's heavy. There's passion here, and real feelings.

"Did you ever tell Oliver about Susan? You said I was the only one who knew."

Every cell in my body grinds to a halt. Who the fuck is Susan?

"I'm sorry," he says, taking my hand. I can't face him, so I stare out at the water, then up at the moon. "I shouldn't have brought that up. I didn't mean to upset you."

"It's okay," I say.

"No, I'm sorry. I have no business dredging up your past. Let's go back to the bar," he says, pulling away. He's being cautious too. It's too much, the two of us out here on the beach alone under the almost-full moon. "We still have to discuss the situation with Oliver. You're the only person who I can trust."

We pick a corner booth in the empty bar, order more tequila, this time *añejo*, neat.

"I didn't want to admit it when you first arrived, but . . ." I slide into the booth beside him. "I *have* been worried about Oliver. Even since before he . . . went off the grid. I actually started looking into Neil Kelly. After Morrow called. He wanted Oliver to invest in this copper mine, Cobre Vista. But I think it might actually be a front for working with the cartel."

Braden clenches his teeth but doesn't say anything, just nods for me to continue.

"I think he's hiding out because he wanted to back out of the deal. And Neil—or the people he answers to—wouldn't take no for an answer."

"Must be a serious threat if he didn't even tell you."

My leg presses against his, and I can't help myself—I imagine assisting the authorities, exposing Oliver's crimes without implicating Isabelle, who, Braden will confirm, was kept in the dark. Braden, my protector.

"I'll be right back," he says, nodding toward the men's room. I could also use some cold water splashed on my face (or a full-body plunge right in the fountain), but I stay behind in the booth and take a long sip of my tequila. While I close my eyes to savor the taste, I hear someone approaching. I expect to see Braden, but instead find that man from dinner, the one in the poorly cut tan suit.

The one who asked Braden about a missing woman. I go stiff.

"There you are. I've been looking all over for you, Liz."

Shit.

My instinct is to flee, but Braden will be back any second—I can't run.

He holds up his phone. For a second, I expect a photo of Isabelle, expect him to say, *I know what you did.*

But the photo is of *me*. It's a photo from the Melanoma Foundation gala. Me talking with Mrs. Reed.

"I . . . I don't know what you're talking about," I say, my brain whirring so loud I can't think. "That's not me."

The man leans in close to me. Too close. "You have dallied with the wrong family, I'm afraid." He opens his jacket just enough to show the butt of his handgun.

Braden will be back any second. I grab the man's wrist. "Give it back!" I yell while I stab at the phone's side button till the screen goes black. "Help! This man stole my phone!" Here comes the maître d'. "Help!" I yell. "He stole my phone."

The maître d' rushes our way, rattling off what sound like powerful insults and threats in Spanish, and the man in the tan suit turns. In that second, my grip fails me, and he wins back his phone before fleeing the hotel.

Returning from the bathroom, Braden rushes over to me, and I feel tears prick the corners of my eyes. He wraps me in his arms and rubs my back, squeezes my shoulders. "What's going on?" he says. "Was that the same man?"

"Yes. He was harassing me." I let myself lean into Braden's warm chest and try to steady my pulse. I was so swept up in trying to preserve my life as Isabelle that I forgot to keep track of who's after Liz. "I need to get out of here, Braden." Which is true. But it's not that simple. The man is probably right outside, waiting for me to leave. "I'm sorry, I don't know why I'm so shaken up. I just need a minute to collect myself. Is your room nearby?"

"Of course, come on. I've got you, Is."

He holds me tight with one arm and ushers me to the safety of his suite.

15

I burrow into the sofa in his suite while he slides open the doors to his oceanfront patio, and the wind lifts the white curtains like sails. I know I shouldn't be here in Braden's room, but I can't exit the resort alone. Not now. Not at night.

How the fuck did Mrs. Reed's hired hand find me here? It's not like he works for Interpol. Or maybe he does, for all I know. Maybe he tracked me through my Liz phone? I should have destroyed that thing long ago. Smashed it, thrown it off the cliff along with Isabelle's and Oliver's bodies . . .

"How are you feeling?" Braden asks, sitting beside me on the small sofa.

"Better, thank you." Braden lays a blanket across me, then moves close enough to tuck himself under the blanket too. "I don't know why I'm getting so worked up over that guy—he was just a scam artist, like you said." Braden strokes my calf reassuringly. Despite the heated energy I've been feeling from him all night, I'm still surprised he's this bold. Reckless, even. For all he knows, Oliver could come storming in here any minute, back from a heli-skiing adventure, even though I think he suspects it's something far worse. Maybe it's this same recklessness that got him and Isabelle into trouble twenty years ago—so much trouble that his own brother cut him out of their life.

But I can't say it's not appealing.

"Of course you're on edge," he says. "With everything going on, with Oliver . . ." I nuzzle close, let the calming rhythm of the waves settle my nerves. "Is, I'm so sorry you have to go through this. You can stay here tonight. I'll make sure you're safe."

"Thank you." It comes out before I can stop myself. Even though Liz is probably safe from the Reeds' fixer, Isabelle—her image, any-way—is anything but safe in this room with Braden. *Come on, Liz. He's supposed to be your brother-in-law, for fuck's sake. You need him as an ally. You can't sleep with him.* But then he reaches around me like he did earlier on the beach and rubs my bare shoulder lightly with the tips of his fingers, and an electric pulse shoots through me.

Pull yourself together, Liz. I wrench myself free and rush to the open window to cool down in the blast of night air.

But Braden simply follows me, and I can feel him standing right behind me, staring at the darkened view. The ocean crashes in the darkness. I'm out of my depth; I want to know what to do next. I want to be guided. For the first time in a very long time, I don't want to be alone. I'm tired of thinking three steps ahead. *When are you gonna stop running, Liz?* my dad asked me the last time I brought him money. Last time I saw him alive. Has to have been five years ago, maybe six. Since then, I've been on the move, leaping from high to high. I'm so used to disappearing, I sometimes think I'll never return.

A gust of cold air sends the curtains flying, and I step backward—into Braden's chest. As if on instinct, Braden's hands land on my hips to steady me, and I turn my head, looking up at him over my shoulder.

"Don't worry, Is. We'll figure this out," he says, so quietly his words whisper against my skin. And then his lips are on my neck. Soft. Hot. On my throat. On my mouth.

I'm instantly lost in it, hungry for it. I turn to face him, giving in to the kiss. There's an urgency, an intensity. Like he's been waiting twenty years for this—for me.

"We shouldn't be doing this," I say, pulling away. Oliver isn't really my husband, and, as far as I can tell, he's a duplicitous womanizer, but it still feels wrong to be doing this with his brother.

"Right."

Braden crosses away from me, toward the open door. I feel instantly cold.

Out on the patio, he sits on the edge of a lounge chair and lights a cigarette. Obviously, something has been chasing him all these years—guilt. Regret. But is it regret over what happened between him and Isabelle, or regret over what could have been? My lips feel swollen from the kiss. I watch his silhouette, and it's like part of me has fully merged with Isabelle. As her, I imagine the regrets he's feeling, the deep stir of emotion, wordless but clearly threaded in every single movement.

I follow Braden outside and lean against the patio wall, knowing that if I get too close, I'll lose control.

Then again, maybe that wouldn't be so bad.

He crushes his cigarette in the ashtray, then exhales several long, purposeful breaths. He runs a hand through that unruly dark hair. "Of course, I'm worried about Oliver. That's why I'm here—not to, you know . . ." He looks up at me. What he means is, *hit on my brother's wife.* "But we both know he's not a good guy."

Another wave rolls toward us, larger than the last, and more powerful; it collapses with a roar.

I choose my words carefully. "I don't love Oliver."

For a moment, the water quiets down, and the moon is reflected cleanly on the black swells, a dazzling orb.

"Did you ever?" Braden is still looking out at the water, his chiseled face in profile.

"I don't know." I drift toward him. My dress rises and then

settles around me when I sit on the chaise next to his, upright and facing the water like him. "I haven't been happy for years." I hate the truth in this; it overwhelms me. Why am I opening up to him?

"This is crazy," he says. "I know it's wrong, but being here with you . . . I didn't expect to feel—*this*. After so long." He's not looking at me, but I can feel the rise and fall of breath in his chest, coming quickly, like he too is afraid of what he's said, of what he'll say next.

Of what he'll do.

"Braden," I whisper. "You don't have to feel guilty. Neither of us does." I take a breath. "Oliver never did." We both know what I mean: that Oliver had mistresses. That their marriage was never a sacred thing, but flawed and broken and full of lies.

What's one more lie, if it's in service of a deeper truth?

Braden and I look at each other, and he smiles like he's been waiting two decades for this moment—eyes wide and bright, cheeks flushed even in the radiant starlight.

Now his hand's on my knee. "Don't you ever wonder what would have happened if we'd . . . if he'd . . . if we could have been to-gether then?"

"Braden," I say again, inches away now, my dress fluttering in the hot, tropical air. Regardless of whatever history existed between Braden and Isabelle, I know that what I'm feeling is not history at all. It's real and it's present and it's *ours*. He turns toward me, and his hand finds my thigh. "Forget about *then*," I whisper. "We're here, now."

The dress feels like nothing—almost nothing. I feel the heat of his hand, the heat of his gaze, running through me. And then the silk is crumpling in his grip as his hands find their way inside my dress, and I turn toward him and . . .

Neither of us can stop it.

He's kissing me again, and his hands are at my waist, beneath the dress, finding my hip bones, grasping at the edge of my thong.

Then I'm on top of him, and we're moving together, my short hair loose and draping forward over him, and I'm transformed in the shadows, fully Liz, fully alive.

"Let's go inside," he says.

And I let him carry me back into his suite.

The blue dress lands like a shimmering puddle on the floor, and the way he moves over my body—it's like we really have known each other forever, and we remember exactly how to fit together . . . where to put our hands. Our tongues.

He kisses me again. "I've wanted you for so long." His Marlboro Red smell triggers all my teenage hormones. I grab his back, pulling him into me, and gasp. He shocks out an "Oh God." Adrenaline hits, an intoxicating fear of getting caught. Of *wanting* to be caught, to be seen, exposed. Wanting everyone to know, to know the truth about me. At last.

• • •

As we lie on our backs, he threads his hand through mine. We listen to the waves and the night birds and the wind. His deep breaths slow, then turn into faint dreamy snores. But I'm too amped up to sleep. Each moment of the night plays on repeat in my mind: the way Braden looked at me at dinner, the pressure of his leg against mine in the booth in the bar . . . I don't want to think about the Reeds' menacing agent, but he's swimming around inside my head too. And something else I can't find yet through the tequila, and the euphoria. Something else about which I need to know more . . . The tragedy that broke Isabelle. That drew Braden to her, made him care.

Who were you, Isabelle?

I slide out of bed and pull on Braden's rumpled white shirt, deliciously fragrant with the smells of tonight—ocean, cigarettes, and sex. I don't want the light from my phone's screen to wake him, so I creep across the suite to the love seat, curl up in the blanket, and open Google.

I don't really know how to find what I'm looking for—Braden mentioned a Susan on the beach. Clearly, something happened to her, and whatever grief she caused was part of what made Isabelle seek refuge in the arms—and the bedroom—of her soon-to-be brother-in-law.

I don't have much to go on, but when I Google "Susan" plus "Isabelle Caldwell" (Isabelle's maiden name), I find an article from 1998 about two teen girls who went missing in Camden, Maine: Susan Warner and Isabelle Caldwell. It's something I must have scrolled past before because it didn't seem relevant, didn't feed into the narrative of what I was looking for. There are plenty of Isabelle Caldwells in the world. But that was before I heard the name "Susan" mentioned in connection with her. Now I'm pretty sure this must be what Braden was referring to. Above the headline, there's a grainy black-and-white side-by-side shot of what looks like best friends on a rocky beach, towels wrapped around them after a swim. I zoom in and there's young Isabelle, smiling, her long dark hair braided and wet.

According to the article, neither girl was ever found. There was an exhaustive search, including divers off the coast of Maine, but no bodies turned up. As I read the details of their backgrounds, I'm especially moved by Isabelle's sad tale. Her mother died in a car crash when she was a baby, then her father overdosed, and she grew up in a variety of foster homes. Susan, on the other hand, grew up with what seem to be normal, upper-middle-class parents. "We deeply mourn the loss of our only daughter," says her mother in the article.

Susan and Isabelle had last been seen swimming in the ocean, and one local claimed she'd spotted the duo on the ferry to

Vinalhaven, dressed for the beach. But it was a crowded summer weekend—they could have been anywhere amidst the swarms of teenagers. The Camden chief of police closed the case after only one month. "From my years of experience, it's my conclusion that both girls must have drowned."

Lazy-ass cop, I think. *If they'd been rich, you would have tried harder.* And clearly Isabelle didn't drown. She's . . . well, she's . . . An image of her battered face flashes in my mind. I return my phone to my purse.

I tiptoe out onto the patio, imagining Isabelle and Susan venturing out for a day at the beach, maybe taking a ferry to an island, laughing in the windswept splashes of water, ogling cute boys. But then what? It's possible they ran off together, that Susan also lived. Maybe her parents weren't as nice and normal as they seemed in the article. Maybe she changed her name, and started a new life, made Isabelle swear an oath never to tell . . . I shiver in Braden's light shirt. But remembering the look on Braden's face when he mentioned her—like he knew how painful it would be for Isabelle to talk about Susan—makes me wonder if she really did drown. And poor teenage Isabelle was left alone. Terrified. Maybe Isabelle wanted out of her shitty life and took the opportunity to get lost. And never be found. That would explain why she eloped, and why there are so few identifiable pictures of Isabelle online. Just like me, she did a good job of covering her tracks.

Except I fucked up and let myself get photographed at that stupid gala. And now I've got the Reeds' guy after me. Eventually, he'll find someone here who will recognize my face as Isabelle; maybe he already *has*. And then I'm really screwed—my Isabelle Beresford and Liz Hastings identities both ruined. That is, if whoever killed Isabelle and Oliver doesn't get to me first.

As I watch the waves roll in and out, I think about how shitty it is for Isabelle's happily ever after to end the way it did. How, even though she and her husband were insanely wealthy, he turned out to be a lying prick, and she still ended up as fish food. Money couldn't solve her problems. But maybe it can solve mine.

I pad back into the suite, formulating a plan. Eventually, I'll figure out how to access Isabelle's fortune. Until then, I can probably get enough for the Tamayo to pay the Reeds back. I just need to talk to the guy when I'm alone and explain that I need a little more time.

A yawn strikes, and I realize just how exhausted I am. I crawl back in next to Braden, hoping to get a few hours of peaceful sleep before I have to deal with the ocean of problems that threaten to consume me.

• • •

And I do sleep, thankfully, since it feels like I've been running on empty for days now. I still stir occasionally, though—can't help it. I sleep light when there's someone in the bed with me. When I wake in the darkness a few hours later, Braden's not in the bed; a breeze filters in from the patio, where he's probably having a smoke. The idea of him out there, a cigarette between his lips, keeping watch on the night, relaxes me, and I'm back asleep again.

Only I'm fighting. Kicking and thrashing in the choppy dark water, something pulling on my leg, like kelp or a giant squid sucking me under. Strong moonlight bleeds through the water, and I see the white soles of kicking feet.

I burst through the surface for air, and there's Isabelle bobbing in the soft swells, her hair braided like in the newspaper picture. I try to call out to her, but water fills my mouth, and the current grabs my cold legs. The moon shines off the black swells. I look again for Isabelle, but I no longer see her white arms swimming or the top of her head or the splash of her feet. I'm alone. A wave smacks the side of my head, and I'm underwater, blinded. I cough up a mouthful of ocean. As hard as I try, I can't stay afloat. I'm underwater again, and my cries turn to desperate gargles, my last gusts of air.

16

I shoot up in bed, drenched in terror sweat. I touch my legs, half expecting to feel the slimy reeds that pulled me under. But my leg is bare and smooth. Still, from my pulse and my blood pressure, it's as if my near escape was real.

I reach my foot across his side of the bed, but Braden's gone.

"Braden?" I say, my eyes squinting in the sun. He's not even in the room. Maybe he went to the gym. Maybe he had work to do, a lawyer in Puerto Vallarta to meet . . . I can't call him, I realize, because I don't even have his phone number. I should just stay put, wait for him to come back—like I'm some kid who lost her mom in the department store. But then another thought hits me: *What if he regrets last night? What if he's gone back to New York?* My skin prickles. I can't just lie in this bed alone. I throw on my dress from last night and leave the suite.

I'm careful as I make my way toward the main building, wary of running into the Reeds' guy. Luckily, there's a crowd of vacationers for me to blend in with, their chattering voices carrying over the birds and the bugs and the waves. I'm just about up to the pool when I'm stopped by a wall of tourists. That's when I hear the walkie-talkie static and see the red lights catching on waxy leaves, the men in collared shirts that read POLICÍA . . .

Fuck.

"What happened?" I ask a woman wearing a thick layer of sun-block. "Why are the police here?"

"There's a dead body in the pool."

Maybe all that zinc got to her head. "What?"

"Yeah, a tall guy. I saw him," she says, like she'll be trauma-tized for the rest of her life. She presses both hands—crossed and trembling—over her heart. "He must have had too much tequila . . . I'm guessing he had a heart attack."

The first thought that shoots through my brain is: *Braden.* Did he go for a morning swim, consumed with his guilt over what we did—another betrayal of his brother? Was my dream of drowning a premonition?

I worm through the crowd up to the police blockade, trying not to panic, and sure enough, floating face up in the pool is a man. *Jesus. They haven't even gotten the body out of the water yet.* I stare, registering, even as one of the cops tries to drag me out of the way. It's not Braden, and I let out a huge breath I didn't know I'd been holding. Then my heart stalls, because even dead, I recognize the man.

It's the Reeds' goon.

Holy fucking shit.

I need to find Braden.

No, actually, I think when I reach the main building, where the concierge can get me a ride back to Casa Esmerelda, *maybe what I need is to just leave.* Because there's no way it's a coincidence. That man threatened me, and now he's dead. The maître d' will tell them all about our altercation, and the police will want to question me if I'm still here.

"Isabelle!"

I flinch, but it's just Tilly. We've reached the Punta Mita resi-dents' parking lot at the same time.

"What are you doing here?" As soon as I've said those words, I realize I should have kept my mouth shut—she'll want to know why I was here too, dressed for company, no less.

"I took a paddleboard yoga class," she says. "Fantastic workout. I feel so Zen now, it's like someone microdosed my smoothie."

"I could use some of that," I say.

"You do look a little rattled. What's up? Cute dress, by the way."

"Thanks. I— They found a dead body at the St. Regis pool. I caught a glimpse of it, and it freaked me out."

She cocks her head at me, as if considering this. "You know," Tilly says, "it's weird—I've never been bothered by that kind of stuff. Honestly, sometimes I feel like I'm missing that normal-human gene. Like, dead animals, gruesome injuries . . . never really affected me."

Images of Isabelle's and Oliver's mutilated corpses fill my mind's eye alongside fresher images of the bloated body of the Reeds' fixer. My empty stomach roils.

"Well, they bother me," I say with a shiver.

Tilly looks almost disappointed, like I've let her down by having what she called the "normal-human gene."

"But that's not why you're really upset." She raises her sunglasses and stares at me, squinting like the scorching sunlight allows her to see into my soul. "I know your little secret."

What? What the hell does that mean? Which of my thousands of secrets is she referring to? I sweat under the heat of the sun.

"I don't—"

"Come on," she cajoles. "I know what you're up to. Same thing you were up to that first day I saw you here in Mexico. Slipping out of a hotel early morning, wearing last night's dress . . . Did someone have a bit of fun last night?"

I breathe a sigh of relief. Thank God, she's just picking up on the fact that I spent the night with a man. "I may have," I say slyly. Let her think I'm just being coy because I'm stepping out on my AWOL husband.

Then, over Tilly's left shoulder, I spot the maître d' from the restaurant last night. He's walking with a few officers toward their squad cars at the other end of the lot. *Shit.* I need to get out of here, fast.

"You want to come back to my place?" I say to Tilly.

"There's an idea." She slides into her golf cart and pats the bench seat for me to climb in beside her. "Then you can tell me about all the mischief you've gotten yourself up to."

• • •

Martina vacates the kitchen when Tilly hops up on the counter like a teenager. "God, I love this kitchen," she says, swinging her dangling legs.

"Thank you." *How can you think about kitchen design when there's a dead body floating in the hotel pool we just fled?* I want to scream. But it's Tilly, so of course she can. *I'm missing that normal-human gene*, she said—well, at least she's self-aware.

She grabs an apple from the bowl beside her, takes a huge bite, then puts it back. She wasn't kidding about feeling like someone spiked her smoothie. This woman has more energy at eight a.m. than other people have all day. She jumps down from the counter and zips to a cabinet across the room.

"I'm going to make you a treat. I'm always ravenous after a night of getting some. Are you starved?" She pulls out a never-before-used pan—it still has a tag on it—that looks like an imprint of six little quiches or tarts. "You have flour and sugar, right?"

I don't know, to be honest. Lupe does all the cooking. He stocked the pantry. He makes the shopping lists for Martina. But Tilly has no trouble finding ingredients and cooking tools, pulling open drawers and cabinets easily, as if she's done it hundreds of times.

"It's perfectly laid out," she says, when I call her on her uncanny familiarity with the space. "Everything is exactly where I would have put it. It's like we share a brain." She sets the flour and the sugar on the island, then grabs two sticks of butter from the fridge. "You have a mixer, don't you? It's okay if you don't—I'm strong enough to stir by hand."

Of that I'm certain. But she won't have to, because she finds the mixer under the island and plugs it in. The cutting boards are in a long cabinet next to the sink.

She skins apples with a peeler she's found. I go to my room to throw on something other than this wrinkled blue silk number, then return in leggings to watch her slice the apples with the precision of a sous chef, the knife flying across the fruit's flesh so fast I'm worried she's going to draw blood.

Lupe wanders in—this is when he usually arrives. He looks like we stole his whole life. "You are baking?" he says with a jowly frown.

"You don't mind, do you?" Tilly says. "Isabelle and I both love to bake. We're having a little girl time."

"So nice," he says, but his English doesn't translate his expression—narrowed eyes, downturned mouth—which clearly says: *Get out of my space.*

"*Gracias,*" I say to Lupe's walking-away back. "This is his domain." I turn to Tilly, but I don't think she heard what I said, because she's thoroughly absorbed in slicing the butter. She carves into the yellow fat with a large fresh knife.

"Nice," she says. "So sharp. It's like it's never been used. Miyabi Kaizens are the best."

And it's true. The ceiling lights reflect in the unspoiled blade, so it looks bewitched—a sword with a mind of its own. I watch, fascinated, as she cuts slice after slice.

"I have an idea." She spins toward me with the knife raised; I catch a slice of myself reflected in its blade.

"Come with me to Brazil." Both her hands, the right one still holding the knife, shoot up with excitement like she's guiding a plane onto a runway.

"What?" I'm so confused. "Brazil? What are you talking about?"

"Brazil. In South America. Don't you want to go?" Her arched eyebrows fall; her smile too.

I didn't jump at her offer, and she isn't pleased.

But her expression softens again and that smile returns. She sets down the knife and grabs my upper arms. "Come on, Isabelle. James heard about some retreat there—some kind of spiritual whatever. He wants to get rid of me. He thinks I'm a psychopath. He actually called me that! At first, I was pissed, but then I looked into it, and, honestly—it's incredible. We can leave now. We can go."

"But I just arrived here in Punta Mita." In actuality, it's been a month, but in the lifespan of Isabelle Beresford that's nothing. "I mean, I'm helping Julia with the regatta auction. I'm pretty busy." She doesn't know the half of it.

The oven dings—it's preheated, hot, and ready to bake Tilly's apple tarts. Waves of heat escape the Wolf range.

Tilly lets go of my arms, but doesn't back down. "Come on, Isabelle. Where's your husband?"

"I . . . he's . . ."

"He's fucking that girl, and we both know it. This place is so over. It's lame."

"This"—I gesture to the kitchen she raved about, then the pool she always enjoys, the ocean view—"is not lame. I love it here."

"You made this, Isabelle. You can do it again. You could escape Oliver before he returns. We'd be free. No fucking husbands. We could start over. Start new. If we go to Brazil, we can be whoever we want. We could be anyone. Or no one at all."

Part of me does want to run away with her. I could escape the

Reeds and Neil Kelly. It's a good idea for me to get out while I can. But then I think about Braden. His hair blowing in the breeze and the way he looks at me with that urgency, and that *knowing*. It's crazy. I can't help it—I already have feelings for that man.

I'm probably just on a morning-after high.

"I can't up and leave. I live here now."

She grabs the dough from the mixer and kneads it into a ball. My phone, left on the coffee table, dings, freeing me from this awkward moment. It's like since she rescued me from Neil the other night, we're suddenly blood sisters. Like I owe her something. "I'll be back," I say.

It's a text from Braden—he's thinking about me too. I'm sorry I missed you this morning. I went for a walk, but then the whole pool area was blocked by the police. Did you see?

The man from last night, I reply.

I know. Can you believe that? Are you okay?

Yes. Thank you. I'm back home now. Connect with you later?

When he "hearts" my last text, memories of last night rush into my body, raising my temperature and pulse. I drift back to the kitchen, filled with thoughts of our bodies and tongues. But then something jabs me in the back. Something sharp.

I whirl around to find Tilly, standing inches from me, her eyes focused and calm.

A knife in her hand.

"Tilly!" I jump and clutch my heart.

Before I can scream at her, she pulls away and bursts into laughter. "Oh my God. I got you so good. You were so scared. Did you think I'd really, like, stab you?" She buckles over she's laughing so hard.

I laugh with her, but it isn't funny. I'm just relieved the tip of that knife is off my back. "For fuck's sake, Tilly." She tosses the knife into the sink, and I think James might be right. Maybe she is as crazy as he claims and exiling her to Brazil is a smart move on his part.

"I know you're right about Brazil," she says, now juggling that ball of dough, and changing my mind—she seems fine again. "Sometimes, I get carried away. Plus, those cliquey bitches will murder you if you don't show up at their regatta."

17

By Friday night, the Sufi Ocean Club has been transformed.

"Isabelle!" Julia races toward me, winding through tables draped with shell-pink tablecloths. Like a gala faerie in her floaty chiffon dress, she swoops right to tweak a flower arrangement, then flutters left to straighten a gold Chiavari chair.

"You're a magician," I say. "Everything looks stunning."

Of all the Punta Mita beach clubs, Sufi Ocean's the least fitting for a charity event. It's on the inlet side of the peninsula. The water's flat here, and the sunset's lost behind the hill. During the day, it's overrun with kids and sand-gunked snorkeling gear; paddleboards and scruffy kayaks clutter the thin strip of sand. I had serious doubts Julia could pull this off. But she'd been adamant: "It has the best view of the boats. Don't you think I could dress it up a bit?" In the end, "dressing it up" entailed a complete top-to-bottom overhaul of the space. Fresh paint applied, crates of rental furniture shipped in, all signs of children erased.

"The chandeliers are ingenious," I say. Strung on fishing wire between the trees, it's like they're levitating. And she was right about the view of the regatta—a hundred-plus sailboats crisscross the darkening water, the tips of their masts catching the last sun of the day.

"I couldn't have done it without your help." She wraps her

freckled arms around me in a tight hug. In truth, I only did the bare minimum to assist in the planning. Early on, I was there to weigh in on fabric swatches and menu options, tamping down some of Julia's more cliché instincts and helping to push the overall aesthetic toward something a bit chicer and more unique. But this past week, I've had other things to focus on . . .

"There you are, Is."

I don't have to turn to know it's Braden. He touches my bare elbow, but only for a second. But then Julia rushes off to greet the next crop of arriving guests, and Braden returns his hand to my lower back.

"You're beautiful," he says. I can't look at him under the pink sky with the sultry music swirling in the humidity while everyone hides their stares.

"Shh. Don't," I say.

Everyone knows he's Oliver's brother—I had to explain why he was here: *Oliver took off on one of his last-minute adventures and sent Braden to manage things in his absence.*

Braden and I stand an inch apart watching the final boat race, and it's hard for me to believe it's been only a week since he arrived.

After the Reeds' man was found dead, Braden checked out of the St. Regis and moved his things into Casa Esmerelda. He claimed that he could never stay in a hotel that allowed a dead body to float in their pool for hours, but I knew he was doing it for me. To protect me. To be close to me. As soon as Martina and Lupe left that first day, we swam in the ocean together at sunset. He carried me out over the waves . . . The next morning, Braden started taking charge of the situation. He called Oliver's lawyers and met with the board of Beresford Capital. He has to comply with a whole list of protocols before he can step in as acting CEO during Oliver's "absence."

"I'm not sure I'm cut out for this," he said to me after his third

Zoom with the board. "I didn't want to take over for Oliver. I didn't come here thinking I would—"

"End up with me?"

I was on the patio, watching cirrus clouds stripe across the hot afternoon sky. I lowered my sunglasses and made Braden sit next to me. It was a rare cloudy day, and the water and sky were both gray.

Braden gave a small smile, placing a hand on my calf. "Honestly, Isabelle, I think a part of me *did* always know I'd end up with you. Not in this way. Not with Oliver missing. My God, no. But you always deserved better." We curled together on the chaise, our legs intertwined, his hands tracing my body, as if to memorize it this time.

We've spent the past week making up for lost time. This morning, when we lay naked in bed, wrapped in the world's softest sheets, the pale curtains billowing gently, casting watery sunlight across the floor, I rolled onto my side, watching him sleep, and felt the urge to take something sharp and rip open my skin, prove to myself I wasn't in a dream, or dead. His lips on my skin, the smell of his hair, his sweat. I've gone and gotten myself addicted yet again to something I can't have. But the craziest part is, maybe I *can have it.* He woke and turned to me. I didn't even hide the fact that I'd been staring. He brushed my hair out of my face. "Isabelle," he whispered, kissing my neck. I wanted to climb on top of him right then, to feel him move under me in the soft morning light, but he was a tease, drawing his fingers down my naked body.

"When did you get that scar?" he asked quietly, his hand finding the thin, rough line near the top of my thigh.

I turned onto my back, not wanting him to stop. "I fell off a horse when—" *When you were in fucking high school, Liz.* I froze, going cold for a brief second. Because presumably, the real Isabelle didn't have this scar when she hooked up with Braden all those years ago. He would have remembered that. But if I told him the real story, the timelines wouldn't align. Keeping everything straight in my head was making me unhinged. "When we were first married," I started over with a decent save. "It was a hundred years ago . . . Don't stop."

"What happened?" he asked, still tracing his fingers up and down along my skin.

"We were in Portugal, horseback riding on the beach. Until I fell, it was beautiful."

"*You're* beautiful," he muttered into my neck, rolling on top of me.

It felt so liberating—the best sex I've had in I don't even know how long. I wanted to tell him the whole truth right then. That the person he's falling for is the real me. *Liz is the one you want*, I wanted to whisper into his ear as he shuddered against me. But of course, I didn't say any such thing. *He likes what he knows*, I told myself as I held on to his shoulders and cried out. *Let that be enough.*

And it was. It is.

• • •

The regatta is winding down, though inside the Sufi Ocean Club, the auction and dance party are only just getting started. Music floats out over us as Braden and I stand side by side on the terrace with the remaining spectators, watching the final boat round the buoy, its numbered white sail shining orange in the dropping sun.

"What a turn," he says quietly, so only I can hear him.

With the soft musk of his cologne so close to me—subtle, the way I prefer it, so I can smell *him* too—I fight the powerful impulse to turn around and kiss him, right there on the deck, where anyone could see us . . . to feel his quick, surprised intake of breath, the edge of his teeth against my lips. I can imagine his hands at my neck and in my hair, his kisses trailing my hot skin, his knee coming between my legs to part them as I'm backed against the terrace wall, and his hands grab me by the waist and he lifts me up, and . . .

But Aimee suddenly appears and pulls me away—from Braden and the fantasy that still has me shivering.

"Isabelle, there you are! The bids are mounting for your piece!"

While Aimee pulls me toward the auction, I look for Braden to see if he's followed us. As if we're perfectly in sync, he appears in the crowd, between two women, and our eyes meet, both of us understanding what needs to be done: The only way to get to the bottom of this is through Neil. He needs to get Neil drunk and talking, find out the extent of Oliver's involvement in Cobre Vista. So far Braden has found no accounts within Beresford Capital connected to this deal. But it's possible Oliver's commitment was only verbal. Funds could have changed hands in secret—off the books.

Neil might even be the hidden name on VH Inc., the shell corp Oliver had been siphoning money to before his death. Braden went to the main Inbursa branch in Puerto Vallarta yesterday, but without Oliver, he couldn't get any new intel.

He also tried to get Neil on the phone several times this week, but Neil kept evading him, which was suspicious in and of itself. For a man who apparently desperately wanted money from Oliver, he sure wasn't interested in talking about it with Oliver's brother. He obviously has something to hide.

Which is why tonight's so important. Because for the next few hours, Neil will be trapped here with the rest of us, and Braden will have plenty of opportunities to corner him. David Morrow has been appeased—at least for now—by Braden's interim leadership. But that's just a Band-Aid. And we still don't know the extent of the danger we're in.

I spy Braden again inside, his shoulders snug in a blue suit jacket with a slightly green hue—the color of deep ocean water—and I'm struck by his determination and stature. When I first met him that morning on the edge of Esmerelda's pool, he was bleary and rumpled, but in the short time since, he's grown into his new role. And I'm glad. Because watching him slice through the throng with the agility of a shark, I feel safe. Even with this copper-mine thing. Even though the Reeds might send someone else down to find me when they get news their guy went kaput in the St. Regis hotel's infinity pool. Whatever happens, I'll have Braden by my side. I know I should feel something—guilt? fear?—but instead I feel invincible. A little high. With an ally as powerful as Braden, can anyone really fuck with me?

"I want the painting you donated, but this douchebag keeps outbidding me," Aimee says, pulling me out of my thoughts. "Can you get me another if he wins it?"

It takes me as second to recalibrate, but I'm fast. "Of course," I tell Aimee. She's a goddess in her sheer yellow dress, and I have the connections to give her what she craves. "I can always call the dealer. I can arrange a private showing if you like."

I cross the dance floor, then enter the club's restaurant, which has been converted into a silent auction gallery. I spot the lavender Bottega mini that Palmer donated—worth $5K, but from the size of the diamonds here, I'm guessing the purse will likely go for eight, maybe ten. They'll write it off as an (illegal) tax deduction; they'll turn greed into altruism. I can't even see my donation the crowd is so thick. Julia, pink from excitement, spins out of the group of bidders entering higher and higher offers into the auction app on their phones.

"Isabelle! The lady of the hour," Julia says, and the pack of desperate art lovers parts. "This is Isabelle Beresford, the generous donor of the painting you're all dying to win."

My donation was less an act of generosity and more an act of last-minute scrambling. I'd forgotten that I promised Julia a piece for the auction, and by the time she politely reminded me about it, there was no way I could tap into my actual art connections to get her something—not on such short notice, and not with the Reeds on my tail. So I improvised. Found a way to make myself the philanthropist of the year while also ridding me of the painting that's haunted me since the day I arrived.

"Ah yes, Tamayo has always been one of my favorite artists," I say to the group, gesturing to the piece, which I can finally spot through the crowd. "I was sad to part with it, but it's for such a good cause." *So long, creep sisters. You can stop staring into my soul and freaking me out.*

"*Mon Dieu.*" Aimee refreshes her phone. "It's up to three hundred thousand."

Julia links onto me like we're childhood friends, and I think about Susan and Isabelle in that photograph. Isabelle made it all the way here from a nothing town in Maine . . . She found her people. And now I've found my people too.

"I'm so grateful you're here." Julia throws her arms around me for a hug. "That dress is insane. You're gorgeous."

"You are!"

She's right about my dress. It's a masterpiece of quiet elegance. When I emerged from my bedroom in the simple burgundy slip dress, Braden almost had an asthma attack.

"So still no Oliver?" Julia asks. "I was hoping he'd be here."

"Me too." I urge her away from the auction frenzy, and the painting's following eyes. "But he just had to go heli-skiing. Apparently, there's a ton of snow this year."

"He would just go without telling you first?" She twists a strand of her long red hair. "If Jeff did that to me, I'd kill him the minute he returned."

"Oliver's an ask-for-forgiveness guy," I say, like I'm so used to this behavior it's no worse than if he'd eaten the last piece of cake.

But Julia recoils at the thought. "God, I hate that. I'm such a rule follower. It makes my skin crawl," she says.

"Same. He and I are very different that way. But I didn't realize until after we were married. I was just a kid—honestly, sometimes it feels like I hardly knew the man before I decided to spend my life with him."

"Well, sometimes opposites attract," Julia says diplomatically.

"Yeah, sometimes . . ."

I'm thinking of Braden, not Oliver, though—of last night, and this morning, and this afternoon.

"Are you okay?" Julia asks.

"I'm so good." Until Palmer and Neil break into my field of vision, and all my sexual energy instantly turns to dread.

"Oh, hey," I say. "You reminded me—I have to go bid on your purse."

"No, I know we're late, but please don't leave yet," Palmer says with hint of a beg. She hugs and kisses me. I'm afraid she'll break down and say *pretty please*. She's suddenly so nice to me when all I did was hold her hair when she puked at her party. I've done that for strangers at bars all over the world. Either that, or she's still burdened with guilt for being all chummy with Oliver's mistress.

"Isabelle," Neil says, with his arm cinched around Palmer's waist.

"Neil."

It's not like he can come for me after the stunt he pulled. He has to behave, or I'll tell Palmer what happened that night. I have Tilly as my witness. Besides, I'm not alone and vulnerable anymore. I have Big, Bad Braden to back me—he would be enraged if he knew what happened at that party, which is why I've kept it to myself. He can't lose control—not now.

"Hi, I'm Braden Beresford." He's suddenly at my elbow, as if summoned by my thoughts, reaching across to shake Neil's hand. "Oliver's brother. I've been trying to reach you, actually."

Just then, the servers begin to plate the tables. "We have to sit," Julia insists. "I don't want to throw off the schedule. We have to set the pace."

We follow orders and find our seats. Braden makes sure he lands the chair next to Neil, and I drag Palmer to sit beside me, so I can hopefully distract her while Braden pries Neil. Aimee's the last to join us—she wouldn't leave the Tamayo painting until the auction closed. She plunks into the seat across from mine like she came in last in a track race.

"It went for four hundred thousand," she says, and the whole table claps.

"Well done, ladies." Jeff kisses his wife.

"A toast to Isabelle," Julia says, and we raise our glasses.

"To art," I say.

"To art."

Under the table, I press my calf into Braden and strain to hear his conversation with Neil, but Palmer's sudden interest in art tricks me into teaching her Art History 101. We're on Cubism when the waiters clear the meal and guests start to abandon the tables to dance. I should be focused on Neil and the task at hand, but I find myself enjoying the night. Some of the families brought their teen-agers and they've had too much to drink. But it's fun to see them sloppy and frolicking—their energy makes me feel young.

"Can we get away with dancing?" I ask Braden. Only Julia and her husband remain with us at the table, plus a woman I've never met who's talking Julia to death.

"They're all plastered—our impropriety won't be noticed." He offers me his hand.

As soon as his fingers wrap around mine, I'm brought back to the moment he touched my scar with such tenderness. Of course, he's also strong, a good dancer, the way guys from old money of-ten are, because they're not afraid to take control—and have been forced to literally waltz in palaces as teenagers when other guys their age were playing video games.

"It wasn't easy, but I got some information out of Neil." Braden's warm breath tingles against the shell of my ear. "You were right about him working with the cartel. He didn't say it outright, but when I started to hint like I knew what he was up to, he basically confirmed it."

I tighten my grip on the back of Braden's neck. "What do we do?"

"I told him I'd do my best to settle the dispute—we're meeting again during the week. I can pay whatever Oliver still owes, but it needs to go directly to Neil—I don't want any Beresford Capital money changing hands with Cobre Vista. And then when Oliver gets back, I have a fucking talk with him about the types of business partners he's getting into bed with." I flinch, both at the choice of phrase, and at the fact that Braden still doesn't know his brother's dead.

But Braden doesn't seem to notice. "There's always a little dark money at play—God knows my dad wasn't a saint either. But Oliver went too far this time. He put *you* in danger. I've been away for too long, letting him run the company without any oversight. I won't do that anymore. I won't leave you alone, Isabelle."

With his hand warm and firm against my lower back, pulling my hips closer to his, I believe him. In fact, I have the strangest thought that this is exactly what he wanted to happen. That he's been waiting for years for an opening, a reason to swoop back in—on his rightful place in the business, and in Isabelle's heart. It makes me wonder . . . I've been so focused on how convenient this has been for me, but I suddenly realize it's convenient for him too.

His eyes sparkle in Julia's stunning chandelier light, and he smiles, and I have to look away or everyone in the room will instantly know about us—if they haven't guessed already. Maybe it really can be as easy as Braden just described . . . Why can't it?

Maybe Oliver and Isabelle weren't killed by Neil Kelly or the cartel. Maybe they didn't even fall to their deaths fighting over the mistress. Maybe it doesn't even fucking matter. Occam's razor, right? The simplest explanation is the best. Maybe I've been letting myself get sucked into a mystery when there never really was one—looking for the lie, for the con, because that's how I've always lived *my* life. Maybe the Beresfords were just killed by a freak rockslide.

The music shifts to a Rihanna medley, and suddenly the dance floor is full, everyone acting as young as those teens smoking on the edge of the water. I've had a few, and it's dark, and for a second, I don't care. Shimmying in the fabulous dress, I dance with Braden as Liz. When I'm close enough, he touches my hips. But I burst away and spin with the other women on the floor. The band plays "Only Girl (In the World)," and Julia joins me, then Aimee, then Palmer. I'm one of the girls. I'm on the inside team.

And then I spot someone who is decidedly *not*.

Tilly is crossing through the light of one of those dangling chandeliers, making her way toward us. I've seen the guest list. I know she didn't buy a ticket. She's not meant to be here. I've barely seen her all week—ever since that bizarre morning when she made apple tarts at Casa Esmerelda and scared the shit out of me. I don't know why, but she stopped coming around. If I hadn't seen her— barely; she was sprinting—on the jogging path last week, I'd have thought she'd followed through with her plan and fled to Brazil. But now she's headed straight for me. I do my best to extricate myself from the committee clutch and meet Tilly at the edge of the dance floor.

"I've missed you," I say. I don't want a scene, and there's something about her expression that screams *scene*. "Come with me," I say. "I need to get some water."

"I'd heard the rumors about you two . . . I didn't believe it. But clearly, I was wrong."

"What are you talking about?" I shout, while I scan for listening ears. It's hard to tell who can hear over the music, but Julia's watching us now.

"He's why you didn't want to come to Brazil, isn't he?" She points to Braden.

"Come on." I take her hand and pull her, but she resists.

"You're fucking your brother-in-law." She laughs, but her tone isn't funny. She's Tilly with the knife again. She's sticking it right in my back. I try to steer her to the beach and the laughing teens who won't give a shit about either of us, but Tilly's stronger, and she wants a drink.

"Tequila. Blanco. Ice." She orders without taking her eyes off me.

"What the fuck, Tilly?" I say an inch from her ear. "Why are you doing this to me?"

"The question is, why are *you* doing this to *me*?"

Braden starts toward us. "Go," I tell him. "I've got this."

But I don't. Tilly's even more off than she was that day in the kitchen. I have no idea what she'll say or do next, especially now that she has a full glass of tequila in her hand.

"I'm not doing anything to you, Tilly. We were just dancing. That's all." But Tilly has no business caring who I'm sleeping with. She's fucked every single man at the Four Seasons, as far as I can tell. Including half the married ones. And half the staff too.

"How can you trust him? There was probably a damn good reason he and Oliver were estranged." Her eyes dart around, then refocus on me, then dart again. "We could have been in another country by now. Instead, you're choosing a man who'd steal his brother's wife," she says.

"Tilly, I had no idea you were even serious about going to Brazil." She literally just implied that I chose Braden over her. She's falling apart. She's unhinged.

She leans around me so she can see the whole venue, then takes off for the restaurant, the only indoor space at the event. I'm just thankful the auction's over and everyone's out here on the dance floor. She can yell at me in private. But before we reach the entrance, out walks the painting with the man who won it for $400K and the two guards carrying it with white gloves.

Tilly whips around to face me and glares. "You know I love that painting," she says. "I could have bought it. But you . . . *you gave it away.*"

I'm floored. My mind is racing trying to keep up with her rant. She thinks she's the center of all my thoughts. I hadn't even considered telling Tilly when I decided to donate the Tamayo; I'd been planning on hocking it to pay off the Reeds' guy before he showed up face down in the St. Regis pool. I had no idea she was so attached to it. "I'm sorry. I didn't think—"

"That's the fucking truth," Tilly cuts in. "You *don't* think, do you? After everything I've done for you—"

"You saved me from Neil, and I'm thankful for that. I am. But you're acting like I owe you my life."

She clenches her hands into fists like she might throw a punch.

"That's enough." Braden inserts himself between us, and Tilly glares at him too. Here come Aimee and Julia and Palmer. They circle behind me like a girl gang. If they were wearing hoops, they'd take them off.

But then—

Screams from the beach cut through the air. Loud, night-piercing screams.

Julia instinctively reaches for her husband, Jeff. I feel Braden come to stand behind me, his hand gripping at the corner of my neck. Even Tilly seems shocked out of her rage.

"What was that?" Aimee voices what we're all thinking.

A number of gala guests rush down to the beach. Our group

follows, and when we get close enough to the shore, I see one of the teenage girls vomiting into the sand.

"Oh my God, oh my God," the vomiting girl says once she's finished emptying the contents of her stomach. She must have fallen into the water because her dress is soaked through. "Right there! Right there!"

"What, honey? Where?" a man—maybe her father—says.

"Right there!" the girl shrieks. Because it's dark, I can only see the outline of whatever it is that's made her scream. The water's nudging something against the sand about the size of one of the round ceramic vases Julia used for the flower arrangements. But that's not right either. I can't make it out. The girl screams again, and even though she's drowned out by the murmurs and shouts of alarm through the crowd, her words, hitched with sobs, are unmistakable. "It's a fucking skull!"

18

"*Estoy bien, gracias*," I say to Martina for the hundredth time when she tries to offer me tea. Like everyone else, she's been worried to death since the little heiress at the gala found what indeed turned out to be a human skull.

All night and morning, *la policía* have been scouring the beaches for any other remains or clues. One skull wouldn't have been enough to identify the body—it had been out there too long and was salt-bleached and bare, no scraps of skin or hair. But this morning, Lupe arrived at Esmerelda with an update from some cousin of his—the police have found additional remains and are close to making an ID.

All of Punta Mita is buzzing with intrigue—the grisly discovery completely overshadowing the gala itself. Julia would have been inconsolable if it weren't for the huge amount of money she raised, thanks mostly to me. I look up at the space on the wall where I painstakingly hung the Tamayo painting that brought me here. Now there's no hint of its existence, no dust rectangle on the bone-white paint. The void sends realization through me: What if I'd never been hired? What if Mrs. Reed had recommended someone else? My mind starts spiraling, back to Chicago, the winter snow I was desperate to escape. I thought I was so slick for nabbing the ruby ring that still sits on my finger. But now I'm wondering which move was the fatal mistake that led me here. What if I'd never met Tilly or agreed to that hike? The painting would still hang on this wall. I wouldn't be worried about human remains or murder charges. The Beresfords would still be dead, but I would be long gone.

I try and assure myself that it would be close to impossible to ID this skull as belonging to Oliver's or Isabelle's corpse, as they would have had to practically *swim* from where I shoved them off the cliffside trail to make it all the way to the Sufi Ocean Club. It's been a month; their bodies would both be decayed beyond recognition, picked apart by predators and ocean pressures, thankfully. And like Tilly said, plenty of people have died in that jungle.

Then again, could there still be DNA on their clothes or hair somewhere?

I feel the panic creeping up my throat as I sit cross-legged on the sectional in the living room, playing out scenarios in my head, trying my hardest to find one that doesn't fuck me and my plans. If it *is* Oliver, maybe they'll rule it an accident. In that case, and that case alone, I can remain Isabelle. I could even be with Braden . . . But I replace that jinxing thought with a horrifying one: What if it's *her*? I could lose everything. I could end up in jail. I'm not well-versed in Mexican law, but I'm damn sure I don't want to go to prison here—or anywhere.

Just then, gravel crunches in the drive. A car, not a golf cart, I can tell from the sound, the harsh final thrust. The doors open— more than one. And then two sets of feet walking. It could be Braden, who left after breakfast hoping to participate in the search for more remains. I tried to prevent him from going, but the haunted look in his eyes when he said, "That could be my brother," stopped me.

There's one sharp knock at the door, and I slip away to the bedroom. Martina will answer it. To settle my nerves, I sit at the vanity and brush my hair with Isabelle's antique brush, rub my thumb over the carved monogram: $S \ldots T \ldots W \ldots$ I hear Martina open the door, and I hope it's Tilly or Aimee—one of the girls popping in for a beach walk. It's not.

"Señora Isabelle?" Martina taps on my door moments later. "The police are here."

There I am in all three mirrors, with my new hair and tan . . . guilty as fuck. I can't move.

"Two detectives, Señora. They have questions for you."

The beach and the jungle are calling—I could run from here. But I'm afraid it's too late. I should have gone to Brazil with Tilly. I could have been a new person by now. Even if it is Oliver, and I get to slide into the role of the bereaved widow, I'll always be on the lookout for someone who knew Isabelle well. Or someone who wants her dead too.

How powerful were those fucking waterfall currents?

Somehow, I stand. It's like I'm on a conveyor belt, the way I move toward the door. I hear rapid Spanish—a woman talking to Martina, a man interjecting: *sí* and *gracias* and *Isabelle Beresford*. And I'm stunned that I'm calmly walking toward what could be the worst moment of my life. But I didn't kill anyone, I remind myself, the manic, problem-solving part of my brain once again kicking in. There might be an actual killer out there, and that's always something I can pivot their attention to. I touch the wall with my hand, checking in with reality. It's cool and solid and safe.

Until it ends. Entering the living room, where two detectives, a man and a woman, stand between me and the front door, feels like jumping out of a plane.

"Mrs. Beresford?" The female detective steps forward, offers me her hand. Her makeup took time, her outfit too. And that slicked-back bun . . . She's meticulous. And she's staring into my eyes.

"*Hola*," I say. "*Como esta?*"

"I'm Detective Quiñones, and this is Detective Ruiz," she continues in English.

"Señora," Ruiz says. He's a watcher and a listener. He'll let his partner scare me into talking with her immaculate eyebrows and pressed navy pants, then watch how I react and take notes. Only his eyes move, and even that's subtle, but he's cataloging the contents of Casa Esmerelda, making lists in his mind.

"Mrs. Beresford . . ." Quiñones addresses me as Isabelle without hesitation, like she fully believes I'm her. "We'd like to ask you a few questions, if you don't mind."

I nod. *Stay calm.* But under my loungewear, I'm sweating like I've already been caught.

"As I'm sure you know, human remains were discovered at the Sufi Ocean Club."

"Is it Oliver?" I cut to the chase. The fear in my voice is genuine, but also useful. If it's him, this is my chance to prove I'm his wife. To show them just how distraught I am by this tragic news.

"What makes you say that?" Ruiz asks.

"My husband has been . . . unaccounted for."

Ruiz pulls out a small notebook and jots something down.

"I'm sorry to tell you this, Mrs. Beresford, but yes." Quiñones's voice is kind, but her face betrays little emotion. "With the help of your brother-in-law, we were able to identify the remains found as your husband's."

I choke out a sob—a real one, of both shock and relief—and Quiñones hands me a tissue, pulled from a little packet in her breast pocket.

"We're very sorry for your loss. As I said, we do have some questions for you . . . You arrived here on"—she opens her phone and reads—"February twenty-second, Delta flight four-oh-six."

"That's right," I say.

"And your husband was not with you?"

"He was supposed to be at a resort, in Bali."

"Supposed to be?" Quiñones turns to Ruiz and gives him a look.

He scribbles again in that notebook, and I'm struck with the urge to rip the pen from his hand and jab it into his neck. I consider mentioning the ski trip I manufactured, as if I could throw them off, but they have his literal remains. And if they haven't searched all his credit cards yet, that lapse on their part might buy me a day or two. I don't need to help them send me to jail.

"I—I guess he didn't make it there. A friend told me that—"

"Would that friend be a David Morrow?" Quiñones asks. *Shit.* "We spoke with Mr. Morrow and he seemed very concerned about your husband. He said he wanted to open a missing person investigation, but that you were against it."

"I—"

"We found more of your husband's remains besides just the skull," Ruiz interrupts. "He appears to have suffered a massive traumatic injury. So many fractured bones . . ." And suddenly it's like I'm there again, hauling their bodies in the jungle, blood on my hands. I might be sick right in front of the detectives. I sit on the sofa before my legs give way or I vomit or faint.

"The streams and rivers up in the hills run into the inlet, so I'm thinking waterfall . . . A fall from that high would explain the cracked skull."

"Stop, please," I say. Tears rush into my eyes, but I hold them back. "He's my husband."

"*Was* your husband," Quiñones says. "Now he's just a bunch of shattered—"

"That's enough," a firm voice rings out.

All three of us turn toward the sound. It's Braden. I must not have heard his car over the blood pounding in my head, because I'm surprised—and very relieved—to find him standing just inside the front door.

"Señor Beresford," Quiñones says. "We were just telling your sister-in-law—"

"I heard the disgusting things you were saying to her," Braden cuts her off, then he rushes to me, and we hug. "I'm sorry, Isabelle." With so much cortisol flooding my veins, it's easy for me to cry. It feels good too—I couldn't contain my tears longer. They've been dying to spill.

"You're the brother?" Ruiz asks.

"The de facto CEO," Quiñones says.

"Right." Ruiz nods. Apparently, this is something they've discussed before.

Braden settles onto the sofa beside me, places a reassuring hand on my knee.

"Do either of you know anything about their plans to go hiking in the area?" Quiñones asks, undeterred.

"What do you mean, 'their'?" Braden says, and I'm seized with panic.

Quiñones looks apologetic for the first time. "We found the remains of a second body, near where we found Mr. Beresford's."

Ice-cold dread floods my veins.

"It was a woman. Her face was smashed in." Quiñones mimes a sharp punch. "Similar cause of death, so our working theory is that they were together when they died. We matched her dental records with what was left of her jaw."

No, no, no, no. This is it. This is how it ends. They've found Isabelle. I'm going to be caught. There's nowhere to run, no way to get out of this jam. *You've done it this time, Liz. You're truly fu—*

"The remains belong to a woman named Madeleine Richards."

Wait—what?

Quiñones registers the confusion on my face.

"Madeleine Richards?" she repeats. "Not familiar at all? No idea who she is?"

"No," I say. I have no idea what any of this is. Beside me, Braden looks equally confused.

Ruiz hands me his phone. "That's Madeleine Richards."

I can't stop the small gasp of air that escapes my mouth. It's Oliver's mistress, the woman in the pictures with Palmer and Neil. Ruiz watches my reaction. So do Martina and Lupe, from where they're loitering by the kitchen island.

"She's from Sayulita—yoga instructor." Ruiz adds, almost leeringly—so I instantly recognize the intentional dig. He's trying to get me to break, forcing the wife to picture the mistress on all fours. *Go fuck yourself, Ruiz.*

"She's been missing for four weeks," Quiñones says.

"Last seen on February twenty-fourth. We also found a condo rented under your husband's name at the Four Seasons, though resort staff have indicated that they believe a woman was staying there . . . Does that mean anything to you?" Ruiz has become an assassin. He throws poisonous darts at their main suspect—a wife so scorned, she murdered the mistress.

I stare at him right back, keeping my face as placid as I can manage. *Come on, Detective. Look at me. Isabelle Beresford isn't a killer. She's a philanthropist with a manicure, for fuck's sake.* But that kernel of confidence is no match for my confusion and fear. Had Oliver and his mistress holed up at the Four Seasons? How should I know? I look down at the photo of Madeleine, and my guts roil. If Quiñones is right, my hands touched this woman's corpse. I threw her over a cliff. She and Isabelle have the same build and hair color. Her face was so battered, I can't be sure, but there's no doubt that it *could* have been Oliver's mistress instead of Isabelle whose body I found on that trail.

The phone starts ringing, and Ruiz snatches it back. *"Hola,"* he says before standing up to take the call. Which is a good thing, because I'm sure he'd be able to read my spiraling thoughts: *What the actual fuck is going on here?*

You didn't kill them, Liz, I remind myself fiercely. *Someone else did.* All I have to do is help them see that. *There's a real killer out there with a motive, and it isn't me.*

"Have you looked into . . ." I blurt out, then stop myself and look to Braden. I don't want to say anything that jeopardizes either of us. He nods. "It's just, I'm worried about the kind of company Oliver might have been spending time with. He mentioned a new business venture, involving Neil Kelly. He told me—last time I saw him, he told me he wanted out, and Neil wasn't happy about it."

Quiñones raises one eyebrow—a sharp, bold line—then jots down Neil Kelly's name. "Thank you, Isabelle. That's a helpful start."

And for a second, I allow myself a breath of relief.

She gazes out toward the ocean, her eyes pausing on the pristine kitchen, then swivels to the bronze statue in the foyer. "Quite a place you have here, Mrs. Beresford. And you, Mr. Beresford"—she turns her focus to Braden—"do you get here often to visit?"

"This is my first time here," Braden says curtly, and his grip on my knee tightens.

"The house is new," I interject uselessly.

"You know," Quiñones says, turning toward Ruiz, who has wrapped up his phone call and rejoined us in the living room, "I'd be pretty pissed if my brother took over the family business and made enough money to splash out on this luxurious home, while I was stuck living in a one-bedroom in Hell's Kitchen. Wouldn't you, Jorge?"

"Excuse me?" Braden stands, and it's like his rumpled shirt presses itself sharp, and every part of him turns into a righteous shield. "My relationship with my brother is none of your business." His voice wavers, and even though I've only inferred Oliver and Braden's shared history, I can tell there's so much hurt there. A lifetime of two brothers unable to get along and the wound of whatever happened between Braden and Isabelle. Not something you could easily explain to the cops.

"On the contrary." Ruiz's hands are on his hips, his stance al-most aggressive—like the two men are facing off. "Your brother is dead, and you are his next of kin. Your relationship to him is very much our business now."

"My brother was found in the ocean. You think he fell on a hike. What on earth would that have to do with me?" Braden's muscles flex beneath his shirt.

Quiñones perches on the arm of the sofa beside me, unruffled, and leans in like we're two gal pals catching up. "Señor Braden is the beneficiary of all of this." She waves her left arm at the house and the view. "His brother—your husband, that is—changed his will two days before he disappeared."

Wait, what did she say? *The fuck?*

"Oh, you didn't know that?" Quiñones clocks my reaction, but it's clear she's not buying it. My head spins. I wish I would faint, or better, that the ground would open and suck me in whole. I'm not saying another word with these two in the room. I stare at the bronze statue of the girl, the book she's reading, the sway of her long hair. I concentrate on her. I can't bring myself to look at Braden, to acknowledge everything that Quiñones and Ruiz are implying.

"From the condition of the bones, we've been able to narrow down the date of their deaths," Quiñones continues, "to one month ago. Right around the time of your supposed arrival, Isabelle." There's a seam in the back of the bronze girl's dress. It's the only sign of the cast into which she was poured. I stare at the line, as if the strength of my gaze could tear the girl apart, right along that seam. "And I must say, you two have seemed awfully close, especially for a brother and sister-in-law who were supposedly estranged—"

"Either charge us with a crime," Braden says coldly, "or leave."

I'm thankful for his protection, for the commanding tone he has taken with them, and yet . . . my mind is still buzzing painfully, and loudly with all this new information. Oliver and his mistress are dead. Oliver rewrote his will—in Braden's name. Braden's here now, taking charge of everything, involving himself in the finances, in the search party, and in . . . Isabelle. Distracting me. Wooing me. Making me go weak over him.

The cold dread that froze my veins turns flaming hot. I believed in Braden and me. I dreamed myself into the worst nightmare of my life.

My brain searches for answers, but keeps landing on a question: *Have I been played?*

"We'll go." Quiñones stands and joins Ruiz near the door. "But you better not try to."

"If you try to leave the country, we will stop you," Ruiz adds.

In my head, I chant, *Go away, go away, go away,* until they finally leave. I hear the front door close and finally tear my eyes away from the bronze girl. Martina and Lupe have fled—scurrying back to whatever chores they'd been neglecting—leaving me alone with Braden.

The man who had the most to gain from Oliver's death.

A man, I realize, with rising alarm, that I hardly know at all.

When I hear the detectives' car pull away, Braden firmly locks the door. When he turns back to face me, his eyes are dark.

19

Braden is walking toward me, and it's like he was wearing a mask that's now removed. I don't recognize him. All the emotion I felt for him has turned to fear.

It's been right in front of me the whole time and I didn't see it. The revelation about Oliver's will makes it obvious. *Stupid, stupid Liz.* With Oliver out of the way, Braden has everything he's ever wanted. The money, the house . . . the girl. Oliver's skull is bagged into evidence, and Braden's in total control.

"Isabelle, I—"

"Stop." I think of all the delusions of my life that have led me here and want to scream. Want to cry.

Stupid Liz.

You walked right into it, Liz.

Here's the thing: you can change your shirt and sneak into the fancy seats, but it won't change your address, or your upbringing, or your destiny—and I let myself believe it could.

"I didn't ask him to change his will, I swear," Braden says, his voice low and steady. "It must be because of the woman they found. He must have been planning to leave you."

He stares at me, willing me to believe him, but his words don't make sense. Even if Oliver *was* planning to leave Isabelle, why would he will everything to his estranged brother? Why not leave it all to his mistress, Madeleine? No—the more likely explanation is that *Oliver* didn't change the will. Someone else did. Braden knew Oliver's password. And he was Oliver's backup at Beresford Capital. Even without the kind of access Braden had through the family business, there are harder crimes to commit than changing the beneficiary on your brother's will.

Oh God. I need to get away from him.

I turn to leave the living room, but before I can, Braden drops to his knees and grabs my shaking hands, squeezing them tight, and I feel the full strength of his grip. All those times in the past few days that I've admired his strength . . . I thought he wanted to protect me. But he could crush me if he wanted to.

He leans in close to me, and I'm sickened by his cigarette smell. "Please, Isabelle, let me explain."

"I need to lie down." The anxious sweat coating my hands finally allows me to slip free. I stumble backward from the sudden release. I use the momentum to escape to my room.

"Isabelle!"

As I trip down the hall and hurry toward Isabelle's suite, I hear Braden call out—"We need to talk, Is. You can't hide from me forever."

I lean against the locked door and try to catch my breath. *Don't cry, Liz. Don't be stupid. Don't fall apart.*

I have to get out of Mexico. I have to get out of this house.

I reach for the bottle of Don Julio 1942 Julia gave me as a gift for helping her with the event. I don't care if it's meant to be sipped—I rip open the fancy packaging and swig straight from the long, slim neck.

Still holding the bottle, I race into the closet and dig out my Liz bag from where I stashed it behind all of Isabelle's designer outfits. I start tossing random items into my bag, as memories of my blissful week with Braden flash through my head. That very first day he found me underwater in the private pool . . . He must have sneaked past the Punta Mita guards. I was too worried about convincing him I was Isabelle to notice that fucking red flag. Then he just happened to catch me in Oliver's study later that day . . . He must have been tracking me the whole time. The thought of his eyes on me makes me squirm now, when before it felt like someone had finally seen me for me.

I take another swig. Around me, all of Isabelle's beautiful clothes sway softly, innocent of all this . . . I want to weep. I grab some of my favorites of hers—they're mine now. I don't want to let go. I shove silks and cashmeres into my bag and swig again. I *am* crying, I realize. Sticky, panicky tears. *Just get out, Liz. Just pack what you need.* But what about what I *want*?

It's not just all these beautiful things I want. It's the beautiful life. It's— It kills me to even have this thought. It's *him*. How I stupidly, stupidly *fell* for him. There's no suitcase big enough to fit my crazy, foolish, childish dream.

I think of that first night in his bed at the St. Regis, and I wipe away tears, as if doing so will erase that night. But of course it doesn't. I still remember. I remember him holding me, kissing me . . . I remember waking up in the middle of the night when he was outside having a cigarette.

Or was he? I suddenly remember only that he was *gone*.

In the middle of the night, gone. The same night that man in the tan suit died of a supposed heart attack.

Oh God. Did *Braden* kill the Reeds' fixer? I can see it now— Braden, driven by his romantic obsession, doing whatever it took to protect his beloved Isabelle.

Sudden knocking on my door sounds like gunshots—rat-tat-tat-tat.

"Isabelle?" Braden hammers away. "Are you okay? I sent Martina and Lupe home early so we could have some privacy."

Fuck. Now we're truly alone. He could do anything, and no

one would know. I try to close my suitcase, but the zipper keeps sticking, and my fingers are fumbling, and—

"Please let me in. I have something I need to tell you. There's so much I need to say."

"Not now," I say. "I—I can't. I can't talk about it."

I hear him slide onto the floor. I can see that his body blocks the light seeping in from the living room. "Isabelle, please hear me."

"Braden, leave me alone. I need to be alone right now." Can I still keep up the charade? *I'm the grieving wife; let me mourn.*

"I can't just leave you alone. Now especially. Don't you get it?"

Focused entirely on trying to keep my movements quiet so he can't guess what I'm doing, I say nothing. He can't stop my escape.

"I love you," he says. And for a moment, I'm frozen in place by those words. The shock of them. Then: "Isabelle. I don't care who knows or what it means. Since I've been here . . . since we've been together . . . I love you and I refuse to deny it anymore."

I need to get the fuck out, but I can't tear myself away. I'm curled in a ball now, knees to my chest, still on the closet floor.

"You don't love me," I tell him. Because how can he?

"Don't do this," he begs. "Don't push me away. After all this time."

After all this time. Has he been planning this? Planning to get rid of Oliver for all these years and finally got up the nerve? It's almost romantic.

As deranged as it sounds, I want to laugh, but I'm trying too hard not to sob, not to shatter. Sure, maybe he loves something, but what he loves isn't me. What he loves isn't even Isabelle. He loves an idea, an ideal he's held in his head.

The guy's a fucking sicko.

The truth is still ricocheting through me: Braden killed them. He killed them to be with me.

And yet some pathetic part of me is sitting here dying to know: Is this what it's like to be adored?

No, Liz, this is what it means to be loved to death.

"From the moment Oliver first brought you home, I knew we were meant to be together. I've never gotten over you. And I never will." Now he's banging on the door. I snap out of it and scramble to my feet. Frantically grab my bag from the closet and go to the door. I can tell from where he knocked that he's standing again. Bright light shoots under the door and pierces the darkness around me. "We've been together day in and day out since I got here. You can't tell me you don't feel it. You can't."

I can't just flee through the balcony and down the beach. I won't move fast enough on the sand. Plus, I need my passport and my Liz phone from Oliver's study, and Braden's blocking the door. Tears spill down my face because I'm trapped again. And all I've wanted this whole time was to be free.

"There's no way you don't feel this too," he says again. "No way."

Now the tears are for the loss of all the emotions I did feel.

"I love you," he repeats.

And the most insane thing is that I loved him too. Yesterday, I was with him at that party, dancing . . . I see him under Julia's chandeliers and my heart breaks because here he is confessing his love.

"I love you too," I tell him. Because I did. For a moment there, I really did.

And also, because I need to stall. I need to think. I need a plan.

My heart swells and my brain fogs and I drift closer to the door.

"Isabelle, I love you. Please let me in."

Isabelle . . .

My swollen heart ruptures like a blister. But it's the reality shock I need. It's not me whom he loves. It's an illusion—the memories that are fueling this obscene breakdown aren't of me. I need to get my passport. I need to get Braden out of my way. And the only way I can think of is risky as fuck. But I don't have a choice. I'm not staying here with him all night. Eventually, he'll break down the door. He'll break *me*.

I leave my bag where I'm standing near the door to the hall and then scurry to the glass doors that lead to the patio. It's so quiet with just the two of us in the house. I whip open the glass door as loudly as I can. With the ocean wind filling my room, I race back to the bedroom door and lie flat so I can look under—sure enough, I see motion, Braden's feet taking off, running for the back of the house. He thinks I'm outside and he's on the hunt.

I grab my bag and dart down the hall, parking the suitcase by the front door. The kitchen's empty, and the doors through which Braden must have just exited are open to the brightly lit pool. I race down the stairs and through the wine cellar. I might have two minutes—three, tops. He's probably made it to the bedroom by now and is cursing me out, but maybe he'll turn and look down the beach, buying me more time. I lunge for the door to Oliver's man cave. My passport's behind the Hemingways, to the right when I enter, under the sailboat in a bottle.

"Isabelle! Where are you?" His voice rings out from the far side of the house.

I rip the books off the shelf and shove my hand into the darkness. But there's nothing there. No passport. No phone. The sweet tequila burns in my gut and makes my head spin. Books fly while I search. Did Lupe come in here? Or worse—did Braden?

Then my hand wraps around my US passport, and I've never been happier to be Elizabeth Dawson in my life. I shove my dead Liz phone into my jeans pocket. Then I pause to listen—I don't hear him in the house. Please let him be out there searching for me still . . . If I time it right, I can grab my bag and take off in his car. It's my only hope.

I rush into the dark wine cellar, feeling my way.

"Isabelle."

Fuck!

I'm blinded when he flips on the light. He's between me and the staircase. I back away, covering my eyes.

"I was just getting a bottle of wine," I say. "It's been such a hard day."

"Wine and a passport?"

He eyes it clutched in my left hand. I stick it in my back pocket while I shrink farther away.

"You can't leave, Isabelle. The detectives made that clear. We're in this together."

"I—I just—"

"I think wine is a good idea." He runs his hands over the bottles, taps them with his fingernails. "It's a lot. I understand that. It's a lot for me too. You think I'm not grieving?"

Grieving what you've done, you fucking psychopath?

"Of course," I say, trying to keep my voice from breaking.

"This is going to sound like the craziest thing I've ever said, but do you ever think things happen for a reason?"

My saliva feels trapped in the back of my throat; I can't swallow. I clutch the wine bottle to my chest, like it can somehow protect me.

"I know it's wrong. It's wrong to say, to even think, but it's also *true*. We belong together, Isabelle. I see the *real* you, and I don't think he ever did."

He reaches for me like he can snare me again with just a touch. "Isabelle."

"Stop saying that."

"But it's true. I love you. Don't you feel the same?"

"Stop calling me Isabelle. You have no idea who I am."

He sighs. "I know."

My breath catches in my chest. I manage to get out: "What do you know?"

"I know you're not Isabelle. I've known for a while."

The wine bottle almost slips from my hand. I take timid steps backward, realizing I'm pretty much up against an actual wall.

"Don't worry. It's okay," he says, moving closer. "I understand— why you wanted to escape. Why you wanted to hide. The past is an ugly thing. I get it. No one needs to know your secret."

"Stay away!" I shriek. But he's touching me anyway, sliding his hand up my arm. I grab a bottle by its cool neck. "Let go of me."

He backs me toward Oliver's office. What will he do to me if he gets me into that room? My foot crosses the threshold. He's pushing me now. "Let go," I say, trying to break free. "Let me go."

"Sus—"

But I don't let him finish whatever he was about to say. My arm takes over, and I swing the bottle so swiftly toward his temple, Braden doesn't even flinch, he's taken so off guard. Green glass shatters; red wine splashes. He crashes into the shelves of wine. "Stay away from me," I yell. "Stay back."

But he staggers up. "Stop this. You're not in your right mind," he tells me, clutching his temple. There's blood. *Oh God.* I dart out of the wine cellar, but he's lunging after me, his arm blocking the stairs, and I wind up in Oliver's office again. *Fuck, fuck.* There's the window I once shimmied through. I just have to slam the door on him—but he slams it open into me, sending me stumbling backward.

"Calm down so we can talk," he says, low and deadly.

"No," I tell him, frantic, reaching out in the darkness of the study.

He grabs me, and I wrestle harder than I've ever wrestled in my life. We hit the chair and it rolls across the room and slams into the open door; we knock over the brass lamp. "Let go of me!" I scream. "Let me go."

"Stop, Isabelle. Jesus, stop! You're fucking insane!"

It's like that word snaps me. It's so dark, and there's an unhinged fury in his tone that terrifies me. When he lunges back toward me, I turn to the bookshelf, frantic, and grab around in the dark for something to defend myself with. My hands land on the copper statue. Just as Braden reaches for me, the sheer panic—the need to survive, to escape—takes over, and I swing.

He falls to the floor in a horrible crash. The heavy copper falls from my hands to the floor in a thud as loud as Braden's was. "Braden?" I step toward him cautiously. There's not even the sound of a groan coming from him, just a heavy, eerie silence. I'm shaking so hard. I can't see through the tears.

His face—oh my God, his gorgeous face. Destroyed just like Isabelle's and Oliver's were.

No, Madeleine's and Oliver's.

I'm in a nightmare, and I can't wake up.

"Braden?" I say again, urgently, desperately. "Braden. Braden. Wake up." But he's not waking up—the copper didn't just make contact. It shot through his temple and into his brain.

What have I done?

What have I done?

I can't breathe. I can't understand what has just happened. I can't think. It isn't real. It's a bad dream, like the dream I had as a kid, the dream of the boiler ticking hotter and hotter. The man who'd hacked up his wife and hidden her in the basement wall. A wave of nausea overtakes me. My vision is so blurred—like that Tamayo painting. I can't see. I can't think. Braden's crumpled on the floor in a deep red puddle, and he's not moving, he's not moving and he's not breathing and *Oh God, what have I done?*

Look what you did, Liz.

How could you do it, Liz?

I kneel in the puddle of cool wine that's slowly filling with his blood.

"Braden . . . Braden . . . Braden . . ." I hold his face, broken now, a vile misarrangement of beauty, blood, and bone. I grab his wrist, but I can't find a pulse. How could there be one?

I know what I've done.

I know what I've done.

I crouch on all fours and retch until there's nothing left but sobs.

20

When I was twelve, I believed—stupidly—that my mother would return.

"Mommy . . ." I cried every night for weeks. "Mommy, please come back." As if she were listening, as if she were near.

"She's done with us," my father said thousands of times. "Stop waiting by the door." "Stop looking out the window." "Stop, Liz. Stop." He never told me where she went or why, even when I begged: *How could she leave us? Where did she go? Tell me, tell me, Daddy. Tell me, please.* Until he finally lost it: "She wanted a new life, Liz. We weren't good enough for her. Do yourself a favor and consider her dead. Get over it. You'll survive."

Get over it. You'll survive.

And until now, I have. But I don't know how I can possibly survive this.

My knees are wet with wine, my face wet with tears. "No, no, no . . ." I shake Braden again, as if his blood might start pumping. It was an accident. I had to fight him off. He was going to attack me. He knew the truth. I had to do it. I'm not a monster. I'm not.

I rub his uncreased brow, and he's sweet Braden again, and I'm broken in two. He knew I wasn't Isabelle. He knew and he loved me still . . .

What have I done?

But even through the fog of shock and grief and horror, a more urgent question enters my mind: *What are you going to do now?*

My bag is packed by the door; Braden's car is in the driveway. All I have to do is get on a plane.

"He killed for the money, not for me," I say like a mantra as I force myself to move away from Braden's body and take the few steps around to Oliver's desk. "He was a liar, calling me Isabelle when he knew I wasn't." It helps me get to the computer and type in "Google Flights." Tickets bought at the counter always raise suspicions, and I can't afford any unnecessary attention on me. Where will I go? Options attack my weak brain: cities and mountains and deserts and swamps . . . My idea of Seattle weeks ago no longer seems far enough. When I type in Brazil, I notice blood all over my hands. Is it Braden's or mine? It doesn't matter. I don't have time to stop. I don't have time to fall apart. I have to get out. I wipe away tears, streaking blood across my face.

While I'm searching for flights that leave in the next couple of hours, an email notification flashes across the screen. At first, I ignore it—I'm done sleuthing the fucking Beresfords. I'm Liz, and I'm getting the fuck out. But then the email's header registers: *Inbursa Banca—Query Regarding VH Inc.*—the shell corp Oliver had wired millions of dollars into.

Curiosity gets the better of me, and I click open the email. It's short, only a few lines of text. But I have to read it twice, because even though the words are in plain English, they make absolutely no sense.

Thank you for your inquiry, Mr. Beresford. We can report that VH Inc. is registered to an Elizabeth Dawson, Chicago, Illinois.

My brain short-circuits. I read it for the third time. That's my name. Elizabeth Dawson. The shell corp Oliver was wiring money to was under my name. How? That makes no sense. The wheels are barely turning. I didn't know Oliver. Didn't even know Isabelle, knew nothing about the Beresfords. I certainly didn't know Braden—whose body is lying five feet away in the darkness, the ambient light from the computer screen catching his legs. For a moment, I think I see them twitch, and a surge of hope and fear threatens to knock me over, but no. It was a trick of the light.

I grab one of Oliver's whiskey bottles and sit back down, taking a swig.

I stare at the screen, blinking. It's still my name in that email.

The feeling of disorientation that rolls through me now brings me back in time. I remember how awful it was, in school, after Bekka betrayed me. After she found out what I'd done, how I'd taken her name and pretended to be her and told all these stories. After she scorned me and told everyone I was a freak. I remember how alone I felt, never certain when I entered a classroom or a dorm hall if the people inside knew about it, thought I was a liar and a freak too. Thought I was a fake, a monster, an outsider, wrong. The anxiety became crippling. I dropped out of school. I spent a good couple of years floating, hovering barely above the surface of things. Working when I could, stealing when I felt like it. The loneliness was a lot. It's what led to the breakdown and the short stint at a ward where they had me in a room with no sharp objects and no strings—not even a shoelace. I had turned myself in, thinking they could help me, that at least I'd find safety from the prison of paranoia that had started to consume me. I thought the UPS guy was a cop. I thought my mother had returned from Boca with a gun. I thought I'd harm myself, and tried. I wanted someone to save me and make the thoughts go away.

But that place, and its puke-yellow walls, left an imprint on me forever, even though I was there only eleven days. It left me with this distant fear. I would never return there again. I wouldn't go back to that place of complete isolation. The irony: I've never felt more mad, more unhinged, than those walls made me feel. Like that little box room was all that was real, and the rest of the world, a filmy, fake illusion.

Now, as the screen's blue light blurs before my eyes, I wonder if it's happening again. "Dissociation," they called it. "Psychotic episode." Such soft words for something that felt like dropping out of reality through a black hole. The terror of it. The not knowing what—if anything—is real.

One of two things is happening:

I'm really and truly losing it again.

Or—this thing is so much bigger than I can possibly grasp.

Either way, somehow, the dead body on the floor is going to save my life, because it is the reminder that I need. It doesn't matter anymore what the truth is. I still need to get out of here.

Channeling Tilly, I decide on a one-way ticket to São Paulo, departing in three hours. Why the fuck not? I fish my credit card from my Liz wallet and begin to type my name into the ticket ordering system. *Elizabeth Dawson.*

But then I stop . . . When I read my name on the screen, I go cold. The police knew the date I arrived in Puerto Vallarta. But I traveled as Liz, not Isabelle . . . so how the fuck did they know I was on that plane?

The airline site flashes a countdown—I'll lose the ticket if I don't buy it now. But my mind is racing, trying to catch up, to find some sort of logic in all this madness.

Why would the detectives know I—know *Isabelle*—was on that flight?

A thought enters my mind almost as a lark, an insane suggestion. And yet.

There really is only one explanation—Isabelle Beresford was on the same fucking flight.

Isabelle Beresford, who I realize with horror, has not yet been found dead or alive.

My pulse pounds, waking up the activity in my liquor-soaked brain.

What if I had it all wrong?

Holy fuck.

What if I had it all wrong?

What if Braden wasn't the killer after all . . .

Oh God no.

I race out of Oliver's office—not tiptoeing or sneaking. Casa Esmerelda's become a prison, cold and empty. Except for . . . Braden, his body on the frigid floor.

I choke on more sobs and gag as I step over his body and hurry to the stairs.

When I reach the first floor, I pause for a moment in front of the empty space where Martina and I hung the Tamayo. The image of the painting fills the void on the wall. Two women, bound together by streaks of blood red. The unsettling feeling I always got looking at the portrait washes over me, stronger than ever before. But this time, mingled with the revulsion is realization. Because I might not know what the fuck is going on, but I've spotted the con.

Isabelle lured me here with that painting. And somehow tricked me into stealing her life.

I'm crying again when I stumble into the bedroom I've convinced myself belongs to me. But everything's hers. It always has been. And there I am, stupid fucking Liz, tripled in her vanity mirrors, wearing Isabelle's clothes, which are covered with Braden's blood. Has she been watching me all this time? Waiting for me to take the fall for Oliver's murder, plus the mistress? And now Braden. I didn't kill Oliver and Madeleine, but—"Braden," I sob. I thought he was trying to kill me. Because I believed he'd killed them too. I replay the past hour—I was fighting for my life. He wouldn't let go of me. I screamed *Let me go*, but he refused.

My legs give, and I'm on the floor, shaking.

Get up. The voice in my head is my father's. *Get out now. Let Isabelle clean up her own mess.*

I touch the passport in my back pocket, make sure it's still there, that it's real. That I'm real.

I tear off Isabelle's clothes and crawl toward the bathroom. By the time I reach the shower, I'm back on my feet.

Turn on the faucet. Get in.

Hot water scalds, and I'm awake again. Capable. *Don't think about Isabelle. Or Braden. Or Oliver. Or your mother. Never think about her. Get to São Paulo. Get on that plane.* Blood runs off me and spirals down the drain. I lather shampoo and scrub my skin, flushing away any cells that aren't mine.

After I turn off the water, I stand for a moment in the thick steam. Once I'm out, I'll be on the move. I have all the steps planned: dress, grab my packed bag, get in the car. Act like everything's normal, be calm, board the plane.

"Come on, Liz. You can do this. Go."

But I still can't help my mind from wandering, from wondering . . . *Where did you go, Isabelle?*

Then I'm toweling off in the foggy bathroom. Then I'm in the closet, reaching for the outfit I picked: chinos, long-sleeved T-shirt, jersey cardigan—all in neutral shades. Completely forgettable. I struggle to tame my tangled wet hair with the soft bristled brush from Isabelle's vanity. My fingers graze over the silver engraving, feeling the familiar letters: sᴛᴡ. Eventually, I manage to pull my hair into a neat ponytail. I wipe a spot clear in one of the mirrors to make sure I look like Liz.

There are so many reflections in this closet—an infinity of mes.

And then one of them speaks.

"You look great, Liz."

"What the fuck?"

It's Tilly. She's dyed her hair brown, to match mine. And her eyes—shining with what looks like unhinged mirth—are now a startling, familiar green.

"Tilly?"

"Wrong again," she says. Her lips curl into a snakelike smile that almost reaches her eyes.

Her *green* eyes. Her dark hair.

"No." The word comes out a whisper as I spin around. "No. You can't be . . ."

Bile rises in my throat, blood pounds in my temples. I'm backed up against the mirror now.

"Oh, I can be."

I try to steady my breathing—the name surfacing to my tongue with ease. "Isabelle."

She smiles, big now, too big. "I was, for a time. I hope you had fun playing Isabelle." She takes a step toward me, her face impossible to read. "But I'm sorry to say this, my little fox. Your time is up."

PART III

PART III

21

At least once a day—lately once an hour—I dream of killing Oliver.

That's normal, I'm sure, to want to kill your spouse. Or at least to wish them dead. Everyone needs a dream.

I spend hours imagining how I could do it. Maybe I'll surprise him at Casa Esmerelda, suffocate him with a pillow while he lounges by that beautiful pool. Puncture his jugular with one of my knitting needles (it's such a cliché, but knitting relaxes me). Or brain him in the shower, leave him naked on the hard, cold tiles. I could creep up behind him in the kitchen and stab him with one of the Miyabi Kaizen knives I bought. "Oliver," I'll say when he's making his coffee with his trendy Moka—*You're not Italian, bro, you're just some dumb schmuck from Connecticut*—"I'm so glad you agreed to these knives." Then I'll plunge it into his neck, the blade severing skin, then muscle, then artery wall. Blood will flow like wine onto that precious white porcelain floor.

But my indulgent little daydreams are impractical, I know.

I've been traveling from one stale charity event to another for months. Bouncing between ballrooms and museums and galleries, writing checks to prove we Beresfords aren't spoiled by our wealth. Tonight, I've braved a Chicago snowstorm to make an appearance at an annual gala for some worthy cause that I honestly can't even remember. Child literacy? Cancer? They all bleed together. The usual moneyed set is here. People I've traded small talk with at five-star spas. Nodded at across lavish rooms. We always pretend to remember each other, even if we don't. I scan the crowd, looking for anything worth getting excited about, but besides a handsome young waiter, it's just the same faces, the same blather.

"My goodness, you're svelte," a middle-aged woman says to her friend.

The friend, a sixtysomething blond woman I vaguely recognize, glances over her shoulder like someone might be listening, but it's not subtle. She wants anyone hovering to hear. "I'm getting the shot. Shh."

It's this season's biggest humblebrag—having so much expendable cash she can spend thousands a month on Ozempic to squeeze into a size two. Maybe even a zero. She'd better be careful—her fingers are so skinny she's about to lose that ring.

I used to relish the way these women clamored for my attention. *Believe it or not,* they *all love me, Mommy. None of them look at me with horror like you used to.* But the novelty has long worn off.

"Thank you," I say to the hot young server when he fills my champagne flute to the top.

"My pleasure."

It's while I'm watching him circle through the crowd that I first spot *her.*

Everyone's clapping for the pointy-boned blond lady, whose name, I learn, is Abigail Reed.

But then, as the applause dies down, my eye is caught by a different woman across the room. She's a half second slower than the rest of the crowd to retake her seat after the standing ovation. And for a moment, all I can see is her.

She's wearing a decent black sheath dress that could use a slight alteration, and that French twist is too fussy, but there's no denying it . . . the dark hair, the green eyes. Her forehead's a little too large, her nose angled and long. But her smile draws you in.

In a sea of attractive faces, hers might not stand out. But I'm enthralled. Because her face looks remarkably like *my* face. Skin that's a bit too pale, eyes a bit too big for her petite, angular face. People have always said I have a distinct look. I have the strangest sensation as I study her, even from afar, that she's stolen something from me. It's as if my reflection shattered through the mirror and decided to seize a life of her own.

After the speeches are done, I back into a corner of the gallery where no one will bother me, so I can watch her. I can't help myself. I've been so atrociously bored by the monotony my life has become; now that I've discovered a shiny new toy, I have to have it.

She tilts her head and raises an eyebrow at that same server with the champagne, and I'm mesmerized. It's like she's wearing a suit of me, a costume, but she hasn't exactly mastered the act. She could be subtler with the hot waiter, but her roughness is refreshing. And sexy . . .

A different waiter shoves a tray at me. "Caviar toast?" he says, blocking my view of my new pet.

"No." I scowl. *Go away or I'll eat your organs like caviar.*

Where is she now? I've lost her. I search the crowd, suddenly hungry. On the hunt. I can feel something within me awakening. I've been good all these years. So good. The doctors told my parents I would never be able to control my urges, and I've proved them all wrong. Who knew I'd grow up to be so well-behaved? But I'm growing tired of these mental restraints. It's just so incredibly dull to limit yourself when you know you're capable of so much more. My skin's buzzing, like I've touched something electric and, after all these years, I've been turned back on.

As I move through the room, determined to find her again, an idea is sparking. I don't yet know exactly what part this woman will play, but I'm certain it's a pivotal role.

When I finally locate her again, Abigail Reed is headed in her direction. My twin, who was just batting her eyelids at the waiter, now has a tear running down her face. Abigail can't resist. I watch in fascination as the dark-haired woman draws Abigail in, wins her over with the subtlest of manipulations—because surely, the sudden waterworks are an act. She hands Abigail a business card. I read *Nice to meet you* off their lips. Then the woman is saying her goodbyes and making her way toward the door.

I hang back while she waits for her coat, then I collect my own while she steals into the freezing-cold night. I'm ready to leave, I text my driver. Because it's all becoming clear to me. This woman, who looks so much like me, is the answer to all my problems. She's the miraculous solution I've been waiting for. She's my ticket out.

Sorry, Ollie, but the clock is ticking.

• • •

I met Oliver skiing out west. For many, skiing is more about the attire than the adventure. They're more interested in hitting an après-ski cocktail than hitting the slopes. But Oliver—at least in those days—wasn't like that. He was a daredevil, an adrenaline junkie, just like me. That day at Alta, we spent hours going off-piste, racing down the wild, ungroomed trails.

"That was the best day of my life," he said over nachos at Goldminer's Daughter. It was standing room only, packed full of powder hounds stripped of our outer layers, all of us glowing from endorphins and beer, everyone smelling of fire-dried sweat.

"You made some beautiful turns," I said, after our second round, and his pride swelled. He'd been clunky out there, awkward and brutish in the delicate snow, but he believed me when I praised his athleticism and grace. It's what he was dying to hear.

I can see his young face now, so much thinner and less entitled. His jaw was sharp, but not aggressive; his chin didn't yet jut. We were steamy, stripped down to our long johns, when I used my fingertips to tousle his helmet-matted hair.

"I was just following you." Then he took my hand and pulled me even closer. It didn't matter that our mouths were sticky with chili and cheese; it was an excellent kiss. He was hooked. And I was pleased. I had been on my own for just over a year at that point, and I didn't mind the security of a wealthy man. I told him my family was dead, and we hastily eloped in Niagara Falls. And for a while, I got everything I wanted from Oliver Beresford. Status, safety, the ability to travel and study art, even pretty decent sex.

But, of course, it couldn't last.

People like me are rarely satisfied for long.

Going on nineteen years of marriage, the only thing that still turned me on about Oliver was when he dominated at work. He'd buy companies, then break them down, and sell off the parts. He'd make a big score and I'd dote on him like when we first met. *Wow, Oliver. You really know when to strike . . . You have your finger on the pulse . . .* Or when he'd break a rule or get his hands dirty with criminals and their money-laundering banks. I'd cook him his favorite dinner, steak au poivre—my God, he was basic—and throw on some naughty lingerie. Though, no matter how much I hinted, the man never once tied me up. All those hours at the gym, and he wouldn't even hold me down.

I don't see how anyone could blame me for losing interest.

The boredom was becoming intolerable, but I might have stuck it out—might have found other ways to entertain myself—if it wasn't for the Morrisons' yappy dog.

On what might have been an ideal (lazy) Saturday morning this fall, Oliver surprised me over breakfast at the Connecticut house with the box of snail and slug bait I thought I'd hidden in the attic. "We don't have snails."

"So? I don't know what that is or where it came from." I returned to my coffee and the crossword on my phone.

"This is the same stuff that killed the Morrisons' chow chow. They were apoplectic when they found out from the vet, Isabelle. Couldn't *imagine* where he'd gotten into the stuff." He dropped the green-and-yellow box in front of me on the island.

"And?"

"Did you . . . I mean, you were always complaining about the noise . . ."

The animal was incessant. Barking day and night. It was enough to drive a person to the brink of madness, despite the acre between our houses. Still, the dog had its friendly moments. It came right up to me, tail wagging, and gratefully licked my offering of poisoned Pup-Peronis through the slats in the fence where our stretch of land ends and theirs begins.

Anyway, Oliver stood there, all furrow-browed, a squeamish look on his face.

I put down my phone and leveled him with a stare. "What are you saying, Oliver? Do you think I actually murdered a dog? Do you realize how insane that sounds?"

Oliver said nothing, just left me with the incriminating box as if facing my weapon of choice would force me to confess. All it did was strengthen my resolve—I needed to act. It had taken him almost two decades, but I could tell that Oliver was finally on to me. You can watch it happen in real time. I've seen it before. They look at you differently, as if they've just seen autopsy photos of a gruesome murder they can never unsee.

After the snail bait, things got uglier. Oliver began asking more questions about my past, poking holes in the stories I'd told him over the years about where I grew up, my lack of family. I caught him taking secret calls with a new lawyer and edging around me silently while I smiled and dressed for dinners out. I knew that now that he'd gotten a glimpse of the real me, it would be only a matter of time before he wanted to leave me. He was probably already drawing up paperwork to divorce me, write me out of his will. We had no children, so his next of kin would be his long-lost brother, Braden. Would he really leave everything to a man he hated just to spite me?

Continuing the docile-and-oblivious-wife act, for which I deserved an Oscar, I coordinated furniture deliveries to the new casa in Mexico, where Oliver had some budding new business ties—and a girlfriend named Maddie. It wasn't until that February, just a few days before I was scheduled to attend the winter gala in Chicago, that he found the article about the Vinalhaven disappearance and snapped.

I was in the kitchen wearing an apron and checking the golden hue on the tarts I'd been baking for Valentine's Day—heart-shaped strips of dough slathered with the black raspberry jam I'd jarred myself over the summer. For the Morrisons, of course. The poor things were still mourning, after all, and I wanted an excuse to pop over and see the fallout from my actions for myself.

But before I knew what was happening, Oliver plodded into the room and grabbed me by the arm. He pushed me hard against the marble island, wagging a pathetic little printout of the article in my face.

"What the fuck is this?" he demanded.

"Ouch, sweetie, you're hurting me." Actually, I kind of liked it. But I didn't want those tarts to burn.

"Don't call me 'sweetie.' Don't call me anything."

"Oliver, really, you're hurting me."

"I want you out of this house." He shoved me harder into the counter.

I had the mixed desire to unbuckle his pants and take him, or push him into the oven with the tarts. Instead, I played scared. "You can't do that."

"I know what you did," he snarled. "Two girls. Both disappeared. Did you—did you kill her?"

"What are you even saying?"

"I can't believe it. I can't believe it," he kept repeating. And then, "You're—you're sick, you know. *Sick*. Broken. You've been lying to me for *years*. Since the very beginning." He was shaking. There were, confusingly, tears in his eyes. "Admit it."

"Admit what?" I risked a glance at the article in his clutch. I'd never taken him for such a little Nancy fucking Drew, and part of me was impressed that he'd finally figured out the truth. But that didn't dull my raging annoyance. He was worse than the yapping dog.

I couldn't deal with it the same way, however. I mean, if the neighbor's dog had owned several hundred million in assets, authorities would've come sniffing around. They sure would have if Oliver suffered a sudden "accident" on my watch. I had to hold out, even though all I wanted to do was push his face down inside the KitchenAid with the meat grinder attachment on.

I'd have to be clever.

People always suspect the wife when a rich man dies. It's such an irritatingly accurate cliché.

At least he hadn't yet figured out what I'd been doing with his money. He'd put that together soon, though, if I wasn't careful. The offshore account I'd been secretly funneling our funds into would need to be renamed.

"Admit it, Isabelle. You're a lying"—he dropped the piece of paper and put his other hand on my throat—"little"—his grip tightened around my neck, throttling—"psychopath."

There it was. The pin that finally burst our twenty-year bubble.

And I had done *so* well. So much better than when I was young and hadn't yet learned to be smart.

"Stop, please." I scratched at his hand. I gasped.

"You disgust me." His angry spit flew. "You took advantage—complete advantage of me. I have all the proof I need to ruin you."

He let go suddenly, and air whooshed back into my lungs.

I rubbed my neck. "Who's the abuser now?" I said, widening my eyes into giant, mortified orbs.

For a second, he looked afraid of what he'd done, as if his hands were not his own. Then he shook his head. "Tomorrow, you're out."

He stormed off to the primary suite, slammed and locked the door. I had taken to sleeping in one of my favorite guest rooms on the third floor anyway—I couldn't stand the smell of him, the sound of him breathing.

That night, after he'd gone to sleep, I reviewed the hidden Google Nest in our kitchen, making sure to download the image of him with his hands around my throat. (You never know what might come in handy later.) Then I unlocked our bedroom from the hall with a dainty little pin and stood over his bed, holding the hammer from the tool set I'd never once seen him use. It felt nice in my hand—the heft of it, the firm rubber of the grip.

I didn't use it, though. I controlled myself. And for that I'm quite proud. The anticipation was enough of a thrill. I stood over him for a good twenty minutes, watching his eyeballs rove while my arm twitched.

Then I went back to the guest room, slammed the hammer down on a framed photo of the two of us at the house in Geneva—glass shattering everywhere—and packed my bags for Chicago.

I really don't think I get enough credit for my patience.

22

I have my driver follow the dark-haired woman's car as it leaves the Hartmann Gallery in Chicago, snow falling between high-rises, a dark fairy tale. I'm chasing my runaway Snow White, except I'm not the queen, I'm the hunter.

We weave carefully through the snow-covered streets, and I find myself thinking of my grandmother Jane. The one who used to hunt deer. An only child, her father raised her like a son. I loved to hold her smooth 35-caliber Remington; it had etched silver details like the monogrammed vanity set she gave me when I turned twelve. I must have been around that same age the first time she took me out deer-stalking. I had few friends (most of the girls my age were put off by my intensity), and even my parents seemed to visibly relax every time Grandmother Jane offered to take me for the afternoon. As if getting me out of the house for even a few hours would be a relief. I knew they hated me. Or, at least, couldn't understand me. But Grandmother Jane never made me feel bad for being different. "You have the clear-eyed focus of a hunter," she used to say.

From the back seat of my own town car, I keep my gaze trained on the Lexus in front of us. I can almost make out my look-alike's French twist through the rear window.

Where are you going, little deer? When will you stop moving long enough for me to take aim and shoot?

Finally, after several blocks, her car pulls over at the Viceroy.

I stay a few steps behind the dark-haired woman entering the hotel, stay far enough away that she can't sense me on her heels, but close enough to see how she makes an effort to skirt the reception desk, her head bowed as she hurries across the lobby. She's just about made it to the elevator unnoticed when suddenly a man rushes out from behind the counter, waving a piece of paper.

"Miss Smith! Elizabeth! We must discuss your bill! You're several weeks past due."

The elevator doors ding open, and the dark-haired woman slips inside. "Sorry, Mr. Hardy! Next time!" The doors slide shut, and like a phantom, she's gone.

The hotel manager returns to his desk, grumbling about no more excuses, and how maybe it's time to get the police involved.

Interesting . . . Seems the little deer is not quite as well-off as the moneyed set she rubbed elbows with tonight.

I decide to stay for a bit, see if she reemerges. I sit at the lobby bar and order a cognac, catching my reflection in the mirrored glass behind the bottles of alcohol. For fun, I pull a hair clip from my coat pocket and twist my short hair into a nubby little updo. It's striking how much we look alike, me and "Elizabeth Smith." But that might not be all we have in common. I pull the event program from my purse and scan the list of donor names. There's no Elizabeth Smith. No Elizabeths at all, in fact. Then I remember someone who might have more information. Someone who comforted the crying dark-haired woman at the gala and came away with her business card. I scroll through my phone contacts until I find Abigail Reed.

"Abigail, hello! It's Isabelle Beresford. So sorry we didn't get to chat tonight, but I had to call you to tell you how stunning you looked in that ochre gown!"

"Oh, *stop*, you're too kind."

"Listen, I won't keep you long. But I met a lovely woman at the event," I say. "A brunette wearing a black dress. And I realize, to my great dismay, that I've lost her card. I think I may have seen you chatting with her. Elizabeth something?"

"Oh, Liz! The art dealer!" Abigail says.

"Yes." *Interesting.*

"She has a lead on a painting. A very prominent artist from the eighties. I'm not supposed to tell. We're going to make a mint. Shh."

"You know me—I'm a vault."

We hang up, and moments later, a photo of a business card arrives on my phone. LIZ HASTINGS—CONSULTANT.

Hastings . . . not Smith . . .

My curiosity grows by the second. It's been a while since I've been tantalized by anything, and I find myself wanting to savor this little mystery.

You're not a deer at all, are you? You're smart and calculating . . . like a fox.

Liz Whoever-She-Is must be at least $10K in the red at the Viceroy—she can't possibly have access to high-level art. I have a feeling Abigail's about to pay for her greediness. Liz has all the markings of a con artist. Which is unanticipated but could work in my favor. People who use multiple names tend to lack connections; no one will miss Elizabeth Hastings if she disappears . . .

A plan begins to take shape. A way to get rid of Oliver—*and* Isabelle Beresford. Can't suspect the wife if she's dead too.

I'll extend my time here in Chicago. Oliver isn't expecting me to join him in Mexico for another week. He's probably on the beach now with that insipid yoga instructor he's been fucking. But after that little stint in the kitchen with the choking, I need to play my cards carefully. I doubt he's capable of real harm, but it's not violence I'm worried about, it's reputation.

Well, and the money, obviously.

I'll keep stalking my little fox until I find the right moment—maybe in some dirty alley with a broken bottle, carving her uncannily similar face into a work of art, or maybe in that unpaid-for room at the Viceroy with two champagne glasses, a heavy dose of Valium, and a tragic fall from the balcony into the traffic on the street below. I haven't decided what kind of story I want to tell with this death—but it needs to be gruesome enough that Liz's shattered face will pass for mine. Plenty of people will attest that Isabelle Beresford was indeed here in Chicago, and if I leave my purse on her corpse to really help sell it, there will be no need for DNA testing. That's step one—kill off "Isabelle." Step two is to snag Liz's ID—assuming she has one—and head down to Punta Mita to take care of all *that*. And voilà, I'm free. "Isabelle" dead. Oliver dealt with. New identity as "Liz" secured. It almost seems too good to be true.

I swallow the rest of my cognac and signal to the Viceroy bartender for another. *Everything in moderation*, Grandmother Jane used to tell me. But I've always had trouble with that advice. When I find something that hooks me, I want *more*. I've learned it can lead to complications, but I still dive in head first.

The more I think about it, the more my little plot *does* seem too good to be true. Killing Liz here in Chicago is risky. She might be using aliases, but still, people know her here. She's been living in this hotel for weeks. Someone might report her missing—if only because of her outstanding bill. Plus, to execute my full vision, I'll need her real name. Her social security number. All of it. Without her name, I can't make the most of her face.

But how can I get this clever fox to reveal herself? Liz found Abigail Reed's weakness; now I need to find whatever that is for Liz. I know she likes money and luxury, and that, for both, she's willing to commit crimes. I know she claims to be an art dealer . . .

I've always been a bit of an art aficionado myself. I love finding unique pieces to furnish our homes. If I left the decor up to Oliver, it would be all dark brown leather and fake trophy gold. He can afford anything in the world, but if he had his druthers, he'd live in a Restoration Hardware store.

I wonder if Liz actually has taste, or if that's just another one of her false fronts. I find myself wanting to ride up the elevator to her room and share a drink with her. Learn more about how she pulls off her cons, where she came from. Maybe it's just a morbid curiosity, wanting to really know the woman whose life I plan to take for my own. But part of me feels something almost like kinship with this woman who shares not only my face, but also my disregard for the rules.

Stop, I tell myself. *She's not your friend. She's not your pet.*

But she *can* be my employee. The idea comes to me in a flash. I'll buy a new piece of art and hire her to handle its installation. I'll fly her to Puerto Vallarta and set her up in Casa Esmerelda— Oliver's never there; he's unaware that I still follow him on his phone. Three weeks and he's only torn himself away from that *down dog* one time. No sensible fox could refuse a tropical beach vacation in a mansion. Clearly, she's wearing out her welcome here at the Viceroy. So there's a good chance she'll be tempted enough by my proffered escape to provide her real information. As soon as I have Liz's real name and her passport info, I can start building my new life.

• • •

The next few days are busy. There are phone calls to make, loose ends to tie up. I make arrangements for separate housing in Punta Mita—can't stay at Casa Esmerelda with Lizzy; a condo at the Four Seasons will have to do. I purchase a painting and arrange for it to be shipped directly to Mexico. This, I admit, I do have fun with. It really doesn't matter what the art is—it's just the bait I need to lure Liz into my trap. But still, I've always admired symbolism. I select a Tamayo—a lushly abstract smear of two female figures, bleeding into one.

I keep tabs on Liz as best I can, trailing her through the snowy Chicago streets whenever she ventures out from the Viceroy. She's accepted my offer of employment, so I don't have to worry too much about her slipping away, but I don't want to leave anything to chance.

While Liz is off getting a new hairdo inspired by yours truly (she must have found my Insta, or Googled my image), I'm doing my own little makeover, pouring peroxide over my dark locks in the hotel bathtub. The fumes are rancid, but it seemed safer to do it myself rather than clue anyone into my new look. The contacts are another necessary evil. I opt for a nondescript brown to obscure the green eyes that Oliver said he could always spot me by.

Finally, I settle into seat 6C on Delta flight 406 and order a glass of champagne. Liz, exactly as I'd hoped, is living it up in first class a few rows ahead of me.

Turn around, I think, while I sip my champagne. I'm sure she wouldn't recognize me from whatever online research she's done, disguised as I am, but part of me wishes she would. I'm even wearing the red scarf she left behind in the house I watched her sneak into, for kicks.

And to see if she'll notice.

Play with me, Little Fox!

Wild animals are impossible to predict; that's what Grandmother said. It's the whole challenge of hunting. The thrill. But I always struggled with that part. I wanted the deer to comply with my imagination, to stop in a clearing and pose. I envisioned myself, rifle cocked, holding a statuesque deer in my crosshairs. She'd show me her regal profile and, right when I was poised to shoot, turn and stare at me with large, wet, black eyes. It never worked out that way—I always ended up shooting the bitch in the back. It wasn't artistic at all.

The seat belt light flashes, and the flight attendants scurry to their jumper seats, and still, you haven't noticed me on your tail. I was certain you'd spot me at the Diptyque counter in Wicker Park yesterday. How close will I need to get for you to notice we're wearing the same scent?

23

The night is warm and clear, with a big half-moon rising over the water. Fireflies lazily blink, dotting the air with their yellow tail lightbulbs, and I wish I had a jar to capture them with, like when I was a child. "Please stop killing them," my mother once cried when she found a lineup of my lanterns of doom. I never poked holes in the lids like you're supposed to and, instead, watched the bugs dim down to death. They would blink less and less. They would fall to the base of the jar. "My God." My mother made that horrified face I can't scrub from my memory when she went looking for more jars of dead bugs and instead found the bird.

It's been several weeks, and I'm *still* here in Mexico. Why haven't I killed you yet, Little Fox?

Yet here I am, twirling on a bar stool, beside a man in an ill-fitting tan suit—the man the Reeds hired to track you down—slowly feeding him roofies and false intel, watching him become bleary-eyed, while you're having your fun romp over in one of the ocean-view suites.

It's starting to feel like I'm the one doing all the work in this relationship, Liz.

You keep escaping me. Compared to you, killing *Oliver* was easy. And Maddie the mistress in her tight little matching lavender bike shorts and bra. Bashing her face in with her phone while she tried to take a selfie—and then a rock to finish the job—was actually pretty fun. Those *uh . . . uh . . . uh . . .* sounds she made as blood gurgled from her mouth. Oliver recognizing me despite the dyed hair and fake eyes was gratifying too. I leapt from behind that tree and his eyelids peeled back and his brow lifted and his whole body froze in awkward awe. I'll never forget that.

It's funny how this whole thing began because that's what I wanted. To kill Oliver and get away with it. You were meant to be the convenient double, the fall girl. And yet now, I haven't thought about him in weeks—all I think about is *you*.

The way you wear my clothes. The way you tilt your head. The way you scan a room, thinking you're seeing what no one else sees. But you don't see me. Not the real me.

You don't see behind the mask. You haven't even thought to look.

My plan had been to bring you right back up to that same lookout spot on Las Mellizas, leave you with the other two bodies. I've always liked symmetry. But it didn't go that way, did it, you lucky thing? Maybe it was divine timing how, when I hung back—so I could catch up and take you by surprise, like with Oliver—another hiker appeared just then and ruined my chance. Someone's watching out for you, Lizzie. It's strange. Maybe you really are special. I was worried for a minute—once I got back down the trail, I couldn't find you anywhere. I would have been so upset if you'd simply stumbled off a ledge on your own. I want to be with you when you die.

But then you emerged at the base of the trail, sweaty and frazzled. I knew I'd have to find another way. Hoping to extract more from your life extension, I gave you my wallet. I was dying to know: How far would you take this? How well would you play into my hand? You looked through my brown contacts while we both clutched the wallet—could you see the challenge in my eyes?

That night, I couldn't stand to be away from you. You could have fled; you could have disappeared. So I spied on you at Esmerelda, hid in the darkness, and watched through the double-paned glass. You had no idea, did you? You skittered from room to room, packing and crying, and getting drunk, you little fox. I could have offed you a million different ways, but I was restrained.

My self-control sure paid off when you surprised me with another plot twist and burst out of the house at dawn. I followed behind while you drove back to the hike in the shadowy light. Trailed you up the mountain. I kept my eyes glued to you this time, didn't let you out of my sight. And it's a good thing too, because, this time, I saw it all. You had gotten lost when we hiked together; now I realized you'd seen the bodies in the underbrush and were returning to the scene. Clever little fox. You took it *so* much further than I ever would have guessed. I killed them, but you shoved their bodies into their graves.

You don't just look like me. You *are* like me.

Aren't you? Sometimes, I'm so sure of it, and then other times . . .

After that, I decided to see how long you'd last as Isabelle, and how far you'd take the charade. I admit, I was taken with you and was rooting for your success. By then, we were a team. So, over the next few weeks, I paved the way for you to become Isabelle. I pointed you out to bartenders and hotel staff and resort residents alike—including those insipid women: Julia, Aimee, Palmer— bragging about what an art aficionado you were. I sold them a dream version of Isabelle who never existed in either of us.

You thought it was your acting that had everyone eating out of your hand. You were a genius, weren't you? Effortlessly stealing my life. Ha!

Every day there were countless opportunities for me to strike. Surfing together in that heavy swell, drinking late-night in town . . . I could have pushed you off your board and held you under the break. I could have slipped some of the Rohypnol in my pocket into your mimosa. I sneaked into Esmerelda to suffocate you with my silk-encased pillow, but instead stood over you for hours watching you sleep. And I balked with the knife.

Now I have to be honest with myself: Is this a list of everything that's gone wrong . . . or a list of excuses for why I haven't killed my pet? Like the fireflies. Like the bird. Except different. I should have killed you, Liz, but, like it or not, I wanted you to live.

Until now.

Because Braden's arrival means I'm potentially fucked. He'll come looking for Isabelle if she goes missing. He'll care. (Especially now that you're in his bedroom having what I'm sure is a thoroughly magical series of orgasms.) No such luck for me. Not that I want Braden again. But you're having fun, and I'm stuck figuring out how to deal with Oliver's brother's sudden appearance while taking care of Liz Dawson's dirty work.

Not that I can blame you. Braden has magic hands. It may have been twenty years ago, but the handful of nights we had together were memorable. I liked him, Little Fox. Believe it or not, I have feelings too. Braden made me feel visible and alive and understood. Or I never would have told him about Susan. Biggest mistake of my life and I didn't even realize it. I didn't tell him the *whole* truth— made it seem like I'd lost her in a terrible accident, which wasn't far off. I *had* lost Susan . . . just not in the way he assumed.

But still, it was too much, and once it was out there, it was this liability I'd never escape. We didn't see him often—he and Oliver didn't get along—but I knew he'd be at the wedding as our witness. So the night before, I slipped into Braden's room with a little party gift. He'd been trying to get clean for months, but with a little help from me, he relapsed epically. Braden was a disaster at the wedding, stumbling, belligerent, even telling Oliver to his face that he and I had fucked. I denied it, and Oliver believed me, of course. He already had about thirty years' worth of distrust of his brother built up. This was clearly just one more unhinged, drug-fueled lie.

I never saw Braden again after that day. Maybe Oliver told him not to show his face around me; maybe he went to rehab. I didn't really care, so long as he stayed gone. Susan or not, Braden was too complicated to keep around. He knew my secret, but worse than that, he'd taken a piece of my heart. He was meant to stay banished.

You've taken a piece of my heart too, Liz.

• • •

"You're sure you know her? Her name is Liz. Liz . . ." The stupid henchman waggles his phone at me, but the screen's off, so I can no longer see the photo of Liz at the Melanoma Foundation event. His brain struggles to compute. "Hastings," he mutters before slumping sideways on a chaise in a configuration of hammocks and loungers hidden in a manicured cluster of jungle plants and trees. It took three roofies and two shots of tequila, but he's finally starting to falter.

"May I see the photo again, please?" I grab the phone from him and hold it up to his quickly slackening face. It opens on a shot from that first night in Chicago, the snow piling up outside, you draped in that black crepe dress. "Yes, it's her. I'll send her a text."

But first I zoom in on the photo. And though I'm under a palm tree at the St. Regis Punta Mita, it's like I'm at that Chicago gallery again, standing just beyond the frame, watching. That moment when I first had an inkling that I was on the starting line of a new life. We hadn't met yet, but we were already sisters. Somehow linked. I study your jawline, your cheekbones, your green eyes . . .

You should be dead by now, Liz.

How ironic that it's up to me to save you now, while you're fucking Braden no less. I laugh. Then I send a text to a random number so Abigail Reed's hired thug—I'm not impressed, Abby—thinks I'm following through on my promise to reach out to my pal Liz. When he was ejected from the restaurant earlier tonight, I followed and told him I'd heard he was looking for someone I might know. "This way," I said, sneaking him back in through the Punta Mita residents' entrance, which no one ever mans at this late hour. I made him wait, hidden, while I grabbed two rounds of shots.

"She's coming," I say now. "I told her to meet me at the lower pool for a nightcap."

"Okay." He manages to stand—thank God—and I offer him an arm to steady him.

"This way."

He stumbles like a fool. I wrap my arm under his ill-fitting suit jacket and finger the gun that will make him more of a suspect than a victim when he's found. "Over here."

Then we're at the pool's edge.

"She's not . . . She's . . ." he says while I lead him down the pool's stairs and into the smooth aqua water. "Hey? What?"

There's that look again. It's remarkable how they know when their end has arrived. Oliver knew it the second he saw me on that jungle hike. He knew what I was capable of. But this man had no idea. Until now.

"Hey. What the—?"

He tries to fight me, but his arms don't work, and his legs buckle. I grip his fatty midsection so he doesn't fall or float—he's not getting away.

"I need to . . . Let me . . . Stop . . ." he says.

"Sorry. But I told you—Liz is a friend of mine."

Then his impaired eyes meet mine. Recognition of the danger he's in dilates his pupils; his brown irises are eclipsed.

I expect he'll sink easily, and drowning him won't take much effort, but when I push down on his shoulders, he manages to use his leg strength to fight back. Fucking drugs are all subpar in this town—a triple dose really should have killed this fuck. I don't

have time for a battle, and I don't want any noise, so I knee him in
the balls. Then, with both hands, I hold his head underwater. He
thrashes and twists while bubbles fly out of his begging mouth, and
I want him to shut it already. This is hard. I'm soaked through and
tired. I knee him in the gut this time, then the face. *Come on, just
die already.* I hold him under with all my weight. I have zero interest
in fucking Braden, but while I'm straddling this gross middle-aged
corpse, I can't help but resent Liz for winning the night. She's up
there coming to Jesus and I'm down here ruining my blowout so
she can live another day as Isabelle Beresford.

Satisfied he's finally croaked, I shove off on my back and float
into the middle of the pool. I gaze at the stars, trying to relax. I
should feel calm—I've removed an obstacle; I've cleared a path—but
a current of anger's building in my veins. I watched her kiss Braden
on the beach (*sloppy seconds, Liz*). I watched him take her back to
his suite. She was scared of the man face down in the shallow end
for good reason—he was about to ruin the life she's worked so hard
to steal. But will she ever thank me for saving her? I think not.

I backstroke a lap to burn off my resentment (*Exercise helps,*
the shrink told my mother), then another, but it doesn't help. No
matter how much you do for someone, they always let you down. I
want to believe Liz is different, but I'm realizing she's as selfish and
clueless as Isabelle. There's nothing worse than an ungrateful best
friend. I close my eyes on the bright stars in the Mexican sky and
taunt myself into my memories.

• • •

The first time I saw Isabelle was the second day of senior year. I had
just arrived at my lunch table and all the girls I called my friends
were pointing and whispering.

"She's the transfer," Alexandra Smolenski said as she pointed to the skinny new student standing near the trays who had skin so pale it was pink. Her dark blond hair had a pink tinge too, like someone had accidentally washed her in hot water with something red. She was new, and I wanted her to be mine.

I strode across the cafeteria with all eyes on me. Miss Pinky was scared, watching me approach.

"I've come to save you," I said. "There's an empty space next to me."

Isabelle Caldwell was so relieved to take the seat at the coveted table, I swear she shed a tear. Alexandra may have been the official leader of our group, but I was the most feared. That seat beside me was always empty because the others respected my space. Or that's what I thought until that day. When I realized that space had remained empty because it was waiting for Isabelle.

We had three classes together—all APs. But she wasn't a nerdy bookworm, oh no. She was just smart. "Come on." I pulled her down to the hall behind the gym locker room and through to the broken emergency exit that led to the patch of brown dead grass where those of us in the know smoked.

"Thank God," she said, lighting up. "How did you know I smoked?" she asked.

"Good guess." It was her self-styled yard-sale clothes, overly worn Docs, and bangs she must have cut with children's safety scissors, something you find in a drawer filled with dried markers and stumpy bits of crayon, wrappers peeled. Scissors dull enough for an orphanage, it turned out. Which was the most exotic origin story I'd ever heard.

"You live here?" she said when I brought her home after school. She'd just turned eighteen and was living in some kind of transitional group apartment above a Rockland corner store. That was both titillating to me—think of the trouble they could get up to—and repulsive—imagine the lice!

"It's not as great as you'd think," I said when she entered our sprawling, flowery manor. "My mother couldn't have another child. Apparently, I destroyed her womb. She almost bled to death. It's too big a house for just me."

She wandered around the ground floor, lightly touching flower-filled vases and the backs of upholstered chairs. I led her upstairs to my room.

"Hi, Cindy," I said to the housekeeper, who did a double take when she passed us in the hall. "This is my new friend Isabelle."

"Nice to meet you, Miss Isabelle," Cindy said. Isabelle was the first friend of mine she'd met. I'd never liked anyone enough to bring them home. Girls like Alexandra wanted to be my friend because my parents were rich. As if my daddy would buy her a car. It was so fake. Everyone in Camden and Glen Cove, even the plain, brainy kids, was full of shit. Except for Isabelle. She was real—so real—and also adept at fitting in. Years of trying to get adopted had made her a shapeshifter like me.

When I loaned Isabelle a Ralph Lauren cashmere cable-knit sweater—pale pink, like her!—she transformed into the sister my mother had failed to produce. She gazed at her reflection while I brushed her hair with my silver brush. "What do you think?" I said.

"You're the best friend I've ever had." Her brown eyes looked sincere in my vanity's mirror, and I was almost moved. I wondered if I'd cry. Or if she would.

After that, we were inseparable. We'd climb out my window and smoke on the roof, speed in my father's car, and scream through open windows. On Sundays, when we'd finished our homework, we'd raid my parents' bar and drink cosmopolitans on the back porch. She never had to be home. And Lord knows no one was watching me. My parents had given up trying to control me long ago.

"Are you still up for adoption?" I asked on my third pink cocktail.

"I think I'm too old," she said. "No one ever wants an old kid."

"You're not too old for me," I said. The sun was setting over the back lawn that led down to the water's edge. "Live with me here."

She stayed the night, and then the next. She was mine. One hundred percent.

Until the night we ventured out to the University of Maine at Augusta to pick up boys. In my clothes, Isabelle was transformed. We found our way to an SAE party, and when we entered, all heads turned. If it wasn't for me, she would have been dirt to them. Poor townie trash. You'd think she'd have thanked me for all my help. I'd adopted her after all. But no one remembers the bottom of the hole you rescue them from. They think they climbed out on their own, and they don't look back.

Around two a.m., she pulled me behind the SAE front hedge, giggly and overexcited.

"Look at him." She pointed to a blond blockhead who was rolling a fresh keg across the lawn with the help of a couple frat brothers. "He's soooo pretty."

I tilted my head and tried to assess the guy objectively. Fair hair, blue eyes. Sharp jaw. Definitely a preppy type. I supposed he was attractive enough, but there was something about his sweet, open face that made me want to vomit. Made me want to wrap the vinyl tubing of the beer line around his neck until those blue eyes popped out of his skull.

"He's awful," I said. "And anyway, you're staying with me."

Standing in the dewy grass with the party behind us, I wanted to force her into my car. I tried to grab her hand, but she backed away.

"I like him," she said. We both watched as he walked a few yards on his hands. His shirt dropped over his face (and off his abs), and he lost his balance and fell. Laughing and snorting like an idiot, he rolled in the grass.

"Did you see that, Isabelle?" he yelled to her. He popped onto one knee. "Come back, Isabelle. Come back."

"You can't leave me," I said, losing control. I hoped she hadn't noticed my disgusting weakness, but she had.

"You didn't really adopt me, Susan," she said, like I'd imagined the whole event. "You don't own me. You think you can have whatever you want, but you can't."

Oh, how I wanted to punch her in the face right there with all those fools watching. I wanted to pummel her. After all I'd done.

A week later, the boy ghosted her—duh—and I welcomed her back as my friend. But the anger and rage I felt when she rejected me at SAE fueled me that final evening when we were swimming in the sound. The sun was setting over the shore while we played like dolphins in the warm summer water. I felt more free in that moment than I ever had. And yet, I knew the moment was fleeting. "If you could go anywhere in the world, where would you go?"

"Where would I go?" she asked, bobbing in water highlighted with purples and reds. "I don't know. I haven't thought about it. I'm just excited to be going to college."

We'd both be leaving town at the end of the summer—I'd gotten into La Sorbonne to study art. Isabelle had received a full-ride scholarship and was headed to the U. of Maine at Augusta, to frat parties and preppy loser boys.

"Come with me to Europe," I said, "or Asia, or South America. You can go anywhere or do anything. What do you most want?" I swam to her. I touched her leg underwater with my foot. But she drifted away.

"What I most want is my own room." She laughed. "But I guess I still have four more years of room-sharing ahead of me." She glanced over my head and back at the coastline. She could see forty miles inland, to the campus in Augusta, and a life that didn't include me.

I circled her so she was facing the open water instead of the shore.

"You understand, don't you?" she said. "Why I'm looking forward to college? With my background, I never thought I'd have a chance to go. I can't wait to just feel . . . normal."

I couldn't have been less impressed. I was offering Paris, and she chose a dorm. She chose "normal."

For better or worse, that was one thing I knew I'd never be.

The sun had slipped behind the houses and trees, and the sky and the water were darkening. We'd floated into the channel, and the current caught our tiring legs.

"Oh my God," she said when she turned. We'd traveled half a mile, at least. She was breathless, exhausted, and the swift inky bay had us in its grasp. The thing about poor kids is, most of the time, they can't swim. Never learned in backyard pools or on vacations to the beach. Isabelle could only doggy-paddle, which is a losing game in the open water. "I won't make it," she cried. I could see she was beginning to panic—the surest way to drown fast.

"We're not that far," I said. "Watch me."

She was like a piece of litter carried out toward the Atlantic on those black swells, but I used my powerful stroke to escape. When I was free of the current, and twenty-five yards closer to the safety of the shore, I stopped and looked back.

"Susan!" she screamed. "Susan! Help. Help."

I could barely hear her, though, she was so far away.

"Swim," I said. "Swim."

She thrashed. She went under. She came up. She went back under. And I watched. "Help. Help," she screamed. "Help."

But I didn't help. She waved at me while she cried out, but she didn't have the strength to hold that arm up for long. *You need that to swim, silly. Don't waste your energy waving at me.*

"Swim, Isabelle," I said. "Like me."

I swam a few more yards, but I couldn't tear myself away. It was like those lightning bugs, slowly fading into black. The white of her face and that desperate hand flashed a few more times, until, like a little flame extinguished, she disappeared. She'd betrayed me, and I'd wanted her gone. I'd cast a spell without knowing it. I'd killed with my powerful mind. I treaded easily while I watched the spot where she'd drowned. I didn't feel cold or out of breath, but rather, like I was doubly alive. Omnipotent. Possessed.

When I reached land, I thought I'd cry or care. Maybe I'd swim back out and try to save her. Maybe I'd call 911. Instead, I found the little pile of our clothes tucked behind a dune and dressed in her monogrammed sweater instead of mine.

Driving home along the waterfront. I kept waiting for something to happen. I'd killed her. Shouldn't that set off some sort of alarm? But there were no police in my rearview. There wasn't anyone behind me at all.

"Hello!" I said when I opened my front door. "Hello." No one was home. "I could have drowned!" I yelled. "I could have drowned, and you wouldn't have cared. You would have been happy. I'd be out of your life."

I grabbed my smallest bag. I didn't want anything from that house. I took only essentials: shorts, a hoodie, my toothbrush, and the clothes I was wearing, Isabelle's monogrammed sweater, my favorite jeans . . . I grabbed the cash I'd been collecting over the years. It was in an envelope taped to the back of the mirror on my vanity. My silver brush and comb set was bulky and impractical, but my grandmother had given it to me, engraved STW. My initials: Susan Tilda Warner. I packed them like tokens—or gravestones—commemorating my old life.

And then I set out alone.

"What's your name?" the trucker I'd flagged down for a ride asked after I told him I was heading west.

"Isabelle." I hadn't planned to do that. I'd just worn her sweater because I missed her, and I wanted her close—the skin cells and sweat on her clothes against my skin. Maybe that sounds strange, since I'm the one who ended her life. But everything was out of my control that night. It was like I was swept up in a river of fate. If only Isabelle had come with me. We could have had the most wonderful life.

Maybe it can be different this time, I think, floating on my back in the St. Regis pool, my dress fanning out around me, the stars overhead winking, brilliant. *Maybe I can find a way to keep Liz.*

24

I reach around and zip up my red dress. This dress is special. It's the dress I'll be wearing on the night Liz and I run away together.

I know the Kellys and their little crew don't want "Tilly Endicott" at their gala; they certainly won't notice what I wear. But I'm wearing it for me, not them.

I'm not used to being left out or ignored—at least, not since my early childhood years when I struggled to make friends. But by the time I got to high school, all those weak kids kept me near as if an ingot of gold might drop out of my pocket. As Susan, I earned their respect—or at least their fear. When I became Isabelle, I learned to control myself, to soften myself, at least on the surface. I managed to be liked—by everyone. Isabelle's always at the top of the guest list. Even my mother would have been impressed. That took patience and skill.

And now, for the past six weeks, I've been Tilly.

Except for the dye job and the contacts, she's just . . . me. A bad seed, all grown up. I smile in the mirror at the truest version of me yet. She's a real cunt, and I like her best.

Maybe that's why I've let this go on for way too long.

The memory of straddling that man and holding him down until the bubbles stopped coming up floats back to me with pride.

I want to confess, Little Fox. I did it for you.

You're seeking refuge in Braden's arms, but I'm your savior, not him.

But still, even with him dead and gone, I was sure Liz would be worried about her little art scheme catching up to her. If they connect the hired man back to Mrs. Reed, she could tell the police who she sent her fixer here to find. It's not like she'll just let that go. She gave Liz a hefty down payment. Plus, the man was sent here to catch a criminal, but wound up dead. Any detective with half a brain would suspect Liz Dawson to be behind the murder.

It's time for Liz to get out of town.

And yet, that day in the kitchen, when I offered up Brazil—a literal paradise, a haven for a small-time criminal like her—she wasn't interested. She needed to get out of here too. Yet she said no.

I should have killed her then—I was so close. She'd rejected my sisterhood. I wanted her dead. But it was like stabbing myself. I couldn't plunge the blade in.

I scared you, Little Fox. I pushed you away.

Just like with Isabelle.

"Pull it together." I inch up to the mirror's surface; my breath leaves a patch of fog over my reflection. As I sweep blush across my cheeks, I look deep into my eyes, afraid that, like my insecurities, my green irises might shine through the fake sheen of brown.

I barely saw Liz all week after the apple tart incident. I let her live—again—and she never even called me. And then *he* fucking moved into my house. Braden, who will no doubt be Liz's plus-one for the gala tonight. I can feel restless fury beginning to percolate in my veins, and force myself to take a deep breath. Now is not the time to let my emotions get the better of me.

I ran every single day this week, logging a hundred miles trying to settle my nerves. (*No, Mother, exercise doesn't help.*) That's the only time I saw Liz, on the jogging path, when I was doing every-thing in my power to get her out of my mind.

Don't you want me anymore? I miss you.

My shallow breaths fog the reflection of my face again, making me appear, disappear, appear again.

Didn't I prove the kind of friend I am when I saved you from Neil?

I won't scare you again, Little Fox. If you come with me, I'll keep you alive.

I smooth down the red sequined dress. I like its weight against my skin, like the thick scales of a snake. It's too daring for Isabelle Beresford. This dress is all me.

I can't believe even here, even now, I'm still finding myself forced to attend another mind-numbing gala. Liz said no to Brazil, but yes to a ladies' committee. It's infuriating, but I still want her to join me on that plane. I thought the real Isabelle could be my pet forever, but she craved normal. She aspired to pastel-pink plain. Not us. Not me and Liz. We want bigger lives. Mansions on the beach, fine food, easy men, and blissful peace. We can have that, together.

I grab my clutch and head for the door.

As I drive to the Sufi Ocean Club in my golf cart, the humid air presses all around me. I know this is my last chance to convince Liz. My last chance to change the ending.

My last chance to save her from myself.

• • •

I hear dance music before I see the beach club. Disco lights spin across the water and the palm trees' shiny fronds. I move through the auction room, and that's when I spot it: the Tamayo. The one I picked out. The portrait of me becoming Liz . . . though it became the story of Liz becoming me, didn't it? Either way, that painting is symbolic. It means something; it holds a coded secret. What the fuck is it doing here out in the open for just anyone to bid on?

Liz sold me out. Sold *us* out.

It hits me, with sudden clarity, how oblivious she truly is. All this time, I thought I was the one luring *her*, training her, tricking her. But she's lured *me*. Made me believe we were the same.

Are we?

I march into the party, fighting off the sting of betrayal, still hoping I have it in me to play nice.

At this point, I just need the truth. I just need to know if she is willing to choose me like I'm willing to choose her.

There she is, dancing like a fool with that gaggle of idiots, singing along to Rihanna. I want to scream:

Run away with me! We can stop pretending!

I'm headed toward her when I spot Braden, all dressed up for Liz.

"He's why you didn't want to come to Brazil, isn't he?" I say, when Liz finally abandons the girls and deigns to actually speak to me. "You're fucking your brother-in-law."

"What the fuck, Tilly?" she whispers, clearly embarrassed by my outburst. Which just makes me angrier. "Why are you doing this to me?"

"The question is, why are you doing this to me?"

I had a *plan*. The hike, the murder . . . But then Liz got involved. She got under my skin and twisted it all around. I set the trap and loaded it with bait, but then somehow, she managed to seduce me with her cunning version of Isabelle.

I fell in love with my own creation.

I'm rambling, I know, the words are spewing out of me, volcanic. *Braden* and *how could you* and *we can still leave*—all in a messy blur. Liz manages to get me to a bar, but the tequila just burns my throat and makes me feel even more lethal. Maybe I'll lure her down to the water or I'll brain her with the blue-and-white ceramic tequila bottle. Fuck all that—I'm so angry, I could choke her right here with my bare hands. Liz shoos away Braden, who's ready to eject me himself.

He reluctantly gives us space, and my eyes trail him across the room. Which is when I see the fucking painting again—this time in the arms of a porter carrying it away. The Tamayo that started it all.

What a fucking ingrate.

I'm seeing red. I want to burn the whole place down.

Just then, the air is pierced by a bloodcurdling scream. For a moment, I think maybe I actually *have* set fire to the room with just my sheer force of will.

But then everyone starts running toward the beach.

There's a girl on the edge of the water shouting and crying. Then I see it nodding against the sand like it's alive.

A skull.

• • •

Oh my God, the chaos. You'd think all those gala guests had skin in the game. Running around frantic, as if *they* were the ones who very likely just had one of their murder victims pop up as yummy fish food. As if *they'd* just been stabbed in the back by a traitor. The rage—at Liz, at myself, at how far I've let things slide—is still pulsing through my skin, just below the surface, and now, *la policía* are in the water with their scuba gear and underwater lights. For fuck's sake. They've already set up operations on the pier and loaded the little harbor with their stupid boats.

They're declaring the whole beach club a crime scene, sending everyone home. I've lost Liz—Braden swooped in and whisked her away in the stampede. I need to get out of here too, and yet everywhere I turn there's an officer blocking the way or a whimpering guest stumbling in heels across my path.

Finally, I manage to make my escape from the madness—though

the quiet that envelops me as I try to jog around the cove, holding my shoes in my hands, does nothing to soothe the screaming in my head.

In all this fuss over a washed-up skull of someone who's *already dead*, no one has any fucking clue about the truth except *me*—but no one's asking little old Tilly. No one even sees me. No one has any idea what I've done, what I'm capable of—or what I'm about to lose.

Because now, with the bodies exposed like this, I really don't have any other choice. Fate is, at last, forcing my hand.

Certain I'm out of view, I finally drop to my knees on the beach. The truth is, I couldn't run farther if I wanted to; the pain, the betrayal, the disappointment, the loss, hit me like a ruptured spleen. Liz left me here on my own, and I'm shocked when I reach up and feel how wet my eyes are. I can't remember the last time I cried. Maybe when Grandma Jane died. Maybe not even then. The tears burn and sting, forcing their way through, making my damn colored contacts sting and blur, making me want to melt into the stand. I crumple over, an ugly moan escaping me.

"Fuck you, Liz," I spit out. *And fuck you too, Tilly. You were a fool to let her walk away from that hike. A total fucking fool. You had to play with her. You had to make her your friend.*

I slam a fist into the murky ocean inlet. I should have left weeks ago, but I was stupid, so stupid, thinking I could let Liz live. "You fucking idiot." I hit myself in the head. "Fuck you. Fuck you. Fuck you." Blow after blow after blow. "Fuck you. Fuck you. Fuck you."

Finally empty, I uncoil and stare up at the dark sky, full of bright, indifferent stars. I fell for Liz, and now I have no option but to kill her. And I don't want to. I don't. Despite everything, I want her in my life. I sob like I never did as a child and choke out horrible, foreign animal sounds.

That's enough, Susan. Remember who you are. Remember.

I summon my tenacity and grit: I made it out of Maine on my

own and created an entire life. And I did that alone. I swat at my tears like they're insects crawling down my face, watery vermin from the depths of my insides. I stand and brush the sand from the sequins. Then I tilt my head to the sky and count the stars that comprise the Big Dipper until my embarrassing tears return to the core of my dark heart. I have no time to waste.

Step aside, Tilly—Susan's back.

I'll have to wait for the right moment. It will be harder now with Braden, and probably the police soon too. But no one knows the house like I do. I return to my golf cart, knowing that if I find an opportunity, it will be my last. I can't hesitate or waffle. "Don't you fucking cry, you stupid fucking baby. Don't you fucking cry."

• • •

By morning, it's as I expected: police parked in front of Esmerelda, no signs of Braden or Liz. *They can't stay forever,* I think. *The police can't know everything yet. They're bound to leave soon, and when they do, I need to be ready.* I return to my condo at the Four Seasons.

It's time.

I squirt the chestnut-brown dye onto the sun-lightened blonde I've become used to. I'm mad at the mistakes I made while being her, but Tilly was honest and raw. I'll miss her and the one friend she made. *No.* I can't let myself think of Liz like that. Not now. Not ever again. The dye stings my scalp to the countdown of my timer. I blink when I pluck the brown contacts from my eyes. It's like washing away decades of artifice, inches of masquerade paint. The timer rings, and I'm in the shower watching the chemical sludge wash from my hair and down the drain.

"There you are," I say to my reflection when I remove my towel and see my true colors on display. The shock sends me into a memory, and I'm a twelve-year-old in my room after a screaming match with my parents, staring at my cold features, my tearless green eyes. "You're evil," my mother had screamed. My father sheltered her in his arms, held her . . . He'd never done that for me. He treated me like I was contagious or filled with venom.

I hiss at myself now, in the Four Seasons mirror, "You were right, Daddy." I'm a viper. Poisonous and ready to strike.

I remember my mother's expressions of horror. How could her little girl be such a monster? How could she have given birth to me? *But even Rosemary loved her demon baby*, I'd thought. "I came out of you!" I screamed from the top of the stairs. "I'm made of you both. If I'm evil, then you are too." I was twelve, and they looked at me like I'd sentenced them to a long, torturous death.

I realize that's how Liz looked at me too when I surprised her at the gala. She wanted to be rid of me. I'd given her a life as Isabelle, and she wanted me gone. Then I hear Isabelle's voice imploring me to understand why she wanted a simple college life and why she turned me down. Here's what I understand: both used me to crawl out of their shitty pasts. I gave them exactly what they wanted, and when I wanted something in return, they both abandoned me. I had a shitty childhood too. Parents who hated me. Prodding doctors and punitive teachers. Isabelle thought she had it so bad, but I'd take dead parents over parents who wanted me to disappear any day.

Once my transformation is complete, I'm back in my cart, speeding toward Casa Esmerelda like a missile.

I punch in the front door code, and I'm inside. The lights are on, but it's still and silent. There's the empty space on the wall where the Tamayo hung. It eggs me on: *Go get the bitch who gave me away. Grab the knife you should have used last week.* Then the bronze girl chimes in: *Finish what you started. Take the life you need.*

Then I spot it: blood.

On the rug and on the porcelain floor. Splattered haphazardly, little drips of it, dragging from the stairs in the kitchen toward the primary suite. I smell it too, the iron in the air, and sweat. Despite myself, the scent of it turns me on a little, lights me on fire. Except . . . what can it mean?

Did someone beat me to it?

Panic.

Where's Braden?

I whirl around to look behind me. But he's not there.

Something faint in the distance—water running.

Someone's in the shower.

I approach my bedroom suite unobstructed.

Inside, a pile of bloodied women's clothing lies in a heap on the floor beside the bed. *What have you done with Braden, Little Fox? Is all this blood why he isn't coming to your rescue? Why he hasn't stopped me and my big, bad knife?*

The bathroom door is wide open; steam billows into the bedroom.

When I'm on the threshold of the en suite, the running water stops. I press my back against the wall and listen. Liz moves to the attached walk-in closet, and I hear the sounds of rummaging, of clothing being tossed haphazardly into a suitcase. *Going somewhere, Little Fox?*

I can't stand it any longer.

"You look great, Liz."

She screams when I step into view. And again, when she sees the knife.

"What the fuck?" she says. "Tilly?"

"Wrong again." I open my eyes and stand in the light, so she sees the green. Watching her brain process the information is riveting.

"No," she says. "No. You can't be . . ."

"Oh, I can be."

"Isabelle."

"I was, for a time."

I walk a few more steps into the closet. Time to move things along.

"I do hope you enjoyed your turn playing Isabelle. But I'm sorry to say this, my little fox. Your time is up."

Liz's eyes are shining with fear, but I can tell she's still calculating, trying to understand my meaning.

"If you're not Isabelle, then who—?" She rushes out of the closet, and I flinch, but she's not heading toward me. She goes to the vanity, grabs my silver brush. "STW," she says, like she's found the key to eternal sunshine, or just the key to staying alive. "You're Susan. Susan Warner."

"Aren't you a smart little fox?" I take another step toward her.

Liz's eyes dart around the room, looking for an escape. But I'm blocking the bedroom doorway, standing between her and freedom. And holding a giant, extra-sharp, brand-new knife.

She brandishes the brush like it's a worthy opponent for my Miyabi. "You killed her, didn't you? In Vinalhaven? You drowned her and stole her identity."

"Wow, Liz, look at you doing the math!" My voice is patronizing, but I am actually a little impressed she's figured it out. *A mind is a terrible thing to waste*, Grandma Jane used to say. Too bad Liz's clever little head can't be saved.

I steady myself, turn my leg muscles into springs, ready to pounce.

"And now . . ." Liz's grip on the hairbrush tightens, her knuckles going white. I see that familiar, dawning horror in her eyes. "Now you're going to do the same thing to me."

"Bingo."

For a brief moment we just stare at each other, one pair of green eyes locking onto another. I can tell what Liz is thinking: she's finally met her match.

And then she lunges for me.

I jump out of the way, and she stumbles forward but manages to grab onto my arm, yanking me backward—and down. We both tumble to the floor, but my grip on the knife is tight. She's not as strong as me, but still she tries, grabbing my wrist, trying to thrust back my arm. I manage to free my other hand and grab her hair. She screams and rolls over on top of me.

Now, do it now.

She's straddling me, almost like we're about to kiss. I'm so thrown off for a second that she manages to leap to her feet. *Fuck.*

She's charging away, toward the doors. I throw myself toward her and grab her from behind, and she swivels, knocking my knife to the floor with a clattering thud, and we're so close again, now weaponless, defenseless, both of us.

"You . . . You're sick. You tricked me," she gasps. "You used me. You . . ."

It feels so good to hear her say it. But I owe her my truth. "No," I say between grunts, trying to wrangle her into stillness. She shoves me back toward my vanity. I tug her to the left, then the right. "You." We scramble. "Used." We spin. "Me."

I'm down, and then she's down, and then we are in the bathroom, which is really a hall of mirrors, reflections everywhere, two brunettes, four eyes, infinitely reflected. A prism of us.

For a moment, I'm stunned, mesmerized. You know that feeling, don't you?

You gaze until your features blur, until you become anyone, or no one. Thrilling. That feeling that you're not alone.

And terrifying: the certainty that you are.

Then, a hard thrust, a loud dulling pain, a mirror shatters as my vision begins to blur and shock moves through my entire being and all I see is *you, you, you.*

Or is it me, me, me?

And now it's just the shattering itself, shards of broken mirror everywhere, long strands of our dark hair, becoming one, and the blood.

So much blood it's dizzying, blinding, bright.

EPILOGUE

In the mirror in the airport bathroom, you study your face. *Everyone does this*, you think, *practices different faces*: pouting like a model, tightening your lips like you have a secret, hurling insults or compliments with only your eyes. Performing the person the world imagines you to be.

Beside you, another woman spritzes her bangs over the slippery sink counter, and an old lady pulls reams and reams of paper towel out of the dispenser. This place is full of women of all ages, going about their lives, their paths intersecting obliviously. Utterly separate. Do they understand how fragile it all is, how tissue-thin?

In the mirror, you dab on lipstick, the color of blood.

Then you fold up the morning's paper beneath your arm—in it, an article about the horrible fate that befell beautiful Casa Esmerelda, up in flames. The two bodies found within: one woman, one man. A lovers' quarrel, perhaps, between Braden Beresford and his sister-in-law, Isabelle.

And it's not the only scandal revealed . . . You can't help but smirk at the thought of Neil Kelly being carted away in cuffs, Palmer's face a pale, outraged O. Neil and Oliver's dealings with a cartel-operated copper mine to the tune of $40 mil are now a poetic prelude to a suspected quadruple murder.

Of course, you know the woman they found in the burning house isn't actually Isabelle Beresford. Then again, she never was.

Hard to tell, though, since the fire ate away at her.

Your hands shake. Your fingers still smell of ash.

In the nearest trash bin, you toss the newspaper, thinking now only of the ruby ring. It makes your heart go icy cold, knowing it's still there in the remains of the villa, a gleaming liability. Much like the red scarf that was left behind at the Thackers' in Chicago: a bread crumb for the curious. A stain of guilt.

In the security line, you hand the TSA officers your photo ID, your passport, all these little plastic cards that vouch for your identity, as if it were a sticky thing. As if a name means anything.

A rose by any other name would smell as sweet.

She didn't smell like roses, though. She smelled like something else. Something wet and alive. Something animal.

Even when she'd gone so very still on that tiled floor.

Every time you blink, you think of her.

Every time you blink, you question which one of you really died.

• • •

The airport is a world of windows, your figure reflected over the wings of taxiing planes, on the glistening black asphalt, under a slanted rain.

You look and look and look until your features blur.

You are everywhere and nowhere.

You melt into the crowd. Swipe your boarding pass over the small red laser beam and hear its reassuring beep. You board the plane and take your first-class seat. You lift into the air. You know somewhere in the vastness below you, her body has turned almost entirely to ash. You know you'll have to live without her now, without Isabelle. Not the real Isabelle, of course, who's been long dead—but the brief, flaming, brilliant dream of her. The one who held everyone in the palm of her hand, including you.

And that's the worst part.

All of this started because you wanted an escape, didn't you? But you should have known better. Should have known that there's nowhere to run. Nowhere to go, no luxury retreat, no alternate identity, no dazzling new life that will ever cure you of the real demon, the one within.

You will be admired, but never loved. Never truly seen. You know you will kill again if you have to, even if it breaks your heart. It's kind of surprising, actually: how easy it is to get away with murder.

If you're being honest, though, it's devastating. How easy it is to disappear.

ACKNOWLEDGMENTS

This book would not exist without the support of many incredible people. First of all, thank you to Lindsay Jamieson, my talented cowriter, for working tirelessly with me to bring this wild idea to life in all its rich, twisted, and disturbing detail. Thank you to Lexa Hillyer for all her creative guidance, story architecting brilliance, and commitment to pulling this off with grace—it's been such a fun ride. Thanks to Jenna Brickley as well for the obsessive detail. All three of you make delicious partners in crime. Special thanks to my editor at Harper, Sarah Stein—a total beast in the thriller space with crucial insights that have made the book stronger. Thanks to Doug Jones and Jonathan Burnham at Harper for seeing and championing the vision early on, as well as to Tina Andreadis, Katie O'Callaghan, Leah Wasielewski, Leslie Cohen, Jocelyn Larnick, Lydia Weaver, Jackie Quaranto, and of course Joanne O'Neill and Caroline Johnson for the stunning cover design. A huge thanks to my amazing team: Kyle Luker (can't function without you, sorry!); Steve Caserta, for his instincts and support; Dave Feldman, for his excellent guidance; everyone at CAA; Stephen Breimer; and Isaac Reuben, for reading more drafts than I'd like to admit and always giving smart, ruthless notes. Thanks also to Lauren Oliver for believing in the terror of doppelgangers; to Mollie Glick, the most killer literary agent; and to Stephen Barbara for helping us get this thing into the right hands at the right times. Thank you to my ride or die, Susan Delmonico, who was with me on the trip where I came up with this idea, and for being the best friend anyone could ever wish for. And most importantly, thank you to the love of my life, my son, whom I live for and who inspires me every day.

ABOUT THE AUTHOR

KRYSTEN RITTER is an actress, a director, and the author of the internationally bestselling novel *Bonfire*, which received a *Publishers Weekly* starred review and which Gillian Flynn called "a beautiful, haunting debut." She's best known for starring in Marvel's *Jessica Jones*.